MW00930486

BLACK FRIDAY

A BOSTON BRAHMIN NOVEL

BOBBY AKART

THANK YOU

Thank you for reading BLACK FRIDAY, a Boston Brahmin novel, by Author Bobby Akart.
We invite you to join Bobby Akart's mailing list to learn about upcoming releases, deals, and appearances. Visit:
BobbyAkart.com

PRAISE FOR BOBBY AKART AND THE BOSTON BRAHMIN SERIES

"This is an excellent stand-alone volume but is even better if you have read the other novels leading up to this one."

"The action and intrigue is highly reminiscent of Tom Clancy with the same depth of research and realism elevating the action to a higher level!"

"… before you know it you're on a rollercoaster of action, betrayal, suspense, and the ride of your life, that you never want to stop!"

"If you think of intelligent action, plot, characters, and realism, you must think of Bobby Akart."

"Bobby Akart is one of the best authors to come along in a long time, and he works his craft very well in his Boston Brahmin series."

"Bobby Akart's writing style is easy to read even for the new reader, yet communicates the tension and emotion experienced by his well-developed characters."

"I love thrillers and Akart writes some of the best."

"Bobby Akart has a knack for making you want to keep turning those pages to see what happens next, right to the end of the book!"

BLACK FRIDAY

A Boston Brahmin novel by
Bobby Akart

Copyright Information

This is a work of fiction. Names, characters, organizations, places, events, and incidents are either the products of the author's imagination or are used fictitiously. Any resemblance to actual persons, living or dead, or actual events is purely coincidental.

© **2021 Wisteria Hall Inc**. All rights reserved. Except as permitted under the U.S. Copyright Act of 1976, no part of this book may be reproduced, distributed, or transmitted in any form or by any means including, but not limited to electronic, mechanical, photocopying, recording, or otherwise, or stored in a database or retrieval system, without the express written permission of Wisteria Hall Inc.

❀ Created with Vellum

OTHER WORKS BY AMAZON CHARTS TOP 25 AUTHOR BOBBY AKART

New Madrid (a disaster thriller)

Odessa (a Gunner Fox trilogy)

Odessa Reborn

Odessa Rising

Odessa Strikes

The Virus Hunters

Virus Hunters I

Virus Hunters II

Virus Hunters III

The Geostorm Series

The Shift

The Pulse

The Collapse

The Flood

The Tempest

The Pioneers

The Asteroid Series (A Gunner Fox trilogy)

Discovery

Diversion

Destruction

The Doomsday Series

Apocalypse

Devil's Homecoming

The Boston Brahmin Series

The Loyal Nine

Cyber Attack

Martial Law

False Flag

The Mechanics

Choose Freedom

Patriot's Farewell (standalone novel)

Black Friday (standalone novel)

Seeds of Liberty (Companion Guide)

The Prepping for Tomorrow Series

Cyber Warfare

EMP: Electromagnetic Pulse

Economic Collapse

DEDICATIONS

With the undying love and support of my wife, Dani, together with the nonstop entertainment of Bullie and Boom, the princesses of the palace, I'm able to tell you these stories. It would be impossible for me to write without them in my heart.

This Boston Brahmin novel is also dedicated to my loyal readers who've been with me from the beginning when I released The Loyal Nine, the first in this series as well as my first novel. Thank you and Choose Freedom, my friends!

A NOTE TO THE READER

Black Friday is written as a standalone novel based upon my six-book Boston Brahmin series. Knowledge of the characters and backstory of the Boston Brahmin series, including my prior standalone *Patriot's Farewell*, will be helpful as you read *Black Friday*.

Whether you've read the Boston Brahmin series already, or if you decide to pick up the story in this time frame, I suggest you read *Previously In The Boston Brahmin Series* found at the back of the book. This will enable you to familiarize yourself with the characters and the events that led to the Boston Brahmin standalone novels *Patriot's Farewell* followed by *Black Friday*.

GO TO *Previously In The Boston Brahmin Series*

EPIGRAPH

"If a civil war is the solution, just remember. There is no honorable way to kill and no subtle way to destroy. Nothing good comes out of war except its ending."
~ John Morgan in *Choose Freedom*

———

"You have to learn the rules of the game and then you play better than anyone else."
~ Albert Einstein

———

"Of all tyrannies, a tyranny sincerely exercised for the good of its victims may be the most oppressive. It would be better to live under robber barons than under omnipotent moral busybodies. The robber baron's cruelty may sometimes sleep, his cupidity may at some point be satiated. But those who torment us for our own good will torment us without end for they do so with the approval of their own conscience."

~ C. S. Lewis, British writer

———————

"Make no mistake, our flag doesn't fly because the wind moves it. It flies with the last breath of each American soldier who dies protecting it. We don't enjoy our freedoms in America just because they're written in the Constitution. We are a free people because there are men and women of our military risking their lives to preserve those freedoms."
~ Henry Winthrop Sargent IV in *Patriot's Farewell*

———————

The duty of a true patriot is to protect his country from its government.
~ Thomas Paine

———————

Choose Freedom!
~ Henry Winthrop Sargent IV

THE ICONIC TOAST TO BOSTON

And this is good old Boston,
The home of the bean and the cod,
Where the Lowells talk to the Cabots,
And the Cabots talk only to God.

PROLOGUE

The Friday after Thanksgiving
4:00 a.m.
The White House
Washington, DC

It began like any other day, albeit with a few wrinkles. Captain Dave Morrell, the head of the president's Secret Service detail, sat in the cool, dimly lit office where he diligently prepared for the First Family's protection. It was the day after an eventful Thanksgiving at the White House. To cap off a tumultuous week, President Henry Winthrop Sargent IV, together with family and close friends, intended to enjoy the long holiday weekend like many Americans.

Morrell had been Sarge's constant companion since their days together on Prescott Peninsula located within the Quabbin Reservoir in Central Massachusetts. Those had been tumultuous times as the nation was thrust into economic and societal collapse. A cyber attack had been orchestrated by John Morgan, the titular head of the Boston Brahmin. Working in concert with the former President of the United States, the devastating attack resulted in the collapse of the nation's power grid.

Their goals were complex and somewhat at odds with one another. Morgan thought the nation was in dire need of a reset to the values he held dear to his heart and upon which the nation was founded. The president, quite simply, wanted more power. The two believed they could have an amiable working relationship as they rebuilt the nation.

They were wrong.

Morgan succumbed to a heart attack within eighteen months of his life-threatening stroke while the Boston Brahmin sought refuge at Prescott Peninsula during the collapse. During that year of unrest and war, Morrell stood by Sarge's side as they protected the Boston Brahmin families from a variety of threats. He was rewarded for his loyalty by placing him in charge of the First Family's Secret Service detail after Sarge was elected president.

Sarge and Morrell had more than a working relationship. They were friends who oftentimes shared a beer or two at the end of a long day. Morrell had become a sounding board for Sarge beyond the inner circle comprised of the Loyal Nine and his other advisers.

Regardless of their close personal relationship, Morrell took his job very seriously. He'd studied the importance of protecting the life of the President of the United States. Even before he was inaugurated, Abraham Lincoln had been the target of assassination plots. Although the Civil War had not officially started, the sabers were rattling on both sides of the Mason-Dixon Line. Despite the threats, like most presidents before him, Lincoln had little use for personal protection, rejecting the offers from friends, police, and the military to accompany him during public appearances.

After Lincoln was assassinated in 1865, there were others who suffered a similar fate. Just a few years later, in 1881, President James Garfield was casually walking through a train station when a man emerged from the small crowd to fatally shoot the president in the back. In 1901, President William McKinley was shot at a reception in Buffalo, New York. He died days later. Then the world mourned when President John Kennedy was assassinated in Dallas, Texas, around Thanksgiving in 1963.

Other tragic deaths were avoided when unsuccessful assassination attempts on Presidents Teddy Roosevelt, Franklin D. Roosevelt, Harry Truman, Gerald Ford, and Ronald Reagan captured the attention of the nation during the twentieth century.

Against that backdrop, Morrell never took his job for granted. For all that Sarge had done in shepherding America back onto her feet, he still had his political detractors. Even as the Sargent administration began to wind down its two terms in office, Morrell was always by Sarge's side whether it was during their morning jogs or late afternoon beers together.

For his part, Morrell had been in the line of fire several times but never hit. He'd been spat upon but never flinched. He'd been cursed out but never let his emotions show. He was the consummate professional who prepared for this day just as he had each day of Sarge's presidency.

Daily, the Secret Service received an average of ten threats against any of its protectees, including the president. To ensure against an attack on a protectee, typically referred to by the acronym AOP, Captain Morrell and his team used a variety of surveillance techniques, tools, strategies, and procedures that were kept secret from the public.

One of those techniques was to keep extensive background files on people who were known threats to the president. For some, killing POTUS would be akin to winning the Powerball Lottery. The vast majority of these potential threats began with a vocal displeasure of government, followed by verbal altercations with other elected officials. Over time, their deluded minds focused on the nation's leading figurehead of politics—the president.

Morrell had often joked his desk was a mere seven feet from the Oval Office. What he didn't disclose was the fact it was located on a lower floor directly under the Oval Office. It wasn't widely known that a secret hidden staircase provided emergency access up to the Oval Office via a trapdoor under the president's desk. Sarge had offered his friend and protector a more prominent office space in the West Wing; however, Morrell turned him down. He needed to maintain a professional decorum coupled with a separation from the hustle and bustle of activity typically found in the West Wing.

Within Horsepower, the name given to Room W-16, the Secret Service Command Post, dozens of agents devoted their lives to protecting the First Family. Morrell was a captain in the US Army, but his official title was Special Agent in Charge, Presidential Protective Division. Technically, he was required to answer his phone with his complete title. However, he'd never done so. When seconds mattered during the protection of the president, he didn't want to waste time spewing out a mouthful of words.

Morrell commanded a team of agents that assisted him in the Presidential Protective Division. The Secret Service was created as an arm of the U.S. Treasury Department, chasing down currency counterfeiters during the Civil War and thereafter. While that was still their duty, the agency was better known for its protection services. The uniformed division worked in concert with Washington's Capitol Police, visibly safeguarding the White House complex and the vice president's residence. The plainclothes agents, like Morrell, devoted their lives to protecting their charges from any clear and present danger, from the ground to the sky.

Even at that hour, his fellow agents occupied cubicles outside his office, where they monitored surveillance cameras and television broadcasts. He was used to the low murmur of voices, tapping of keyboards, and radio chatter from the Capitol Police scanners. Their job was to protect the president, which necessarily required cooperation between local law enforcement, not only in Washington but wherever the president's travels took him for the day.

Morrell was primarily responsible for the protection of the president and his family. Other protectees, presidents past and the president-elect, fell under someone else's purview. That morning, *Professor*, the Secret Service's code name for Sarge because of his past teachings at the Harvard Kennedy School of Government, was still in residence. *Scribe*, the code name for Julia because of her career as a journalist for the *Boston Herald*, was also in the Executive Residence.

Unlike most presidential couples, Sarge and Julia slept together in the same bedroom. Oftentimes, because the president had to be called to duty at odd hours of the night, he preferred his wife to sleep in one of the other three bedrooms in the Executive Residence. That was not the case for Sarge and Julia, who were inseparable.

Inseparable, except for today.

Morrell rubbed his temples as he contemplated the challenge facing his team on that day. The president and his closest buddies were destined for a day of hunting. The First Lady, the vice president, and the White House chief of staff's wife, together with their children, were going to engage in a great American tradition—mall shopping on Black Friday.

PART I

The day after Thanksgiving—Black Friday
November 2024, early morning

CHAPTER ONE

5:00 a.m.
The Executive Residence
The White House
Washington, DC

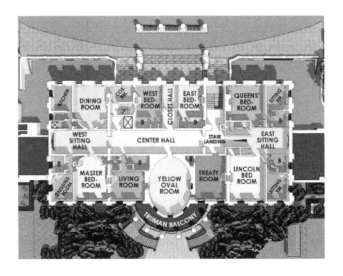

Sarge slept in fits and starts, driving a sleeping Julia crazy throughout most of the night. To be sure, he'd faced many challenges throughout his presidency that might cause anyone in his position to endure a sleepless night or two. However, the tense confrontation he'd had with his fellow Boston Brahmin the night before weighed heavily on his mind.

He exhaled and stretched his arms, trying to let out some nervous energy and release the tension that had plagued him all night. He desperately needed to run and contemplated calling Morrell to tell him of the change in plans. The two men enjoyed their morning jaunts around the National Mall and the Capitol Reflection Pool.

Sarge shook his head as if to dispel the thought. Morrell's job would be challenging enough that day without POTUS suddenly changing up his schedule. He leaned over to check on his bride, the mother of his three children, and the love of his life. Julia was sleeping peacefully, and he didn't dare wake her.

He pulled on his dark crimson sweatpants and a gray tee shirt, both of which were emblazoned with the Harvard University logo, his alma mater. Next, he worked up a good sweat on the treadmill located at the far end of the Executive Residence in a converted sitting room. There were plenty of places to sit in the White House, so Sarge had made a morning gym out of the space.

Afterwards, he ducked into the kitchen, where the staff was prepping breakfast for Julia and the kids. Sarge was a light eater in the morning, generally grabbing a muffin or a bagel and his beloved iced chocolate mocha latte. Throughout the years, both before, during, and after the collapse of America, Sarge's lips had never touched a cup of hot coffee. He wasn't anti-coffee by any means. He simply liked it cold with a strong chocolatey taste.

While he munched on a blueberry muffin that was to die for, he stared absently out the window toward Blair House across from Lafayette Park. A light snow had fallen throughout the night, leaving about three inches on the ground. The President's Guest House, as it was known, had hosted several members of the Boston

Brahmin inner circle as the First Family hosted their final Thanksgiving in the White House.

In the sitting hall that separated the dining room and the master bedroom, multiple television monitors were mounted on the walls flanking the tall, arched window. This was the Sargents' family room. The exquisite furnishings that ordinarily hosted visiting dignitaries fortunate enough to be allowed into the First Family's residence had been removed and replaced with slipcovered furniture surrounded by toy boxes. The Sargents' children, ages three through seven, were not unlike any other kids their age. They needed a place to play, flop, and, well, be kids.

A member of the staff offered him another blueberry muffin, warmed and dripping with melted butter. On most days, he'd politely decline. However, this was the start of a three-day weekend of fun with his family and friends. They'd be eating, drinking, and putting the stresses of running a nation behind them before undertaking the task of winding down their administration. With a shrug and a smile, Sarge graciously accepted and took a man-size bite out of the muffin.

One by one, Sarge grabbed the remotes and powered on the monitors. *Why do you torture yourself, pal?* he asked himself as the talking heads of the cable news networks filled the screens.

After the cyber attack took down the nation's power grid, America had been thrust into a brutal, seven-month-long struggle to survive. While most Americans fought for food and clean water, others, like the Boston Brahmin, fought for the heart and soul of the country. After the former president called in the United Nations peacekeeping forces to quash any dissent to his authority, Sarge led patriots across the nation in a battle over tyranny.

The victory, although partial, was hard fought. The former president, who'd polarized the nation on so many issues, retreated to his home state of Hawaii. From there, he managed to convince Hawaii, California, Oregon, and Washington, along with parts of Nevada and Arizona, to secede from the Union. Despite Sarge's efforts at a hastily called Constitutional Convention in St. Louis, the Pacific States of America broke away, leaving the nation divided.

In addition to getting the country back on its feet, Sarge's goal was to bring the fifty states back together. He'd negotiated with the former president without success. He'd made veiled economic and military threats to resolve the issue, but the Pacific States controlled a significant amount of military assets in both California and Hawaii.

As a result, in the last year of Sarge's administration and as a new president was being elected to replace him, the Pacific Statehood Act made its way through Congress. Sarge wanted a clean bill, free of extraneous issues or conditions. In his mind, a straight up and down vote that either allowed the Pacific States to return to the United States or not was appropriate.

Instead, as was often the case in Washington, lawmakers overplayed their hand. The economic and social issues insisted upon by the former president as a condition precedent to reunification were included in the bill. The very cause of the nation's polarization prior to the collapse was about to be codified into law.

The vote was close, but forces unknown to Sarge played a hand in the bill's passage. Now, he was faced with the prospect of a veto that might destroy the positive legacy he'd established while in the White House. His bringing America back from collapse would be overshadowed if not forgotten if he left office with the nation divided.

With a long sigh, he finished his muffin and took a long sip of his iced coffee. His eyes darted from screen to screen, studying who was being interviewed and what the topic of conversation was. He shook his head in dismay, not surprised in the least at how the coverage portrayed the news of the day.

CHAPTER TWO

6:00 a.m.
The Executive Residence
The White House
Washington, DC

His success in staring down the Chinese over the Straits of Taiwan and rescuing the American ambassador hardly got a mention on the news networks. China was America's greatest geopolitical threat. They had been for many decades. While the Russians were a threat to Europe and America's allies in the region, it was Communist China that had the capability of attacking the United States militarily and winning. Many had pointed to Beijing's provocations in the South China Sea as the potential flashpoint. Sarge disagreed. If America came to blows with China, it would be over Taiwan's sovereignty.

The six news networks were all over the board that morning. The *Today* show provided a color-coded map revealing the change in the balance of power within Congress once the Pacific Statehood Act was passed into law. The talking heads were salivating over the blue wave from the Pacific, as they called it, sweeping over U.S. politics.

Good Morning America focused on the presidential election that had just been held and the effect passage of the act would have on the new administration's ability to govern. The president-elect, Stanford Rawlins, was a Southern democrat governor from South Carolina who had been instrumental in bringing the coalition of Southern states to the table during the Constitutional Convention. It was a daunting task, as the former Confederate states would have been just fine re-forming their perceived glory days.

Rawlins was the handpicked choice of the Boston Brahmin. A democrat whose economic policies and international worldview were considered moderate, Rawlins had no desire to advance the social issues pursued by the far-left wing of his party. Most importantly, Rawlins understood his role and where his allegiances stood—to Sarge and the Boston Brahmin.

Interestingly, CNN also covered the presidential election of three weeks ago but from a different perspective, one that Sarge was puzzled by. As of that Friday, Virginia's thirteen electoral votes had not been officially cast for Rawlins yet. Not that it mattered. His victory was substantial, and the thirteen electors couldn't sway the result. However, it was the reason for the breaking news that caught Sarge's eye. CNN's chyron read VOTING IRREGULARITIES TAINT RESULTS.

Sarge read the closed-captioning on the CNN screen to get a sense of what issues had been raised. To be sure, the Boston Brahmin had the wherewithal to steer any election, both foreign and domestic, to achieve the desired result. However, in the case of Rawlins's victory in early November, they didn't see the need. President-elect Rawlins was deemed to be a sure thing.

Now, investigative reporters at CNN were suggesting otherwise. Moreover, it was their lead story. Sarge made a mental note to discuss this with his chief-of-staff and longtime friend, Donald Quinn, when they gathered in the Oval Office following his morning briefing.

Newsmax had several constitutional pundits on that morning, discussing the Pacific Statehood vote and the complex maneuverings that must've taken place to gain its passage. They viewed the passage as a win for the president. Sarge disagreed. He hadn't won yet.

When he took office in the throes of the nation's collapse, his focus was to bring stability to a nation that had reached the precipice of anarchy. It was back to the basics, as he'd told Donald on day two of his presidency.

His first priority was to secure the southern border from any potential geopolitical threats. America was at its weakest and ripe for attack. While its governing apparatus was in disarray, any number of nations could've taken advantage, as the UN tried, and caused the United States of America to cease to exist.

Sarge had appealed to the patriotic nature of its military leadership. He ensured the members of the armed services were paid and fed. The show of strength and solidarity was intended to warn off the Pacific States from expanding its territory while dispelling any notion of America's international foes attacking our shores.

With the nation secured, his next priority was to bring back the nation's economy, beginning with reestablishing the gold standard for America's currency. His mentor, John Morgan, had helped in that regard by storing gold and silver bullion at One Prescott Peninsula, the name given to their secure location as the collapse unfolded. Through Donald's efforts, the Boston Brahmin had liquidated domestic holdings into precious metals that would later become the basis for returning to the gold-backed dollar. A king's ransom in super-priority U.S Treasury bonds was issued in exchange for the bullion, making the Boston Brahmin the nation's single largest debtholder. With China being relegated to ordinary creditor status, they no longer held the U.S. by the throat financially.

With the dollar respected once again, Sarge issued executive orders designed to overturn any regulations from the prior administration that hampered the engines of manufacturing. For too many years, American business was unable to compete with China and other overseas manufacturers because they didn't operate on a level playing field. By eliminating the shackles on American production related to environmental and social matters, Sarge started with a clean slate. America's economy roared back to life, and within two years, the nation was at full employment.

As he neared the end of his presidency, he was disheartened to see how the country was falling back into its old ways that caused so much discord between Americans. He'd often lamented to Julia that people's memories were short. They'd forgotten how close they were to starvation as they fought one another over food. As criminal opportunists ran amok, violent crimes destroyed lives. And the threat of becoming subservient to a foreign power was real.

With the passage of the Pacific Statehood Act, he was concerned the return to rancor would be accelerated. His successor, President-elect Rawlins, was firmly against the act, as passed, although many others in his party were pushing it. Rawlins was firmly aligned with Sarge on the matter. His vice-presidential choice was as well. In an odd twist, the Republican candidate for president believed reunification was necessary regardless of the minutiae, as he called it, concerning social issues. It made for an interesting series of debates in which one might scratch his head as to which candidate leaned left or right.

Sarge leaned forward and studied the closed-captioning. In just a matter of weeks, he'd be sitting at home, in Boston, doing the same thing. Only he wouldn't be the president. He would, however, be pulling the strings.

Suddenly, Julia appeared behind him; lighting from the lamps gave away her approach by casting a shadow across the wall. Sarge leaned back and accepted a good morning kiss from the woman who'd been his rock throughout the last eight difficult years.

"Good morning, Mr. President," she said softly as she kissed his neck. "You slipped out of bed without telling me."

"I thought you needed a few more winks. I'm pretty sure I rolled around a lot last night."

"You did. A little more than usual, I might add. Methinks your confrontation with Gardner weighed on your mind more than you let on when we went to sleep."

Sarge nodded and sighed. "None of us expect to agree one hundred percent on any matter of importance. If we did, we'd fail. However, until Gardner became more active following his father's death, the dynamic has changed. I'm in the midst of a power struggle that Gardner has orchestrated for some time. I'm pissed at myself for not recognizing it and for being late to the game."

Julia hugged his neck and walked around to join him on the couch. She glanced at the televisions before turning to look her husband in the eye. "Well, based on last night's tossing and turning, I think you're prepared to be fully engaged. Here's the thing. As president, you've been, quite honestly, distracted."

Sarge laughed. "You think?"

"Yeah, Mr. President. It took a lot out of you to save America. Now you can focus your attention on the Boston Brahmin and any adversaries within the ranks who might try to make a power move against you."

"Like Gardner Lowell," added Sarge.

Julia chuckled. "Don't forget about mommy dearest. Constance put him up to this and is most likely the driving force behind all of it. She's been resentful of John's move to install you as the head of the Boston Brahmin since the beginning."

Sarge took a deep breath and squeezed his wife's hand. "I'll be battling new wars soon. It'll be a piece of cake compared to these last eight years."

Sarge said the words. However, he wasn't convinced. Neither was Julia.

CHAPTER THREE

7:00 a.m.
The Executive Residence
The White House
Washington, DC

While Sarge took a shower and got dressed for the day, Julia began the daily task of wrangling the children out of bed. For the first time in American history, three children had been born to a sitting president. In 1893, Esther Cleveland was the first child of a sitting president to be born in the White House.

The Sargents' first baby had been born on Inauguration Day seven and a half years prior. Henry Winthrop Sargent V, Win, was now growing up to become an astute young man. He certainly marched in his father's footsteps, revering all aspects of Sarge's life. Win proudly self-proclaimed himself to be *big-brother-in-chief* to his siblings.

After Sarge's reelection to a second term, Julia became pregnant with their daughter, Rose. She embodied her mother in every way. Her mannerisms. Her looks. Her eyes and their ability to melt Sarge into a ball of mush. Rose would never be a daddy's girl. She was

Julia's mini-me and would most likely grow up to hold her father in the palm of her hand.

Then along came Francis. The three-year-old toddler insisted upon being called Frank because it sounded rough and tough. He was wise beyond his years and capable of holding his own with any argument involving his siblings, or an adult for that matter. As Sarge often put it, Frank was a walking, talking middle finger who would do great things one day—albeit dangerous ones. Of that, Sarge was certain.

The kids were remarkably cooperative that morning as Julia rousted them out of their slumber. "You guys need to get ready. Susan and the girls will be here soon for our big shopping outing."

Susan Quinn, one of the Loyal Nine and Donald's wife, was a frequent visitor to the Executive Residence and a dear friend of Julia's. The Quinn daughters—Penny, who was nineteen, and Rebecca, age fifteen—were favorite playmates of the Sargent kids because they were almost adults, as Frank had declared one day. Penny had begun attending Wellesley back in Boston a year ago. Becca adored Rose, frequently referring to her as Princess Rose.

"Mom, where are we going shopping?" asked Rose, who would later conspire with Becca to choose their favorite stores.

"It's the largest shopping mall in the East," replied Julia as she adjusted Rose's pretty-in-pink dress. All the kids had to be well dressed, as the First Family, sans Sarge, would be on full display on the biggest shopping day of the year. "It's located in Pennsylvania."

"Where, Mom?" asked Win, who had his cell phone at the ready with Google Maps open. He fashioned himself a knowledgeable trip planner because he could navigate the routes.

"King of Prussia," she replied.

"Russia! No way!" shouted Rose. "It's too cold in Russia."

"You like the cold," said Frank, inserting himself into the conversation.

"Not that cold," Rose countered. "That's, um, well, Russia is polar-bear cold."

Julia, who often had difficulty getting a word in when the kids were on a roll, intervened to explain. "Guys, King of Prussia. Not Russia. It's a town outside Philadelphia."

"Oh," said Rose, who was genuinely dejected at not traveling to the *real Russia*. Plus, she actually liked cold weather, which prompted her to race away from the group to the nearest window. "It snowed some more!"

Her exclamation caused Win and Frank to join her by the windows. The three faces were pressed against the glass, taking in the unusually early snowfall in the District.

"Are you guys on Santa watch already?" Sarge surprised the kids as he snuck into the room unannounced.

"Daddy!" yelled Rose joyously as if she hadn't seen her father in weeks. She began to run toward him to get a hug when she suddenly stopped in her tracks. The young fashionista had a puzzled look on her face. "Where's your suit, Daddy?"

Julia took a few steps toward her husband. "Yes, Mr. President. Good question."

Sarge studied his attire from head to toe. "It's casual Friday."

"I see," she said with a chuckle. She approached him to get a closer look. She adjusted his shirt and patted him on the chest. "Well, at least it matches."

Sarge was dressed in camouflage clothing and boots. Following the morning briefing, he and his entourage would board Marine One for Western Maryland before meeting up with the Loyal Nine families at Camp David for a weekend getaway.

"Mom, I wanna go hunting with Dad," said Win with a hint of whine in his voice.

Sarge detected his son's disappointment and addressed the issue instead of making Julia the bad guy. "Not this time, Win. This is a new location for us, and we have some business to discuss."

"Dad, I have a high security clearance," Win insisted.

"Me too," interjected Frank, who pushed his way past his brother to stand directly in front of Sarge. The young boy scowled as he tried to exert his will over his father.

Sarge made eye contact with Julia, who gave him that *whatcha gonna do, boy* look. Sarge turned his attention to his sons. Fortunately, Rose wanted no part of hunting unless it was for pretty dresses or yacht clothing from Vineyard Vines, Becca's favorite.

"Listen, you two. We've got a big weekend ahead at Camp David. I'll do the hunting, and how about you two help me cook the deer meat?"

"But I want to shoot my rifle," said Win.

Sarge scowled. This was a tough sell. He enjoyed taking Win on his hunting trips. His experiences during the collapse had taught him the importance of being prepared for the worst side of society to rear its ugly head. Win should be able to protect himself whether he was seven or seventeen.

"Okay, I'll make you a deal." Sarge knelt down in front of his boys. "Win, I'll arrange for you and Uncle Drew to do some target practice together. Frank, we'll bring along your Red Ryder." Sarge had given Frank a Daisy Red Ryder BB gun for his third birthday. Julia had not jumped for joy over the present but certainly understood Sarge's reasoning.

"I'll get it!" said Frank. After a moment, Win nodded in agreement. Drew always let him shoot the big guns, too.

The kids hustled off to the dining room for breakfast, leaving Sarge and Julia alone. She took a sip of coffee and asked, "Hanson Briscoe? Are you sure about this?"

Sarge grimaced and shook his head back and forth like a pendulum. "Well, no, not really. Briscoe does have roots to the Founding Fathers, just like we do. Hell, he was a descendent of John Hanson, the president of the First Continental Congress. Some argue he was the first president of the United States. Not George Washington."

Julia scowled. "That's all well and good, but he's connected to George Trowbridge. We've never been able to trust his motives, and at times, it's uncertain where he stands."

Sarge laughed. "That's the problem with all those Yalies. They're squirrely."

Sarge was making reference to the Eastern U.S. elites led by the

Trowbridge family who went to college at Yale. Yale and Harvard alumni were natural rivals, both in terms of school spirit and business. Over the years, Trowbridge interests had conflicted with those of the Boston Brahmin on occasion. There wasn't necessarily any bad blood between the two groups although John Morgan had warned Sarge to keep his distance. His decision to accept Briscoe's longstanding invitation to hunt his property at Monocacy Farm was a way for Sarge to lay the groundwork for a future working relationship with the group. Plus, it was on the way to Camp David.

Sarge glanced at his watch. It was almost time for the Presidential Daily Briefing, and he wanted to catch up with his vice president before they got started. He kissed his wife, stopped to provide each of his children a peck on the cheek, and exited the Executive Residence with a little extra spring in his step.

CHAPTER FOUR

8:30 a.m.
The Executive Residence
The White House
Washington, DC

The Executive Residence erupted into chaos. As Susan Quinn and her daughters made their way to the stair landing outside the Treaty Room, Rose sought out her best teenage friend. She and Becca locked eyes before the two soul mates erupted in excitement.

Julia came rushing out of the master bedroom, where she was putting the final touches on her outfit for the day. She was going to keep it simple with a pair of khakis and a Vermont Flannel shirt. She was slipping on her L.L.Bean shoes over her woolen socks as she joined the joyous reunion.

"Girls, we just saw each other yesterday, remember?" said Susan with a laugh. She and Julia hugged one another and then admired each other's attire. Susan commented first. "Khakis and flannel. Perfect."

Julia returned the compliment. "Cords and a sweater. Well done. We don't want to give the media anything to criticize."

"Oh, they'll find something anyway. For one thing, the DC locals will question why we went shopping in Pennsylvania instead of here."

"They'll knock our use of a chopper to get there, calling us elitist," Julia added. "You know, I never expected them to bow down and kiss our asses. However, at least be fair, considering what our husbands went through to keep Black Friday as a, um, a thing."

Julia led Susan to the coffee bar while the kids compared their shopping lists. Susan continued. "I remember that last Thanksgiving at 1PP with all of the families. We thought Black Friday was a thing of the past."

Julia took a sip of coffee and nodded. "Heck, we thought America was a thing of the past. Yet here we are. The nation is back, and shopping is too."

"So are the plans the same?" asked Susan. "The mall. Camp David. Back on Monday morning?"

"I think so," replied Julia. She was never certain of anything. Sarge could be pulled away without notice at any time of day. That morning, she'd prayed for an uneventful weekend so they could enjoy some time with their friends.

"When do we leave?" asked Susan.

"Abbie is gonna sit in on the PDB this morning and then join us on the South Lawn. Captain Morrell arranged for us to fly on the backup Marine One and land right by the mall at Lockheed Martin's heliport adjacent to the mall property."

"That's convenient," said Susan. "I bet Dave is pulling his hair out today."

Julia laughed. "He doesn't have much left after eight years of this. He was appreciative that we gave him a heads-up about our plans. It'll be a tough assignment to secure the mall anyway, much less on Black Friday."

Susan, who lived with the constant threats because her husband was Sarge's chief of staff, had learned to have complete confidence in the Secret Service personnel to protect her family. "I have my shopping list. Donald has lost quite a bit of weight in the last year."

"I've noticed. Is he okay?"

"At first, we thought it was stress. The White House docs told us it might be the onset of celiac disease. They've modified his diet to combat the effects of the disease. The hard part is making him follow their suggestions."

Julia gave her dear friend a hug. "In a couple of months, we'll be regular old people again. Less stress and very little public scrutiny. We can take better care of our minds and bodies when we're out of this fishbowl."

Susan nodded and dropped her head. She'd been feeling the pressures alongside her husband, who was carrying the weight of managing a presidency as well as the financial burdens of the Boston Brahmin on his shoulders.

"I'll miss Camp David," Julia continued in an attempt to change the subject. "It kind of reminds me of Quabbin Reservoir. Other than the guards, it had become a family gathering place for us. A place where we could hide away from the outside world."

"I like the family part the best. It's so rare for us to be alone with just the Loyal Nine. I know we're part of a bigger picture, but I will always look at our group as different."

Julia understood. "In a way, I wish there was a way out of the Boston Brahmin relationship. They exist for a singular purpose and that is to manipulate things. That's stressful in and of itself."

"Don't we know it. The thing is," began Susan, "the Boston Brahmin is all business, especially for the members of the old men's club like Cabot and Lodge. The Loyal Nine is different. We're friends and family first."

"Don't forget about God and country," added Julia. She offered words of encouragement. "Listen, eight more weeks until it's over. Right?"

Neither wife would ever admit to their husbands that the presidency weighed so heavily on them. They'd been supportive throughout because they were patriots first and wives second. However, that didn't stop them from longing for the political off-ramp.

CHAPTER FIVE

8:30 a.m.
The Lowell Estate
Wellesley, Massachusetts

The Boston Brahmin had existed as a secretive group of powerful business leaders, politicians, military officers, and philanthropists since the founding of America. They were stealthy. Working in the shadows. Unseen patriots who were mostly direct lineal descendents of the Founding Fathers and the Sons of Liberty—brave men who risked their lives to break away from tyrannical rule to form America.

For two hundred fifty years, they gathered together to forge a path for the nation. They were everywhere and played a part in most aspects of Americans' lives. Many people never had an inkling that a shadow government, a cabal of this nature, even existed. Yet the names of the Boston Brahmin were etched throughout history as instrumental in the nation's founding—Lowell, Cabot, Lodge, Winthrop, Peabody, Endicott, Bradlee, and Sargent.

For decades prior to Sarge's election as president, the Boston Brahmin had been led by John Adams Morgan, a kingmaker of sorts whose invisible hand of power held a firm grip on the nation's political and financial affairs. His closest confidants were Walter Cabot and Lawrence Lowell.

Cabot, a direct descendent of John Cabot, a shipbuilder during the time of the Revolutionary War, was tied to virtually every major defense contractor in the nation. He had long since retired, but he was still active in the dealings of the Boston Brahmin. His counterpart, Lawrence Lowell, was a direct descendent of John Lowell, a federal judge in the the First Continental Congress. He was one of a long line of powerful attorneys who shaped the law and was instrumental in Supreme Court nominees over the years. Following his death years ago, he'd left behind his wife, Constance, and children, the oldest of which was Gardner Lowell.

Before Morgan's death, the vaunted leader of the Boston Brahmin executive council had made it clear that Sarge would succeed him in guiding the group through the twenty-first century. This decision, coupled with the death of Lawrence Lowell, had resulted in a power struggle within the Boston Brahmin. With Sarge's ascendency to the highest office in the land, he'd cemented his role as the formal head of the Boston Brahmin.

That didn't mean Constance Lowell and her son, Gardner, had to like it. For years, despite Sarge's accomplishments, an underlying jealousy had festered beneath the surface. Both Constance and Gardner worked behind the scenes to undermine Sarge when possible and to poison his accomplishments in the minds of their fellow Brahmin, especially the elderly Walter Cabot.

Yesterday, on Thanksgiving Day, following a frenetic rescue of the U.S. ambassador to Taiwan and the aftermath of the political machinations surrounding the Pacific Statehood Act, Sarge took the opportunity to bring the Boston Brahmin together in the Solarium, a place of relaxation on the top floor of the Executive Residence. He wanted to reassure his fellow Brahmin that they would profit greatly from his last seven weeks in office as a lame duck president. It was time to reward his associates for their sacrifices and efforts in rebuilding the nation.

Only Gardner Lowell voiced his displeasure with Sarge and his promises. Vociferously, in fact. The two argued, and Sarge found himself defending his decisions to Gardner while the others tried not to take sides. Sarge had sensed Gardner's jealousy in the past and expected this confrontation would occur at some point.

After the back-and-forth, Sarge brought the hostilities to an end by saying, "The point is none of us can enjoy the luxury of operating outside the group—going rogue, if you will. This group has been established to establish certain goals, and I've been charged with the responsibility of achieving them. Thus far, I've not failed any of you."

His words were true and accurate. He'd done an incredible job of stewarding their interests through the recovery and setting them up for years of financial gain. To drive the point home, Sarge demanded an up or down vote of confidence. He offered to step aside if his fellow Brahmin voted nay. Unanimously, with even Gardner choking out the word yea, Sarge received the affirmation he needed to move on.

Not unexpectedly, Gardner wasn't prepared to put the past behind them. He hissed in Sarge's ear as he pushed his way past his nemesis to exit the Solarium, "It's not over." Sarge was quick with his response. "It is for today."

Now, it was the day after Thanksgiving, and Gardner was still fuming over his rebuke.

Constance, the Lowell family matriarch, had more backbone and political cunning than her deceased husband. Lawrence had been an exceptional, high-power lawyer who'd made a name for himself around the world. Gardner followed in his father's footsteps and became an accomplished international lawyer who advocated on behalf of foreign governments when they dealt with Washington. Neither had the toughness and grit that Constance possessed. Nor were they capable of controlling their emotions.

She settled into a chair across from Gardner at the breakfast table, glaring at her son, who was acting like a petulant brat.

"I can't believe he defied me like that, Mother!" Gardner complained as he sipped his tea.

Following the confrontation in the Solarium, Gardner had returned to the suite the Lowells occupied at the Trump International Hotel on Pennsylvania Avenue. They'd checked out and immediately departed for the family estate in Wellesley, an affluent suburb of Boston.

Constance tried to calm her son down while appeasing him at the same time. "It was too soon. We're only now laying the groundwork for his removal from the Brahmin completely. We went to Washington to defeat his wishes on the Statehood Act. We accomplished our mission."

Gardner was still fuming, but he managed a deep breath followed by an equally exaggerated exhale. He reminded himself of the accomplishment.

"I made that happen," he muttered.

"Yes, son, you did. It was a magnificent manipulation that caught them all off guard. Over time, our fellow Brahmin will see that it was you who brought the Pacific States back into the fold, and as a result, their wealth will increase exponentially."

"Far more than the hollow promises Sarge made last night," added Gardner.

Constance managed a smile. Gardner was just like her deceased husband. He needed constant reassurance to do her bidding. "Yes, son. When the time comes, you will disclose to the executive council the methods you deployed to achieve this great political win for them. You will be able to point out Sarge's ineptitude in his attempts to defeat the vote."

Gardner furrowed his brow and became pensive. He leaned back in his chair and stared into the garden, where snow covered the plant life.

"You're right, Mother. However, I've made promises. Checks that, at present, I can't afford to cash. Everything I've planned depends on a major restructuring, an upheaval, within the hierarchy of the Boston Brahmin. My plan, um, our plan doesn't have a place at the table for Henry Winthrop Sargent IV."

Constance stood and walked around the table to grip her son by the shoulders. She patted him on the back and leaned into his ear to whisper, "We've discussed this. Your traps are being set. You shall have your restructuring. You simply have to be patient." She patted him on the back again and left the room without another word.

Suddenly, Gardner's burner phone began to vibrate, indicating an incoming call from one of three sources. A sly grin came across his face when he saw the caller identification. Gardner Lowell was many things. Patient was not one of them.

CHAPTER SIX

8:45 a.m.
The Lowell Estate
Wellesley, Massachusetts

"Talk to me," he demanded from the caller without so much as a hello. Gardner understood diplomacy. He'd made a career of navigating the relationships between presidents and kings, dictators and clergy. His underlings, however, were not deserving of common courtesies.

The terms operative and fixer were often used in the world of shadowy dealings. In government, operatives were nameless, faceless individuals who performed off-the-books activities that included assassinations, blackmail, and other forms of subterfuge to gain political advantage. For corporations or high-profile individuals, a fixer was a trusted person or entity who, well, fixed things. It could be a CEO who got caught dipping his wick in the wrong inkwell. It might be the son of a politician who was caught driving a hundred and ten miles per hour through a school zone. The tasks varied, but they had one thing in common—surreptitious action.

A family as powerful as the Lowells had to call upon both operatives and fixers in order to maintain their wealth and power. Oftentimes, they called upon resources utilized by the Boston Brahmin. However, in Gardner's quest to unseat Sarge from the executive council and otherwise destroy his life, he had to rely upon an outsider.

The man he'd entrusted with such matters for many years was known to him as Mr. West. The seventyish, gaunt man resembled an undertaker more than he did someone's vision of an operative. On the rare occasions Gardner met with Mr. West in person, he was always dressed the same. Black suit, starched white shirt and a solid black tie. His neatly combed white hair gave away his age although his pale, mostly wrinkle-free faced seemed to defy the aging process.

Regardless, the man got results for Gardner and had performed admirably during the manipulation of the Pacific Statehood votes. A congressman from Indiana. A senator from Iowa. A congressman from Georgia. Mr. West made bribes, removed obstacles, and in the rare event nonviolent methods of coercion were unsuccessful, all other options were on the table.

As soon as Gardner had exited the White House and the network of surveillance devices it employed, he phoned Mr. West and let him know he intended to step up his efforts against one particular adversary. Mr. West was not surprised, nor intimidated, by the requests made of him. He assured his employer that the asset was in place to accomplish his goals.

"Arrangements have been made, sir," the man's gravelly voice responded. "As per our agreement, means and methods will not be disclosed to you in order to maintain a modicum of plausible deniability."

"Agreed. When will I receive confirmation?"

"Not from me. The news reports will suffice."

Gardner smiled again. By design, the two men limited their telephonic communications to less than one minute. After a call was placed between them, the burner phones would be destroyed and a new one chosen from more than a dozen in each man's possession. Likewise, personal meetings between the two were conducted in locations capable of blocking NSA satellite surveillance.

Gardner was extremely careful in carrying out his plan of dethroning Sarge. Whatever took place could not lead back to him. He needed to be viewed by the Boston Brahmin as the savior who was perfectly suited to pick up the pieces.

Feeling better about his day, he decided to play dad to his grandson and namesake, Gardner Percival Lowell II, who would one day follow in his footsteps. Yesterday, he'd stood up to the Sargent boy Win and called his father a weak president. Gardner was inwardly incensed that his son had admonished the young Percy in front of the others. It was that show of weakness that confirmed his decision to keep his son out of Brahmin business.

Perhaps walking the estate in the snow, a little grandfather-grandson time, would enable Gardner to continue grooming the young boy for great things.

CHAPTER SEVEN

8:45 a.m.
The West Wing
The White House
Washington, DC

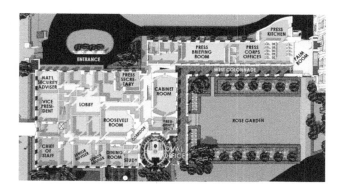

While the West Wing was being built in 1902, President Theodore Roosevelt's office was temporarily located in the present-day location of the Roosevelt Room. It was so named by President Richard Nixon in honor of both Roosevelts—Theodore for building the West Wing and Franklin for its expansion years later. The windowless room in the center of the West Wing had always been an all-purpose conference room used by the White House staff and, now, for the president's daily briefings. It had been upgraded over the last several years to include a wall of televisions and a large screen for multimedia presentations.

Because of the three attempts to assassinate Sarge during his two terms in office, he preferred to utilize the Roosevelt Room for meetings with foreign dignitaries, opting to stay closer to home and the protection afforded him on U.S. soil.

Every day, whether weekend or holiday, the director of National Intelligence and his team prepared the Presidential Daily Brief, commonly referred to by the acronym PDB. It consisted of reports from the nation's intelligence community. Sarge and Donald requested the meeting be divided into international and domestic issues.

Regarding foreign affairs, Sarge preferred to be briefed followed by a roundtable discussion among the senior officials concerning the issues of the day. As to domestic affairs, he preferred to keep his decision-making process close to the vest, frequently adjourning to the Oval Office with his closest confidants. Namely, Donald, his chief of staff; General Francis Crowninshield Bradlee, or Brad; and Dr. John Joseph Warren, affectionately known as J.J.

The three men were part of the Loyal Nine, the close group of friends who fought together to save the nation during the collapse. Of the Loyal Nine, only Sarge held a place within the upper echelon of the Boston Brahmin. That did not, however, prevent him from sharing those secret discussions with his loyal friends and advisors.

Sarge was met outside the hallway by his longtime White House secretary, Betty Greer. Betty had remained loyal and faithful to her president, and incredibly, she didn't burn out from the rigors of the job. Standing next to Betty was Donald, who, as always, seemed to have an armful of binders and reports to dole out at the briefing.

Betty had a large grin on her face. "You're looking dapper this morning, Mr. President." She and Sarge had that kind of relationship after eight years.

Sarge laughed. "You know, Betty, you and Julia seem to have some kind of special wiring between your brains. She had a similar reaction to my attire."

"We girls have to stick together," she said before becoming more serious. "Sir, I have several phone calls from members of Congress. The House Minority Leader would like to schedule a ceremonial signing of the Pacific Statehood Act into law."

"I'm sure he would," said Sarge with a glance toward his friend and compatriot Donald. "Wait until I'm on Marine One, and then let him know that the PDB ran long, so there was no time to broach the subject with me. How's that?"

Betty smiled. "I'll tell him to pound sand if you'd like. I don't have much use for the man."

"I couldn't agree more," said Donald. "He's chompin' at the bit to get the reins of power once the Pacific states are readmitted. He can wait a little while longer."

Sarge winked at Donald. Maybe a *lotta while longer*.

Betty addressed another matter. "Sir, the White House staff will be operating on a skeleton crew over the weekend. Um, would you like me to come in to—"

"No way, Betty. In fact, I know you. Don't make me contact Morrell to revoke your access privileges until Monday morning."

She raised her hands in surrender. "Okay. Okay. You're the boss. As soon as you're wheels up, I'm outta here. I have grandkids I haven't seen in months."

Sarge and Donald said their goodbyes to Betty. Donald handed Sarge his copy of the PDB and then gestured toward the door. "There's nothing earth-shattering in there today. Most of it is follow-up on the Taiwan matter and Beijing's response to our perceived outrageous intervention in the region."

Sarge smiled and nodded. He'd been a thorn in China's side since the beginning of his presidency. The economic collapse that resulted from the power grid being taken down by the cyber attacks had burdened the recovery effort for years. China had assumed they'd turn to them for consumer goods to get America back on her feet. Sarge had had a better idea.

He felt the nation had become beholden to China, who held much of America's debt. Rather than continuing to rely on foreign goods to sell to U.S. consumers, Sarge worked with Congress to rewrite labor laws, repeal overly restrictive environmental regulations, and instituted tort reforms to reduce the litigation burdens on business. As a result of his agenda being passed, American manufacturers and suppliers could compete on an even playing field with China and other foreign nations.

An ancillary effect of Sarge's policies was a monumental shift in where other nations purchased their consumer products. Sarge immediately sought treaties with the nations of Europe and Asia so they'd become less reliant on Chinese products as well. Soon, America's engines of prosperity were roaring, and for the first time, the nation exported a much larger number of goods than it imported.

As he entered the Roosevelt room, Sarge thumbed through the binder to the highlights section that he insisted on being included in each briefing. If there was a topic of interest that he wanted to see fleshed out, he'd bring it up first. On this day, the reaction of the Chinese appeared to dominate the briefing.

"Good morning, all," said Sarge as he entered the room. Everyone stood from the chairs out of respect and returned the greeting. Sarge glanced around to see who was in attendance and saw a couple of new faces as well as one who had been absent for several weeks.

"Good morning, Mr. President," greeted Vice President Abigail Morgan Jackson. Abbie was a longtime friend of Sarge's, and the two had once had a brief relationship until her father, Sarge's godfather John Morgan, discouraged it. Abbie had been elected senator from New York and immediately became a vice presidential hopeful. The campaign came to a screeching halt as the cyber attack occurred just months before election day.

"Well, Abbie, this is certainly a pleasure. I didn't really expect you to be here this morning."

"Well, sir, I have plans to further stimulate the economy today. I thought I'd attend the PDB before I set out."

Sarge eased into his chair and whispered to Abbie, "I take it Drew made it home okay."

She nodded. "He claims he slept on the transports. However, Drew also complained about King snoring so loudly that he almost asked the pilots to roll down the windows on the C130 to drown out the noise."

Sarge smiled. He'd come to rely heavily upon Drew Jackson, a former operative who'd worked with Sarge's deceased brother, Steven. Drew headed up a covert unit of operatives at Aegis, the Boston Brahmin's security company. It was through Drew's efforts that the U.S. ambassador to Taiwan had been recovered after being taken against his will.

While Drew was not one of the original Loyal Nine, he had been welcomed into the group after the death of Steven. He was never envisioned as a replacement for Sarge's brother; however, the two men were out of the same mold. And now the Loyal Nine were technically just eight.

Katie O'Shea, the ninth member and Steven's girlfriend, was an intelligence operative and an inside spy who'd infiltrated the prior administration. She'd been isolated from the group after Sarge learned she'd become disgruntled with Morgan's decision to place Sarge at the head of the Boston Brahmin. Katie firmly believed Steven was more deserving of the job, or at least a seat at the table of the powerful Brahmin. Her constant badgering of Steven had caused him to lose focus, which might have resulted in his death.

After she was alienated from the Loyal Nine, Katie had been assigned to Aegis. She had been killed in a terrorist attack in Berlin while running a security detail for an associate of the Boston Brahmin, an international financier. It was a freak occurrence that was deemed unavoidable. Half of her team and a number of civilians were also killed.

Sarge put his arm around Abbie's shoulder as he spoke. "Julia and Susan are probably upstairs if you'd rather join them."

"No way. I'm gonna use my high security clearance to find out the details of what Drew went through in Taiwan. He won't tell me anything, as usual."

Sarge furrowed his brow. "You guys have that deal, right?"

"Yes, sort of a don't ask, don't tell arrangement. I won't tell him about the politics of our jobs, and he won't tell me about getting shot at or almost dying."

"It's worked well for eight years, and considering your pregnancy, it's for the best. Don't you agree?"

Abbie sighed and unconsciously rubbed her seven-month-pregnant belly. She and Drew were expecting their first child together in late January just as their administration was coming to an end.

"Of course, you're right. I feel like such a wuss."

"You're being smart and avoiding stressful situations. Doctor's orders, and mine." Then Sarge paused and disclosed to Abbie a decision he'd made that morning. "Abbie, this is for your ears only. Understood?"

Her eyes tried to pierce Sarge's mind to determine what was coming next. "Of course."

"Do not repeat this to Drew, but I'm sidelining him until our term in office ends. Sure, he'll have things to do to prepare us for life after the White House. In the meantime, I will not put him in harm's way."

Abbie licked her lips, and it appeared she was on the verge of tears. Relieved, she mouthed the words *thank you* before hastily standing and excusing herself. She regained her composure long enough to wish everyone a relaxing long weekend with their families and friends. As soon as she exited, the Secret Service moved into the hallway and shut the door.

Sarge got started. "Let's talk about the aftermath of Taiwan first. I see a couple of new faces. I assume you two are from State?" Sarge was referring to the State Department.

The two young Asian men nodded in unison. One of them sat a little taller in his chair. "Yes, Mr. President. I'm Brandon Keltic, and this is my assistant, Ming Wang."

Sarge glanced around the room at the other attendees and then gestured to the newcomer, indicating he should get started. "Let's go, Brandon."

CHAPTER EIGHT

9:00 a.m.
The Oval Office
The White House
Washington, DC

The Oval Office has been the center of power for American presidents since its construction was completed in 1909. Three eleven-foot-tall windows overlooked the snow-covered South Lawn and patio just outside. The room had been decorated to Sarge's liking, including the nineteenth-century partner's desk. The oak desk with leather inlay was exquisitely adorned with brass appointments. When Winthrop Sargent Gilman, one of Sarge's ancestors, opened his bank in the early 1900s, this had been his desk. It had been passed along through the years to Sarge's father and ultimately to him.

Sarge entered the Oval Office with Donald following the PDB. The first thing they noticed was the easel standing near Sarge's desk with a dry-erase board perched on it. It had been there for days, as the Oval Office had become the center of the battle to defeat the Pacific Statehood Act.

"I need to get Ocampo to remove this damn thing," said Donald as he approached the easel. Marcos Ocampo, a former student of Sarge's at the Harvard Kennedy School of Government, was a valued member of the White House communications team.

"No. Hang on a minute." Sarge studied the board and tilted his head as he viewed the numbers.

At the eleventh hour, and even as the vote was taking place in both the House and the Senate, a few surprises had caught Sarge off guard. He hadn't admitted this to Julia earlier, but another one of the reasons he was tossing and turning in bed last night was the haunting feeling that he'd been outmaneuvered.

Sarge had been a political novice when he entered public service as president-elect in the midst of the nation's collapse. However, he applied common sense and the principles of the Constitution to bring the nation back to greatness. Yet despite his on-the-job experience, somehow he'd missed the fact that somebody powerful was behind the scenes, causing votes to switch.

Naturally, following the previous night's encounter with Gardner Lowell, he presumed the culprit was within the ranks of the Boston Brahmin. He hoped to talk with Donald, J.J., and Brad while they were hunting to determine what Gardner's angle was. Despite the loss, Sarge had an ace in the hole in the form of the pocket veto. He simply needed to clear his head this weekend with family and friends to look at the ramifications of his decision from all angles.

CURRENT HOUSE

R-46% D-45% L-6% S-3%

NEW HOUSE

D-48% R-47% L-3% S-2%

CURRENT SENATE

R-49 D-45 I-6

NEW SENATE

R-48 D-46 I-6

Donald walked up to the dry-erase board and ran his fingers along the numbers. "We knew it would be close. Honestly, Sarge, I don't know why we lost those votes. Those who defected weren't even on our radar."

"Have we gotten soft? You know, lackadaisical as our term ends?"

"I don't think so," replied Donald with a somewhat reassuring tone. "We kicked Beijing's ass yesterday."

"And they're pissed. Suits me just fine. If this had been eight years ago, I would've never been as bold as we were."

"Rawlins is gonna have to deal with them, I'm afraid," added Donald.

"Unless they pull some crap in the next two months, anyway," said Sarge as he approached the board. He pointed at the percentages related to the new political makeup of the house and senate after passage. "Here's what we learned. A republican senator flipped for no reason. I'm thinking she was bought. The question is whether her political loyalties have shifted to the left."

"I can bring her in for a chat," offered Donald.

"Maybe. Let's wait a week or so. However, if she's shifted to the dems, and the independents find a reason to vote with the left, then suddenly Rawlins isn't facing a divided government."

"That was our check and balance," interjected Donald. "If he has both houses, as a democrat, he might be tempted to go off the reservation."

"Exactly," said Sarge. "Certainly, we know where his skeletons are hiding and where the bodies are buried. Enough to keep him in line, I hope. However, I don't want to hover over his presidency with an iron fist. It fosters resentment."

Donald started laughing. "You sounded exactly like John Morgan just now." Then Donald used his best Boston Brahmin accent to imitate Morgan. "Well said, Henry. You slug that Southerner with your iron fist as often as you deem fit."

Sarge burst out laughing, as he always did when Donald imitated Morgan. As the two men laughed, a gentle knock on the door was followed by Betty sticking her head through the crack.

"Mr. President, if you two are not in a deep conversation, may General Bradlee and Dr. Warren join you?"

Sarge calmed down and waved his arm toward her. "Absolutely, bring them in."

Brad and J.J. entered the Oval Office. They had changed out of their business attire into hunting gear.

"Well, it appears three of us know how to dress for deer hunting," said Brad with a chuckle as he pointed at Donald, who was wearing a gray pinstripe suit and red power tie befitting his political ideology.

Donald tugged at his lapels. "I'm a professional, General, and will remain so clothed until we are aboard Marine One."

J.J. pointed toward the snowy exterior. "Speaking of which, shouldn't we be airborne? It's supposed to get colder as the day goes on, with more snowfall possible."

Sarge glanced at the South Lawn and nodded. "I agree. There's nothing that needs to be discussed or decided standing in the Oval. The sooner we hit the woods and bag our limit, the sooner we'll be by the fire at Shangri-la."

Brad was confused. "Shangri-la? Why did you call it that?"

Sarge gestured for the men to follow him out of the Oval Office. "When FDR built the retreat with WPA money during the Great Depression, he thought it would be appropriate to call it Shangri-la. Ike became president and thought the reference was elitist considering people were still suffering in the aftermath of the Depression. As a result, the military man formally changed the name to Camp David, a nod to his career as a general and to honor his grandson, David."

"Geez, you'd think I'd know that," said Brad, an ardent student of military history.

Sarge slapped the back of his close friend, who'd led the charge to evict the United Nations peacekeeping forces out of the nation during the collapse. "It was a political move, which is my area of expertise. You keep finding ways to win battles, like in Taiwan, and I'll maneuver the political minefields. Deal?"

"Deal," replied Brad.

CHAPTER NINE

10:00 a.m.
White House Helipad
South Lawn
Washington, DC

One of the more awe-inspiring sights that any visitor to Washington might catch a glimpse of is the arrival of Marine One to the South Lawn. The president's helicopter arrives in a loud, masterfully choreographed manner that exudes the pomp and spectacle befitting the highest office in the land.

Marine One approaches the White House from the south, roaring up the Potomac, its powerful rotors drawing the attention of most anyone on the ground. After gracefully hooking around the Washington Monument, it descends toward a huge flowerbed shaped like the number 1 near the southwestern corner of the White House. Even when the ground was covered in snow, White House landscape personnel ensured the pilot had the capability to identify his landing zone.

The helicopter itself was striking. Its white top was rarely seen by those on the ground. Its massive size surprised most. Landing a helicopter the length of an eighteen-wheeler on the tight confines of the White House grounds isn't an easy feat. And, on this particular day, several exact duplicates of Marine One arrived near simultaneously, much to the delight of tourists who'd descended upon the District for the long Thanksgiving weekend. At the thunderous sound of their approach, pedestrians fortunate enough to be walking along the fence line on E Street NW had the best vantage point to view their arrival.

The grounds crew had cleared the snow and put into place the large red disks with a white plus sign in the middle for the pilots to expertly set their wheels on at landing. A highly specialized team of Marine pilots continuously trained for the delicate act of landing the behemoth chopper on the tiny, temporary helipad on the South Lawn.

As was always the case, despite inclement weather, a press gaggle had gathered near the White House along the service road separating the West Wing from the helipad. Most times, reporters would shout their questions at the president and simply receive a wave and a smile in response.

White House communications teams had become more disciplined over the years in controlling the messaging disseminated to the news media. Sarge, however, was a rare exception. He never shied away from the opportunity to speak with the media. He was firm in his convictions and unapologetic about his political stance on every issue. All he asked from the media was that they fairly report his positions without mischaracterization or omission.

It was the largest entourage of travelers to exit the White House for the waiting helicopters that anyone could remember. Sarge and Julia, with their three children, led the way, followed by Abbie and her husband, soon-to-be-father Drew. The ever-present chief of staff, Donald, was accompanied by Susan and the girls. Lastly, the bachelors brought up the rear. Neither Brad nor J.J. had found the right woman to marry although both had taken some time for social interaction. The guys were committed to their career and country with neither particularly focused on having a private life.

As Sarge passed the press pool, several questions were shouted in his direction. He glanced back at Donald, who shrugged. Or perhaps he shivered, as he was still dressed in his suit with his hunting gear stowed in a duffel bag over his shoulder. Sarge stopped and squeezed Julia's hand.

"These guys have braved the cold to get a quote or two. I'm gonna speak with them for a moment."

Julia leaned in and kissed her husband on the cheek, an affectionate gesture that drew what sounded like a thousand clicks from the media shutterbugs. "Have fun with the boys today."

"I will. Thank you for stimulating the economy, as Abbie calls power shopping on Black Friday."

Julia laughed and gave him a playful slug. "We're simply patriots doing our part, Mr. President. Now, go greet your adoring friends in the news media."

"Yeah, right," said Sarge sarcastically. "I love you!"

"Love you back!"

"See ya later, Dad!" shouted Win.

"Love you, Daddy!" Rose yelled to her father before throwing him a kiss.

Frank simply gave his dad a thumbs-up, followed by a salute.

Sarge was feeling the love as he wandered toward the reporters. Donald said his goodbyes to his family and joined Sarge while keeping a respectful distance. The media began to shout their questions, and the first one was a doozy.

"Mr. President, should the U.S. be willing to go to war with China in order to defend Taiwan?"

Sarge shook off the cold and was fully engaged now. He expected questions about what he had planned for the day or whether he'd enjoyed his Thanksgiving dinner. Instead, he felt like he was making an impromptu appearance behind the podium in the White House press room.

"Well, first of all, good morning to you all. I trust you had a nice

Thanksgiving with your friends and family. Yesterday was a little more exciting than we might normally expect on a holiday, and I'd hoped to give you guys an uneventful long weekend to recharge your batteries."

"What about Taiwan, sir?" the reporter from the *Washington Post* pressed on.

Sarge smiled and chose his words carefully. He knew Beijing was listening. They'd tested his mettle in those early days of the nation's recovery and quickly learned Sarge was not going to bow down to the economic stranglehold they held over America.

"For roughly eighty years, Taiwan has existed in a gray area, geopolitically speaking. Taipei governs itself like an independent nation, as they should. They are a thriving democracy with a strong economy.

"However, China has always insisted that the island is part of its territory. Because of Beijing's political strength and its economic grip on much of the world, governments have been fearful of standing up to the Chinese. I can understand others' hesitancy, but we chose a different path.

"Prior to the collapse, Washington had pursued a noncommittal policy toward Taiwan. In a way, one might call it strategic ambiguity. By that, I mean our nation's leadership tried to maintain a strong economic and political partnership with Taiwan while recognizing China's claim that the island is part of its territory." Sarge paused for a moment as he considered his words carefully. He didn't want to push China into a war just as a new administration was set to enter the White House.

"While I pulled America away from her reliance on Chinese goods from an economic standpoint, geopolitically, I remained neutral on Taiwan. That changed when our ambassador was kidnapped, followed by rapid troop deployments by the People's Liberation Army to the shores along the Straits of Taiwan. I deployed our ships as a deterrent to Beijing making a mistake. As far as I'm concerned, any overt hostilities toward Taiwan will demand a full-blown military response from my administration."

Donald stepped forward in an attempt to get Sarge's attention. He knew opening this door might result in a long, drawn-out press conference that the two of them had not prepared for. Before he could reach out to Sarge, another reporter fired off a question.

"Mr. President, the House Minority Leader issued a statement moments ago that you will be conducting a ceremony in the White House next week to sign the Pacific Statehood Act. Can you confirm this for us?"

Sarge didn't hesitate. "I don't know any of the details of my schedule for next week. Right now, I'm focused on spending time with my friends and family after a very hectic week. I suggest the Minority Leader, and all of you, do the same." Sarge began to wander away before another question was shouted his way.

"Mr. President! Would you like to comment on the alleged voting irregularities being reported in Virginia? Are you aware of similar questions being raised in Wisconsin, Michigan, and Pennsylvania?"

Sarge turned to Donald, whose face was scrunched into a scowl. He had not looked into the Virginia matter and was completely unaware of three other states claiming similar issues. Sarge was about to speak when Donald stepped in.

"We have no comment at this time on the election results. The states have until December 8 to certify their votes, and I expect they'll use all due diligence to ensure accuracy. Now, if you don't mind, the president has earned a few days off. Thank you all, and we'll see you on Monday."

Donald hustled Sarge toward Marine One. As soon as they were safely on board, the other chopper lifted off en route to King of Prussia and a shopping excursion. Sarge's helicopter prepared to lift off, but his mind was still firmly planted on the ground in front of the reporters. He studied Donald for a moment before addressing the issue.

"What am I missing? The vote for Rawlins was solid. Sure, the usual four or five states were determinative of the outcome.

However, he won them all. Virginia was never in question, nor does it matter in terms of the electoral count."

Donald raised his hands to calm Sarge down. "I know. I know. The issues being raised are in Loudoun County and Fairfax County. It's the damn mail-in balloting provisions in Virginia. Apparently, there are larger number of ballots being challenged by the GOP."

"Donald, how do we get them to stand down? We can't take a position on this. GOP leadership would never understand why we threw in for Rawlins, a Southern democrat."

"I understand. I'll have to think it through. What bothers me now is the fact three other states may have challenges. Those are enough electoral votes to throw the entire outcome into dispute."

Sarge leaned back into his seat and exhaled. This was supposed to be a no-stress kinda day.

PART II

The Hunters
November 2024, mid-morning

CHAPTER TEN

10:10 a.m.
Undisclosed Location

Her real name was not Rikki; however, it was the nickname by which she was known. It was also one she'd earned many years ago as a Marine sniper. She'd been deployed on missions throughout the Middle Eastern theater, using her unparalleled fusion of skills such as situational awareness, weapons proficiency, and knowledge of ballistics and physics to undertake the impossible to achieve her goal—kill a human target.

She'd been credited with over a hundred kill shots. However, it was one in particular that gained the respect of her comrades and the nickname so richly deserved.

From six hundred yards away, a high-value target raced across a dirt-covered street in Kabul, Afghanistan. At a rapid pace of four miles per hour, he was nothing more than a low-resolution dot a few inches high. Even when viewed through her state-of-the-art, high-powered scope, a human-sized, stationary target on a calm day presented a physics problem that might appear humanly impossible to solve.

Not so for Rikki, although she would, in fact, face the impossible. The variables that made the shot daunting included the usual considerations of distance, elevation, air temperatures, and wind speed. Her mind raced as she factored in calculations related to her gun barrel's temperature, the type of ammunition she'd chosen, and now, the target's irrational behavior of darting from one side of the street to the other.

The man was either paranoid or had somehow become aware of Rikki's sniper hide. Regardless, he'd made himself a moving target that confounded Rikki in her efforts to take the shot. Outside the city, Alpha Company, a contingent of the Marine's finest, were prepared to enter that part of Kabul to flush out a nest of Taliban fighters who were holding Americans hostage. Talks had broken down with the prior administration, and the military solution was the only option.

Rikki was tasked with finding an overwatch position to protect Alpha Company's advance into the neighborhood. Then her directives changed. An Air Force reconnaissance drone had identified a high-ranking Taliban leader as being in the area. A message was sent to her with several close-up pictures of the target so he could be easily identified. The rescue operation was placed on hold while Rikki searched the streets for the man.

And there he was, darting down the street, hell-bent on getting to somewhere rather than seeking protective cover. It was a mistake on his part.

Rikki's training and mental discipline coolly took over as she followed the man through her scope. She was waiting for that opportunity, however brief, when her prey stopped long enough for her to take the shot.

Her weapon of choice at the time was an L115A3 long rifle made by Accuracy International, a company established by two-time Olympic shooting gold medalist Malcolm Cooper. With its $38,000 price tag, it was pricey even by U.S. military standards. For most operations, it suited Rikki's needs perfectly. The weapon was designed to achieve a first-round hit at seven hundred yards and was capable of shooting harassing fire at the enemy at more than a thousand yards.

Rikki's opportunity to shoot presented itself. Seven hundred yards away, her target came to a stop between an abandoned American Humvee and a smallish Hyundai sedan. The man appeared winded and was gasping for air.

She recognized that the shot was near the outside recognized range of her rifle. She was slightly out of adjustment in her scope, and because of the man's constant movement, her position was far from optimal.

Her best opportunity arose as she tried to take the shot through the windshield of the Hyundai and out the driver's side window, which was rolled down. She gently squeezed the trigger, sending the first round soaring toward her target. Before the windshield exploded into bits and pieces of glass, Rikki had reloaded and prepared for a second opportunity.

Through her scope, she saw blood fly as the bullet ripped through her target's shoulder. It was not, however, a kill shot. The man had dropped behind the car near the left front tire. Rikki could see his foot protruding from his loose pants.

Then she did something that earned her the unique nickname. She trained her rifle on the fender of the armor-plated Humvee. Once again, with unparalleled confidence and calm, she gently squeezed the trigger. She knew the moment the rifle slammed into her shoulder that she'd pulled off the impossible. As the heavy-caliber bullet sped toward the fender of the Humvee, her trained mind was able to visualize the result in mere milliseconds. It was a brief moment in time that the mind was incapable of comprehending. The result was a perfectly placed shot designed to ricochet off the armored vehicle to strike the target center mass.

The bullet struck the Taliban leader with sufficient force to explode into his chest and pierce his heart. He was killed instantly, and the sniper earned her nickname—Rikki, for the incredible ricocheted kill shot.

With each subsequent assignment, she came to expect the

unexpected, both in terms of the assigned target and the conditions under which she'd take the shot. She was a private contractor now. A gun for hire with allegiances to no one other than those who paid her in cryptocurrency. Her reputation was stellar, and her anonymity was priceless.

On this day, she'd kill someone on American soil. A fellow American, a first for her. The price she was being paid was enormous. She'd insisted on that. The target was certainly high profile. But to Rikki, it was just another challenge for the consummate hunter of human beings. He would be yet another target within her sights to be eliminated.

CHAPTER ELEVEN

11:11 a.m.
Monocacy Farm
South of Frederick, Maryland

The rotors of Marine One slowed, leaving fine particles of powdery snow flying in swirls around the chopper. While Sarge and his fellow hunters waited, a second, identical helicopter landed in the snowy field of Monocacy Farm barely a hundred yards away. This was a protocol followed by the security team and Marine Helicopter Squadron One, known as HMX-1, which accompanied the president.

Captain Morrell, a native of Canada and now an American citizen, hopped out of the second chopper together with several armed security personnel. A Marine sergeant in formal dress left the second chopper and took a position at attention near the base of the staircase while the armed Secret Service agents formed a protective perimeter around Marine One. Once he was satisfied that the president was safe to exit, Morrell gave the order, and the chunky door of the Sikorsky VH-92 helicopter opened.

Drew, Brad and J.J. led the way, followed by Donald and then

Sarge, who was the last to exit. Standing at the perimeter of the clearing was Hanson Briscoe, their host and the owner of Monocacy Farm. Briscoe, an unabashed conservative and front man for a politically well-placed political contingent, had been aligned with the Boston Brahmin on several business dealings in the past. Despite the loose relationship between the Brahmin and Briscoe's *Bonesmen*, the name given to the men who were part of the ranks of Yale's Skull & Bones organization, Sarge had never completely trusted Briscoe or his close associate George Trowbridge.

In any event, with his administration coming to an end, it was time for Sarge to strengthen those ties as he transitioned from public figure to the head of the powerful Brahmin. For years, Briscoe had offered his farm as a hunting refuge for Sarge. Its close proximity to Camp David, also located in Frederick County, made it an ideal hunting spot despite the snowfall. As the group landed, the sun began to shine, betraying the weather forecast, rendering their surroundings beautiful, yet almost an almost blinding white.

After dismounting from his horse, Briscoe ambled through the snow, a large leather jacket with a fur-lined collar pulled tight around his upper body. A brown leather cowboy hat sat atop his grayish-white hair. For the aristocrat that he was, his attire made him look more like a rancher.

Sarge was the first to greet Briscoe, as the others had never met him. During the fundraising for his reelection, Sarge had been approached by Briscoe and George Trowbridge, an influential entrepreneur from Connecticut. Both had ponied up some big bucks to Sarge's coffers but never asked for a favor in return. At first, Sarge had considered that refreshing but later, after reflection, realized they were laying bets he was the man to lead the Boston Brahmin through the twenty-first century.

"Hey, cowboy!" Sarge yelled across the field as the rotors of both choppers stopped their movement. "Do you have horses for all of us?"

"Sorry, Mr. President. My horses don't like the cold," he said with a laugh. He pointed toward the two choppers. "Plus, these two beasts would've scared the living daylights out of them."

The two men shook hands, and Sarge made the introductions to the rest of the hunting party. Briscoe led them toward the edge of the clearing, where several four-wheelers were awaiting the hunting party. Two members of the Secret Service had unloaded the hunters' weapons and ammunition together with other gear.

"This is my kind of horse," said Donald, who picked up the pace and kicked his way through the snow.

"You're such a city boy," said Drew with a hint of his East Tennessee accent. He'd grown up on a farm in the small community of Muddy Pond on the Cumberland Plateau. The thought of hunting using four-wheelers stifled his sense of adventure. Hunting was a walking man's sport.

"Accountant by trade and seeker of creature comforts at heart," Donald shot back.

All of them were accustomed to the cold, having grown up in Massachusetts, except for the Tennessean.

Sarge thought for a moment and turned around to take in his surroundings. He addressed Briscoe. "Harlan, this is your farm, so we'll follow your lead. However, is there any reason why we can't start our hunt from here? The terrain and nearby streams might make it favorable for chasing whitetail."

The military guys burst out laughing. Talk between young guys in the barracks ranked second only to a men's locker room when it came to sexual innuendo. It took Sarge a moment to pick up on the intentional misinterpretation of what he said.

"Wait. That didn't come out right. You guys know what I mean. Nobody's chasing any tail in this group."

Briscoe didn't get the reference, so he responded to Sarge's question. "Actually, you're right. The Monocacy River meanders through my property just to the north of here. It's about a two-mile walk. There's an old logging trail that I keep clear for the four-wheelers that will lead you there. On the other side, there are some dips and saddles marking the start of one small ridge connected to another."

"Deer love hollows and gullies," interjected Drew, the expert in the group. "It's not cold enough yet to freeze over any ponds. If we can work the river and head out of the flatland into a hollow, we'll have some pretty good luck."

Sarge turned to Morrell. "Dave, does that work for your team?"

"I don't like any of it, Mr. President. That said, having hunted whitetail myself, I know we can't get out ahead of you guys. We'll have to flank you and follow to the rear."

Sarge looked around the clearing at Morrell's team. "I see the bright orange vests. That'll make them easy to spot so we don't make a mistake and shoot one of them. I think we'll set out from here. What do you guys think?"

"Works for me," replied Donald.

Brad and J.J. nodded their agreement and gave Sarge a thumbs-up.

Drew reached into a four-wheeler and retrieved his MK 17 battle rifle. The automatic weapon had been a mainstay of U.S. Special Operations Forces. Drew's weapon of choice had a sixteen-inch barrel that was easily exchanged to alter its role from sniper rifle to battle rifle or for close-quarters combat use.

"Hey! That's cheating!" Donald complained as he pointed at Drew's imposing choice of weapon.

"I'm not hunting today," said Drew calmly as he checked his rifle and slammed in a full twenty-round magazine. "I'll be your hunting guide and protector. Those guys can only cover our six. Somebody has to maintain an eye on any threats ahead of us."

"Well, I feel a lot better," said Morrell truthfully.

Sarge shrugged. "Suit yourself, Drew. I appreciate it, but I was counting on you to actually shoot a deer. The rest of us will probably be talking and enjoying a shot of Glenlivet from time to time. You know, to keep warm."

"I feel a chill," said Donald with a grin. He looked to Brad and J.J. "How 'bout you guys?"

"Brrr," J.J. quickly responded. The group's Armageddon doctor knew the last thing anyone should do in a cold environment was drink alcohol, but he enjoyed playing along with Donald. Today was about camaraderie with his friends, not survival in the wilderness.

The guys, except Drew, shared a shot of scotch whisky and headed up the trail. Briscoe wished them luck and confirmed Morrell had directions to his home. He asked Sarge and his guests to join him for a drink when the hunt was over.

With Drew leading the way and Morrell bringing up the rear, the guys began their slow, steady march up the hill toward the Monocacy River, where they looked forward to doing battle with the deer population of Western Maryland.

CHAPTER TWELVE

12:25 p.m.
Monocacy Farm
South of Frederick, Maryland

"Okay, seriously. Are we lost, or is this damn logging trail drawing us into a *Twilight Zone* episode?" asked Donald as he huffed and puffed his way through the snow. He'd trailed the others, taking advantage of their footprints, which packed down the snow as they walked.

Drew, an expert tracker, understood the woods of the eastern United States as well as anybody. His experience allowed him to easily recognize deer magnets on a map, as well as on the ground. Ditches and gullies led their way to the river and grew in width as they approached. He could sense the moisture in the air generated by the running water.

"Not much longer," he reassured Donald. "You know, we could've gone turkey hunting back home. It would've been easier for the occasional hunter." He was clearly referring to Donald and Sarge, who hadn't complained but, as leader of the free world, didn't have much time for recreational endeavors. In fact, this was his first outing in four years.

Brad laughed. "Yeah, we should've gone turkey hunting last week. We could've filled the dinner table with our own birds."

"I think we just missed turkey hunting season," said Drew.

Donald caught up to the guys and took a deep breath. As always, Donald had to consider the political ramifications of everything Sarge did. "Well, we were a little busy, so there wouldn't have been time. Besides, the optics would've been horrible."

"How so?" asked J.J.

Donald laughed. "Okay, follow me on this. The great hunters go out into the wilderness to slaughter a dozen turkeys. Then the day before Thanksgiving, the president here has to mosey out onto the East Lawn to pardon Lenny, the ceremonial turkey from West Virginia. Those would've been two congressmen's votes down the tubes."

"Besides," added Sarge, "the media would crucify us. Pardon one after killing the others? PETA would be in front of the White House, waving signs calling me a murderer. They'd be worse than the damn fossil-fuel haters."

"You guys are right," said Brad. "Honestly, I thought all that absurd bullshit would've been left behind after the collapse. You know, we, as Americans, should appreciate the lives we've made for ourselves. Why must we tear down our country?"

The men grew silent for a moment as they contemplated Brad's words. John Morgan had believed the nation was in need of a hard reset. The cyber attack was supposed to be a controlled method of bringing America to her knees only to return her to her former glory. Things had gotten out of hand, and the United Nations had been ushered in by the former president. It had made for some difficult times during the recovery process.

"This is why I opposed the Pacific Statehood Act in its present form," said Sarge. "I wanted a clean bill. One that didn't allow the rogue states, and their tyrannical president, the ability to dictate their terms of surrender. It doesn't work like that."

Drew subtly shook his head in disbelief. They'd discussed politics the entire two-mile trek up through the snow except for the brief discussion about turkey hunting. Even that had a political slant to it. He was glad he and Abbie had their unwritten rule about keeping their respective careers to themselves. He raised his nose in the air and studied the treetops. The breeze had picked up slightly, indicating there was an opening ahead. He was right.

"Guys, I see water," he said. Drew picked up the pace as the Monocacy River came into view. It was moving briskly through the landscape, its banks slightly swollen due to the rains followed by snowfall. As they crested the rise to overlook the water, the calming sound of the river flowing caused the group to stop their chatter.

All of them stood together, quietly taking in the beauty of Briscoe's land. The historic property was located near the city of Frederick, Maryland. In July of 1864, the Battle of Monocacy had been fought nearby as well as in these woods. It was a major part of the Confederates' Valley Campaign to turn the tide of the Civil War.

The goal of the South was to capture Washington and influence the election of 1864 in their favor. While the Confederates won the battle, they lost the war, as they say. The Union soldiers, outnumbered three to one by Confederate General Early's Second Corp, held the line long enough for reinforcements to encircle Washington in a defensive formation. Although most of the Union soldiers perished, they bought time and prevented a likely Confederate incursion into the nation's capital.

It was not one of the largest battles of the Civil War, but it had a major impact on the outcome. Sarge, a student of history, was the first to break the silence as he relayed the history of the Battle of Monocacy to his fellow hunters. It was a reverent moment as the men reflected on battles won and lost, both in times of war against foreign enemies and on U.S. soil, as during the War between the States and the battle for the heart of America just eight years prior.

Drew eased along the banks of the river until he spotted the wooden bridge that crossed a narrow point of the water. Morrell wandered away from the group for a moment and touched base with his Secret Service agents who'd trailed the hunting party to the rear and a hundred yards into the woods on both sides of them. He was thankful for the hunters taking a break so his men who didn't have the benefit of a cleared trail could catch up.

With Drew and Morrell satisfied that the group could proceed, they led everyone along the river's edge along the bank. Because the bridge was somewhat rickety, they agreed to cross one at a time. Drew spoke to them as they made their way over the bridge, which was in need of repair.

"Okay, it's time to get to work, guys, or we're gonna have to stop by McDonald's on the way to Camp David."

"Oh, sweet Jesus," said Donald. "Susan would never let me hear the end of it."

"The kids would be pretty happy," Sarge pointed out.

Brad wasn't too concerned. The military man had spent most of his adult life eating MREs. "I'm sure there's a grocery store along the way. We could just buy some Boston butt and throw it on the spit. A little barbecue sauce and we're golden." Boston butt was pork tenderloin from around the shoulder. During Revolutionary times, the butt was considered a delicacy. Over the years, it was often referred to as Boston butt.

"There's no sport in that," interjected J.J. "Drew's right, gentlemen. It's time to do our duty and prepare our muskets!"

This drew laughs from the guys, who made their way across the rickety bridge, careful not to step through a broken plank. Sarge urged everyone to go ahead of him. Then, contrary to Drew's suggestion, he crossed with the dutiful Morrell just a few feet behind him.

Minutes after their arrival on the other side of the river, the bridge suddenly became impassable.

PART III

The Shoppers
November 2024, late morning

CHAPTER THIRTEEN

11:30 a.m.
King of Prussia Mall
Northwest of Philadelphia, Pennsylvania

"I'm glad you came along with us, Abbie," said Julia. She patted her friend on the knee and studied Abbie's belly with a knowing look. She'd been seven months pregnant herself. Three times, in fact. It was too early to look to the end and that glorious day when the baby she was carrying felt like it weighed a couple of hundred pounds. However, most expectant mothers found themselves checking the calendar several times a day and wondering, or hoping, she'd miscalculated her due date.

"Yeah, Abbie," added Susan, who was in a chipper mood that morning. "If it weren't for you, we'd have to ride in one of those airport shuttle buses or even a Greyhound."

The last eight years had taken its toll on all of the Loyal Nine, but Susan seemed to have been the worse for wear as a result. Donald had performed admirably on many fronts, all of which were stressful. Julia imagined that stress had inserted itself into their home life, such that it was. She'd already spoken to Sarge about a long overdue vacation for the Quinns.

"I see how it is," said Abbie jokingly. She, too, was grateful for the comfort of an exact duplicate of Marine One that was afforded her as the Vice President of the United States.

Today's activities had posed a challenge for the Secret Service as well as the Marines' HMX-1 operation. Under certain circumstances, as a security measure, Marine One might fly in a group of as many as five identical helicopters. One would carry the president or, as in this case, the vice president. The others would serve as decoys.

Watching them depart the White House grounds was quite a spectacle. As they took off, the helicopters would shift in formation to obscure the location of the president. The Secret Service referred to this as the presidential shell game to confuse any would-be terrorists who wanted to attack the president's transportation with surface-to-air missiles.

One decoy had accompanied Sarge to Monocacy Farm, and two had flanked the chopper carrying Abbie, Julia, Susan and the children. As they'd approached their landing zone in unison, the decoys hovered while the helicopter carrying the precious cargo landed on a well-secured helipad inside the Lockheed Martin complex adjacent to the mall.

Like the president, Abbie had her own version of the heavily armored limousine commonly referred to as the Beast. Her limo had been delivered to Lockheed Martin days ago as part of the advance team who prepared for her visit to the King of Prussia Mall. A contingent of fortified Chevy Suburbans operated by the Secret Service were also standing by to ferry the shoppers the short distance from the defense contractor's facility to the mall.

The Secret Service faced greater challenges today than they had in Sarge's eight years in office. The shopping mall was expected to be packed, as the nation was enjoying the best economy since the collapse. Most pundits recognized that the nation had never seen low employment and high incomes without inflation in American history. As the vehicles had approached the mall, the amount of consumer spending taking place was readily apparent.

And the shoppers were in a frenzy, making protection of the vice president and First Lady, together with their entourage, very difficult. Plus, the King of Prussia Mall was the largest retail space in the U.S., with more than four hundred mostly upscale retailers filling every available space.

All of the ladies had enjoyed shopping on Newbury Street located west of Boston Common and within walking distance from Julia's home with Sarge at 100 Beacon. They had not returned as a group to Boston in years. In fact, this was only the second opportunity to have a girls' day out since Sarge had been elected president. That might have accounted for Susan's good spirits. It was rare that the leading ladies of the Loyal Nine were able to spend any quality time together.

Although they had not formally booked a tour, a service for groups of ten or more by Simon Properties was offered to provide the ladies a personal shopper during their visit to the mall. They made their way to the mall offices with the Secret Service in tow. From there, they let the mall management team know what their favorite stores were, and a game plan was quickly put together.

"Okay, Julia, I have a big ask," said Abbie as the group tour organizers went over their suggestions with the Secret Service team.

Julia was caught off guard by Abbie's serious demeanor. She stretched out her reply. "O-kay."

"I haven't mentioned this to Drew because we both agreed that we wanted to be surprised, you know, when the baby comes."

"I remember."

"Well, maybe it's just me being a rookie mother, but I really do believe our baby is a boy." She was beaming from ear to ear.

Susan overheard the conversation and joined in. "I've had two girls, so I have some insight into this."

"Well, my two boys and Rose kinda give me a variety of

experiences," added Julia. "What makes you think you're having a boy."

Abbie stood a little taller and swayed her belly back and forth. "I look like I've swallowed a pumpkin. And have you noticed how low he is? At first, I was hoping that meant he was ready to eject himself and we could call it a day. Now, after looking on the internet and talking to my ob-gyn, I think it's a boy."

Susan turned to Julia. "Whadya think? Were Win and Frank baby pumpkins?"

"More like boulders," said Julia with a laugh. "Have you seen Frank's broad shoulders? They're the reason I told Sarge four children was completely out of the question."

Abbie remained serious. "Okay, let me ask you this. When you carried Win and Frank, did you crave salty foods like chips and such?"

Julia nodded and laughed. She gestured as she spoke. "Yup, and get this. The White House staff fed me Sour Skittles and Sour Patch Kids Extreme candy. Do you guys remember how much my weight blew up with Frank? It was the darn cravings."

"Now I'm convinced," said Abbie, who nodded her head vigorously as she cradled her baby-bump-turned-basketball. "Which leads me to my request."

"Go ahead. What is it?"

"May I have the boys with me as we shop? I feel like I need to get some experience with the little guys."

Julia practically jumped into the air with delight. "Oh, my God. Yes. Win, bring your brother over here." Win stopped eavesdropping on the discussion between mall security and their own Secret Service team. While Frank was the epitome of brawn considering his toddler age, Win was very cerebral for a seven-year-old. He took Frank's hand and gave him a tug so he could join his mother.

"Sure, Mom."

"Okay, listen up. Aunt Abbie needs some shopper assistants

because she needs to buy a Christmas gift for your dad. Would you mind hanging with her today? You know, to help her out."

Win shrugged. "Sure, but that's easy. I think he wants—"

Julia politely interrupted him. "Now, giving Aunt Abbie a list wouldn't be very much fun, would it? You are about to learn that shopping is like hunting. Instead of tromping around in the woods in the cold, you are battling the crowds to find the best deal on the perfect gift. It's not that easy. You'll see."

Win looked up at Abbie and then glanced at her tummy. The kid surmised there was a boy in there. After Abbie began to show, Sarge and Julia had had *the talk* with Win, although they'd deftly avoided answering the *how* questions.

"Sure," he replied before turning to Abbie. "Can we hit the LEGO store?"

Abbie stifled a laugh. "Um, do you think your dad might want a toy from the LEGO store?"

"They do have a model of the White House. He might want to take it home when we move out. As a reminder of how nice it was to live there."

Abbie smiled and gave Julia a knowing glance. The two had joked once before that Win would be president someday. Now she was sure of it.

CHAPTER FOURTEEN

Noon
King of Prussia Mall
West of Philadelphia, Pennsylvania

The group of honored guests were not only enjoying their shopping time together, but they also were appreciating the shows of adoration and support from the throngs of onlookers. Julia was a rock star among the group, as she'd been a very active proponent of Sarge's policies. She often campaigned on behalf of politicians loyal to her husband. Abbie was being given considerable attention due to her pregnancy. Susan was more than satisfied taking a back seat to the two easily recognizable women. She was taking several pictures with her iPhone to share with the group once they arrived at Camp David.

At the Nordstrom Court just outside their main-floor entrance, a huge Christmas display was seen by the kids, who immediately realized Santa Claus had come to town. Frank pulled Win's arm, who in turn pulled Abbie away from the adoring Pennsylvanians. Even the Quinn girls, who had outgrown the whole concept of

Santa Claus, were delighted to see the jolly old soul who looked as realistic a Santa as they could remember.

The mall personnel were able to convince those waiting in line to allow the First Family and their guests to take a number of photos with Santa. In addition to the professional photographer doing his job, hundreds of people crowded around Santa's display while others hung over the balcony railings above to video record the spectacle on the camera phones. Shoppers and honored dignitaries alike enjoyed Santa's hospitality as well as the discount coupons he handed out to them.

"Seriously? We have coupons to Vineyard Vines!" exclaimed Becca Quinn. "Mom, this is like free money."

Susan laughed. She was about to add something to the effect of a penny saved was a penny earned, but her oldest daughter, Penny, hated when they recited Benjamin Franklin's axiom, often used by her parents to tamp down her tendency to want to buy things. Susan thought better of it but nevertheless decided to take advantage of the fortuitous present from Santa.

Susan couldn't resist. "Hey, girls, Vineyard Vines is right over there. Shall we spend some to save some?"

Julia began laughing as she playfully covered Rose's ears with both hands. "Susan Quinn, do not teach my child such things. I need to teach her frugality." The women laughed and exchanged fist bumps.

"Well, the boys and I are off to the LEGO store," said Abbie. Until now, they'd shopped together with the assistance of the mall's personal shoppers. All of their purchases were gathered together at the mall's offices and then examined by Secret Service personnel before being placed into one of the agency's Chevy Suburbans.

"Yeah!" Win and Frank shouted in unison.

Abbie smiled and shrugged. "Okay, they're not that much different from my big boy, Drew. He gets excited the same way about Bass Pro Shops."

"Where are you guys going?" asked Susan as she gently tugged on Rose's long locks.

"Well, I'd like to get Rose her first Alex and Ani bracelet if they're not too large. Probably one with her birthstone. Then we'll stroll over to Pottery Barn. They have a leather cigar book that I want to get Sarge for his office at 73 Tremont. I'm sure there will be many an afternoon when he'll invite the guys over to hang out on the balcony overlooking Boston Common. They can pick out their favorite cigars from the book."

"All right!" exclaimed Susan. "Let's do this. When and where should we meet up?"

Julia turned to Morrell's assistant, a woman who was a seasoned veteran of the agency and a frequent companion of the First Lady when she traveled. "Whadya think? Three o'clock. At the mall office."

"Yes, ma'am. No later, please. That will allow us time to regroup, board the choppers, and arrive at our destination by dark."

Abbie nodded her agreement. "That's plenty of time for us, right, guys?"

Win and Frank shrugged but generally agreed.

With that, the trio of women split off on their separate quests to find gifts for themselves and others. Susan was the only one of the three who didn't have any awestruck constituents with her. That was fine, as she enjoyed spending time with her daughters like the old days. Well, at least as far back as she could remember.

Then she suddenly stopped, and a chill came over her. The last time she and the girls had shopped at Vineyard Vines, a riot broke out at the mall. If not for the quick thinking of Donald, they might have been hurt. Susan tried to shake off the foreboding thoughts. Nonetheless, after a glance over her shoulder to search for Julia and Abbie, she firmly grasped her grown daughters by the hand and led them to the store as if they were nine years younger.

CHAPTER FIFTEEN

12:15 p.m.
King of Prussia Mall
West of Philadelphia, Pennsylvania

Julia was truly enjoying her time alone with Rose. As her mini-me grew up, she saw how easily her daughter could take on her mannerisms and gestures. The two even dressed similarly. Naturally, Julia purchased Rose's clothing; however, she allowed her child to be involved in the decision-making process. Her daughter chose to emulate her mother, which flattered Julia. She hoped they could maintain the kind of relationship Susan had with her daughters. Mothers and daughters were notorious for butting heads as the years passed.

At Alex and Ani, Rose insisted upon buying a shiny gold wire bangle bracelet with a rose-colored birthstone even though she was not born in October. It was rose and that was that, she'd affirmatively stated to her mom when the choice was made. Julia applauded her strong-willed daughter for her choice. Rather than giving in to the salesclerk's suggestion that she choose her actual birthstone, Rose stuck with her first choice.

With the bracelet firmly in place on her wrist, she and Julia walked hand in hand through the mall to Pottery Barn. The crowd of onlookers dissipated somewhat as the afternoon wore on. From time to time, Julia stopped to allow a photograph of her with Rose. However, the Secret Service warned her against personal contact with the other mall shoppers. While there were no specific threats on that day, Julia agreed out of an abundance of caution.

Because she was a prolific campaigner over two years, whether it was for Sarge's reelection or during the midterm elections, Julia was used to large crowds of people vying to get her attention. Today, she was a little less approachable because she was alone with Rose. She'd entrusted her sons to Abbie, who, by virtue of being vice president, garnered more Secret Service protection than she did as First Lady. Poor Susan, who'd quipped earlier that she was the lowly chief of staff's wife, only received a protection detail of three operatives. One for her and each of the girls.

After some shoe shopping at Kids Foot Locker and the purchase of a dozen golf balls for Donald, they finally made their way into Pottery Barn, Julia's favorite home décor store prior to the collapse.

The store was decked out in Christmas décor. Near the front entrance, a ten-foot-tall artificial tree had been adorned with white ornaments made of glass coupled with white felt ornaments of various animals. She pointed toward a plush deer ornament with a large rack of antlers. She gently grasped it as she thought of Sarge. She loved her husband and found herself missing him. It was not unusual for them to be apart for days as he performed his presidential duties or when she hit the campaign trail. That didn't stop her from missing him.

"Hey, Mom. I like this tree better," said Rose, who pulled away from Julia in a flash. She rushed through the displays of Pottery Barn to a tree decorated in red and gold with more traditional-style ornaments. "See? These ornaments are like toys. We should get this one for Frank."

She held up a wooden toy soldier. Julia smiled at her daughter. She certainly nailed the appropriate gift for her little brother.

As she admired her daughter, a sudden movement caught her eye. The two Secret Service agents stationed inside near the dual front entrances to the store moved briskly into the openings. Then, inexplicably, they went flying past her.

Well, at least parts of them did.

PART IV

The Hunted
November 2024, Afternoon

CHAPTER SIXTEEN

12:30 p.m.
Undisclosed Location

Rikki was used to being mission support. Her job was to protect the operatives moving into position or engaging the enemy in battle. Sometimes her goal was to harass the enemy by suppressing their fire with her own. Other times, a specific target was identified. It might be a machine-gun nest or even the enemy's commanding officer.

Then there were the political targets. Not necessarily enemy combatants on the field of battle but, rather, they wielded their might with words and actions in the legislative world. Today, she was tasked with removing a powerful political figure, one that wasn't necessarily out of alignment with her political views. However, she now worked in the private sector. Whether it was heads of state or a business executive, when called upon, she'd do her duty. For a fee, of course, because after all, a gal had to pay the bills.

Elevated high above the ground in the sturdy limbs of a mature white pine tree, Rikki watched and patiently waited for her opportunity. The scope of her rifle was trained on the location where she anticipated the target to appear if he was still alive. The shot would be challenging but doable. She had the benefit of height, and although the weather conditions were not optimal, the wind wasn't gusting like it had during her Middle East deployments.

Rikki was the proverbial plan B. The backup plan to what her employers considered to be a more solid and viable method of eliminating the target. If she were required to squeeze the trigger, it would be because the target arrived alive, only to be killed by her bullet.

When she insisted upon being paid in full, in advance, regardless of whether she pulled the trigger, there was no argument from her new employer. Cost, he'd explained, was not a factor. Rikki recalled making a weak attempt at a joke. The mysterious man who'd reached out to her didn't bother to smile. In fact, his expressionless face haunted her at night to the point she'd be glad when this job was over.

She focused her thoughts back to the task at hand. She'd been told in advance that the timing of the mission was fluid. In other words, once the other hit team made their move, the entire operation could turn into a shit show, leaving her the last opportunity to accomplish their goal.

Playing gently through her AirPods was her favorite playlist consisting of country beach music, which stood in sharp contrast to the cold, snowy conditions that surrounded her. Rikki had grown up on the beaches of Galveston, Texas. She was Texas country through and through but not in the *buckle bunny* sense. Sure, her good looks would allow her to play the part, but she'd had no respect for girls like that growing up. She'd preferred to hunt hogs, deer, and just about anything that roamed the fields and woods of Texas.

After high school, she'd set her sights on enlisting in the military. She was an excellent marksman and dreamed about the opportunity to fire the advanced weapons used in America's armed forces. She went to the Baybrook Recruiting Station on West Nasa Road in nearby Webster and signed up. She never told her mother of her plans, and her father had been gone for years.

It was her steely demeanor and excellent training that brought her to this point in her life. So, with the discipline instilled in her during her stint with the Marines, Rikki waited, her head slowly keeping pace with the beat of the music.

CHAPTER SEVENTEEN

12:30 p.m.
King of Prussia Mall
West of Philadelphia, Pennsylvania

"All teams, green light. Go!" The woman's voice filled the earpieces of more than a dozen operatives under her command. They'd trained for two weeks, spending twenty hours a day planning, practicing, and analyzing all angles of their multipronged attack. It was possible they'd never be called upon to undertake the mission. But now they were ready to engage.

She'd stalked her prey upon their arrival at the mall. Her team blended in well with the shoppers, and their trained eyes easily identified the Secret Service detail assigned to the targets. In order to accomplish her goal, she chose to change clothing to match her primary target. While the group was playing footsies with Santa and his elves, she dashed into nearby Nordstrom and purchased color-matched attire to the First Lady. She then notified her teams of the change. When she made her move, she didn't want to be killed by friendly fire.

As she was changing clothes, she'd received word that the targets had split into three distinctive groups. This unexpected turn of events complicated the mission, but after giving it some thought, she saw this as beneficial. The primary target was to remain unharmed. The others, except the children if possible, could be eliminated.

She'd disguised her appearance on the off chance some of the Secret Service agents assigned to the First Lady might recognize her. When she vetted her team for the operation, she'd made sure none of them had worked directly with the agents assigned to the First Family. Some members of her team had worked within the prior administration and were carried over to the new one for a short period of time before leaving to work for a private contractor in California. They made for ideal recruits because of their knowledge of the methods used to protect the family of the president.

As the opportunity to move in approached, she wrestled with what to do with the young child, Rose. Would she become collateral damage? Would that actually be a benefit in their negotiations? Although it was not her decision to make, she'd have to make a judgment call as events unfolded to determine the little girl's fate.

As the first explosion rocked the mall and immediately obliterated the two Secret Service agents guarding the First Lady, she took on the role of actress, intentionally disguising her more familiar role as operative and, well, family friend. It would be a tough sell but one she'd rehearsed over and over and over.

CHAPTER EIGHTEEN

12:30 p.m.
Vineyard Vines
King of Prussia Mall
West of Philadelphia, Pennsylvania

It had been more than a year, since Penny had departed for college, that the three Quinn women had gone shopping together. Penny was no longer interested in the preppy, spending-the-weekend-at-the-Cape look. Her college classmates preferred shopping at places like Abercrombie & Fitch or Free People. With the promise of her favorite clothing stores being next up on the agenda, she endured Becca's gleeful shopping spree at Vineyard Vines.

They were at the rear of the store, perusing the long-sleeved polo shirts, when the first explosion rocked the King of Prussia Mall. A cacophony of screams rose to a crescendo as the sounds of panicked shoppers stampeding for the exits provided a glimpse of what was to come.

When the second bomb exploded, the incendiary effect filled the air with the smell of gas and fire. Susan saw the flash just outside the store in the center atrium closest to the Sephora entrance.

The Secret Service agents from her protective detail had been stationed at the front of the store just inside the entrance. Their first reaction was to take several steps into the atrium to determine the origin of the blast. Their natural reaction turned out to be a deadly mistake.

Automatic gunfire from above rained bullets upon them, killing them instantly. Susan, who huddled at the rear of the store with her girls as the carnage broke out, quickly considered her options.

Many years had separated her days as a warrior on the grounds of Quabbin Reservoir and the streets of Boston. However, she'd never forget that afternoon at the mall in Newton near their home when protestors from Black Lives Matter harassed shoppers until they were turned upon. The result was a squabble that quickly escalated into several fistfights.

Ironically that day, they had been with Donald shopping in the Vineyard Vines store. Her husband, through quick thinking under pressure, had noticed that the frightened store personnel had disappeared. He'd rushed to the entrance of the store, and with Susan's help, they'd lowered the steel-reinforced security gate.

Today, Susan didn't hesitate. "Girls, listen very carefully. Find a place in the storeroom to hide. But separately, do you understand me?" She didn't want to admit verbally that her daughters were a larger, easier target if they huddled together.

"Mom, what about—?"

Susan cut Penny off. "Go. Now!" She shoved them toward the rear of the store as a herd of employees and customers raced past. Susan had to dodge the hysterical women as they almost knocked her into a display table.

Keeping her head low, she ran toward the entrance. Her eyes darted in all directions to determine if the gunmen were making their way inside. There was no doubt in her mind that she was a target of the assassins every bit as much as Julia and Abbie were. If not for her natural instincts to protect her daughters, Susan would've rushed into the mall in an effort to protect her dear friends.

Instead, she relied upon her prior experience and used the clothing racks as cover to locate the operating mechanism of the security gate. *There!* she shouted in her mind as she spotted the two push buttons. Red for close, green for open. Unfortunately, they were covered by a hard plastic case with a small padlock. There was no time to locate a key. She'd have to break the casing.

Behind her was a rolling rack holding the retailer's Christmas collection of long-sleeve tee shirts. She ripped at them, frantically tearing them off the hangers until the rack was light enough for her to pick up and use as a club. More gunfire erupted as bullets ripped up the tile floor in the mall common area, tearing holes until the bullets ricocheted into the store.

Susan fell to the floor in fear for her life. After she quickly regained her composure, she picked up the rack, turned it upside down, and began to bludgeon the case until it broke. Then she slapped the red button hard with the palm of her hand.

The closed security gate wouldn't stop the gunmen from shooting out the plate-glass window. However, it might deter them or perhaps confuse them long enough for her to find a way to escape with the girls. The gate hadn't completely closed before Susan, now completely alone in the front of the store, began racing toward the back storage room, knocking down racks of clothes and mannequins as she went.

CHAPTER NINETEEN

12:30 p.m.
LEGO Store
King of Prussia Mall
West of Philadelphia, Pennsylvania

Win and Frank were beside themselves as they tugged Abbie to and
fro inside the LEGO store. After locating the White House replica
and handing it to the clerk for safekeeping, the boys quickly began
to shop for themselves.

Abbie tried to stay close to them as they darted from one display
to another. Then she picked up on how the mothers in the store
handled it. They found a relatively safe place near the front of the
store where they could guard the only exit in case one of their
children decided to make a run for it with a Super Mario set. They
were also able to keep tabs on which LEGO sets interested them the
most, making mental notes for Christmas gifts.

The head of the Secret Service detail assigned to Abbie and the
rest of the group remained with her as the second-highest-ranking
government official in America. Outside the entirely plate-glass
storefront, two agents flanked the door like the Queen's Guard

might at Buckingham Palace. Their job was not to be obscure but actually quite the opposite. The four agents plus the detail leader wanted to be highly visible as a deterrent against someone impulsively attacking the vice president.

When the first bomb blast rocked the mall's interior, Abbie's protective detail converged on the entrance. They were immediately swarmed by kids and store customers trying to run out into the mall, who in turn crashed into other frantic shoppers seeking safety inside the store.

The agents turned and formed a protective barrier, using their best efforts to stem the tide of people flowing inside. Their goal was to limit the entry of any threats to the vice president. It was the security team leader who first noticed the threat was already among them.

"Gun!" she shouted as a nondescript man to her right pulled a sidearm from a concealed holster under his jacket. He took aim at Abbie but was shot in the chest twice by the agent before he fired wildly into the floor. The bullets bounced off the yellow polished concrete and skipped across the floor before embedding into the tiny legs and bodies of the children gathered around their parents, seeking safety.

Frank had broken away from Win and rushed toward the display window out of curiosity. He'd almost reached the Disney display where Abbie was pinned against the wall by one of the Secret Service agents. Win chased after his brother and grabbed his arm. He spun Frank around and sandwiched his brother's body to cover Abbie just as automatic gunfire obliterated the entire storefront.

Large shards of plate glass flew inward. Win, who shielded Frank and Abbie in a bear hug, screamed in agony as several jagged pieces of glass embedded in his back and lower legs. Frank shrieked in pain as small pieces of glass peppered his exposed hands.

Instinctively, an agent protecting Abbie rushed to reach for the boys. His decision resulted in his death as more gunfire rang out, ripping into his body. Those bullets that missed blasted the wall full of plastic LEGO projects, sending the multicolored parts flying through the air.

Abbie dropped to her knees, knocking Win and Frank down as well. The three of them were sprawled out on the floor. Abbie immediately noticed Win's Harvard sweatshirt was soaked in blood. Frank lay perfectly still, eyes focused on the entrance, seemingly unaware that his hands were covered in blood, as bits of glass had torn into them.

Amidst the shouting and cries for help, Abbie could hear the excited voices of the Secret Service agents communicating with one another. Their earpieces were no longer capable of being heard with the gunfire, explosions and crazed shoppers screaming.

"Scribe team! Report!" the lead agent shouted into her radio in vain. "Scribe team, come in!" She knelt on the floor with her back to Abbie and the boys, her handgun trained on the entrance, scanning from side to side for a potential hostile.

"Win, are you okay?" Abbie asked in the calmest voice she could muster.

"It stings," he replied weakly. "I'm, um, I'm so wet."

Abbie turned him slightly to get a look at his back. Several large, triangular pieces of glass had embedded in his back. She hesitated to remove them, but she was afraid that all of the activity from the frightened shoppers might cause further damage.

She whispered in his ear, "This might hurt a little, but I have to pull the glass out. Okay?"

Win managed a nod, and then his eyes met Frank's. The toddler's bloody hands reached over to Win's. The boys held hands while Abbie extracted the larger pieces of plate glass. She decided against removing his sweatshirt for now, as she was unsure how much glass had torn through the lightweight cotton material.

"Madam Vice President, I can't raise anybody on the radio."

Abbie's eyes grew wide as she looked past the head of her detail. The two remaining Secret Service agents were engaged in a gun battle with men using the stem wall at the front of the Victoria's

Secret store for cover. Seconds later, one of the agents took a bullet to the head, causing blood to spray inside the LEGO store.

"What about Julia?"

"I don't know. You're my priority right now. We need to exit through the back of the store."

Abbie nodded and tried to stand. Suddenly, sharp pains shot through her midsection as excruciating cramps enveloped her baby.

"No. No. No." Her voice was filled with agony and fear. Begging for her baby to be safe. However, the pain got worse. She gazed upon the boys, and her eyes stared at the agent, pleading to get them to safety. All of them, both born and unborn.

CHAPTER TWENTY

12:35 p.m.
Pottery Barn
King of Prussia Mall
West of Philadelphia, Pennsylvania

Pottery Barn was wall-to-wall full of shoppers as the blast obliterated the entrance and turned her Secret Service personnel into a bloody mess of body parts. Several shoppers either died or were dismembered as the force of the bomb took out those in the entry, and its concussive effect shattered glass displays around the walls of the store.

"Mommy!" Rose shouted in a high-pitched voice.

It both frightened Julia and gave her a slight sense of relief as well. Her daughter was alive. Julia still visualized where Rose had been standing with the toy soldier in her hand. Despite the darkened interior caused by the blast destroying virtually all the ceiling light fixtures, Julia was able to make out the traditionally decorated Christmas tree, which had been knocked over onto a sofa.

"Stay down, honey. I'm coming to you." Julia knew better than to say her daughter's name. If this attack was directed at her and the First Family, then their assailants would appreciate her pointing out their targets for them.

Julia disregarded the pain she felt as she crawled across bits and pieces of broken glass, large and small. Shards from the front entrance were scattered about, their jagged edges embedded in bodies and fabric pieces all around her. The most painful cuts came from the glassware that had crashed to the polished concrete floor. Finally, Julia tried to avoid the fine mist of fluorescent light bulbs that floated through the air. She pulled her shirt over her mouth and nose to avoid breathing in the mercury gas within the compact fluorescent bulbs.

A chaotic stampede of surviving shoppers complicated matters. Some tried to exit through the front door while others rushed to the rear. When gunfire erupted in the mall's atrium, a deluge of people pushed into the store despite the dead bodies that blocked the way.

Julia did her best to crawl across the goo and glass to get to Rose. She desperately wished she had a gun and contemplated searching the body parts for the Secret Service agents' weapons. However, her priority was Rose, who called out her name again.

"Mommy, over here by the tree!"

Julia changed course and turned left toward where the tree had fallen. Seconds later, she arrived by Rose's side.

"Honey, are you hurt?"

Rose broke down crying now that she was safely in her mother's arms. For some young children, remaining brave is your only option until your parent is there to protect you, at which time you can let your emotions out. Through her sobs, Rose was able to confirm that she was unharmed. While Julia hugged her child, she began to scan her surroundings.

The combination of panicked people and dust and smoke filling the air made it hard to determine what her best options were. For the moment, she and Rose pushed themselves backwards against a display shelf and watched the pandemonium, both inside the darkened store and outside in the mall atrium.

"Mommy, what should we do?" asked Rose.

Julia looked down to her daughter and squeezed her tight. Then she rolled her eyes and shook her head side to side. *How do I answer a question that I don't have the answer to?*

It'll be okay.

We'll wait for help.

I don't know, honey, somebody's trying to kill us.

None of the above, thought Julia. "Rose, let's go out the back. It's too crazy out there." Julia stood and helped Rose to her feet. Just as they turned to walk toward the back of the store, a flashlight illuminated the interior. Its beam moved from one body to the next, pausing slightly on each of the dead's faces or remains.

Julia pulled Rose behind the display and whispered in her ear to stay quiet. Julia wanted to believe the Secret Service had arrived to protect them, but she couldn't be sure until they identified themselves.

The beam of light moved closer toward their location. Julia became mistrustful of the person's intentions. They never called out to determine if anybody needed help. If the person was with the Secret Service, why didn't they shout her name, or at least her code name—Scribe.

Julia's palms grew sweaty, mixing with the gooey blood she'd accumulated while crawling across the floor. She pulled Rose to the side of her and gently nudged her around the display as the flashlight began shining on the bodies near them. Slowly, they eased out of sight and made a quick dash for the cash wrap at the side of the store.

Both she and Rose were on their knees, hiding behind the concrete countertop that protruded slightly from the cabinet. To enhance their ability to hide, she slowly pulled out the short, wide cabinet drawers that held unprinted newspaper used by Pottery Barn employees to wrap fragile home décor. With the drawers pulled out, she thought she could hide from her assailants. And if it was the Secret Service, they'd call out to her by name.

Seconds seemed like hours as she anxiously awaited something to happen. The sound of movement inside the store had dissipated, as either people had already escaped through the rear of the store or others were not allowed in, an indication that the Secret Service or mall security had managed to gain control of the situation.

The gunshots became few and far between except for in the distance. Julia realized that this attack was not some random terrorist incident. She was certain she and her friends were the targets. She became nervous once again, worried for Abbie and her sons. Fearful that Susan and the girls were also in the line of fire. Her anxiety caused her hands to shake as she huddled behind the cash wrap, waiting for the person who'd entered the store with the flashlight to identify themselves.

Seconds later, she got her answer.

"Julia? Are you here?"

CHAPTER TWENTY-ONE

12:40 p.m.
Vineyard Vines
King of Prussia Mall
West of Philadelphia, Pennsylvania

"Girls! Where are you?" Susan frantically pushed her way past several customers cowering near the doorway in the darkness. Over a dozen people, including all the store personnel, were crammed into the stockroom at the rear of the Vineyard Vines location. They'd made the choice to turn out the lights in an effort to hide from the attackers.

"Mommy! Over here!" shouted Becca, who could barely be heard over the crying and frightened voices surrounding them.

Susan didn't care about others' feelings or common courtesy at the moment. She brusquely forced herself past anyone between her and the sound of her daughter's voice. When the three were reunited, they held each other, allowing their relief to transfer between their bodies. Once Susan confirmed they were unharmed, she turned her attention to their plight, shouting her questions to be heard over the sniveling.

"Is there a manager in here? Why haven't you people left?"

"I'm the assistant!" A young woman's voice came from the far recesses of the stockroom.

"Isn't there an emergency exit?" A logical question.

"Yes, but it's locked."

Susan fought the natural urge to go see for herself. She didn't want to drag her daughters through the packed-in group.

"Nobody locks an emergency exit! Push the panic bar!"

"We already tried. Somehow, it's locked."

"Where's the damn key?" Susan had become angry and aggravated. Just like their prior experience at Chestnut Hill so many years ago, the staff of the store was neither prepared for, nor did they have the inclination to deal with, an emergency.

"Um, either Shelley the manager has it, or it's in the register."

Susan rolled her eyes and forced herself to not lose her mind on this young girl. Sarcastically, she asked, "And where is Shelley?"

"She's still at lunch with her boyfriend," the young woman replied. Her voice had calmed somewhat.

"Okay, okay," began Susan, who tried a different tack with the assistant manager. Blasting her verbally might just result in the poor thing having a nervous breakdown. "You need to check the register for a key."

The girl didn't respond immediately, so Susan pressed her. "Did you hear me?"

"Yes," she replied sheepishly before adding, "Um, I don't want to die."

"Listen to me. There are gunmen out there who want to kill us. We have to get out of here, so we need that key!"

No response, but the level of anxiety shot up in the storeroom as the realities of what was unfolding in the mall struck them. Susan took a deep breath, squeezed the girls' hands, and made a decision.

"I'll go with you, okay? Just come forward, and the two of us will get the key."

"You will?" The young woman's voice was childlike now. Susan began to wonder if she was Penny's age. She certainly had regressed to a girl of Becca's age.

"Yes. Come on up. We'll run to the register. You open it, and I'll keep a lookout. Please. We have to hurry."

Suddenly, words of encouragement, albeit self-serving, flowed in the direction of the young assistant manager.

"Yeah, Kaitlin, you can do it."

"It's the only way. We all wanna get out of here."

Susan picked up on the assistant manager's name. "Kaitlin, is it? Come on. You and me. We'll hit the register, grab the key, and out we'll go."

Susan could sense the group was parting to make way for Kaitlin to move toward the front of the stockroom. She turned to Penny and Becca and whispered her instructions to them to slowly ease toward the emergency exit. If necessary, they'd throw everyone else in harm's way if that was what it took to escape death.

"Here I am," Kaitlin announced as she joined Susan near the storeroom door.

"I'm Susan. Please stay calm. We're gonna do this together, okay?"

The young woman nodded, the ambient light from the store's interior illuminating the abject fear on her face. A round, porthole-style window allowed a limited view of the dressing room area. The interior of the store wasn't visible from that vantage point.

Susan put a firm grip on the young woman's hand both to provide her security and to keep her from bolting back into the perceived safety of the storeroom. She eased the door open and dragged Kaitlin along with her. They both inched along the wall that separated the dressing rooms and the back wall of the retail portion of the store.

The sounds of gunfire and people screaming permeated the store. Kaitlin tried to pull back; however, Susan held her firmly in her grasp.

"Stay with me, Kaitlin. I closed the roll-down gate. If anybody was in here, they would've come back to the storeroom, right?"

Once again, Kaitlin nodded, too fearful to speak. Keeping their bodies low, Susan led the young woman along the wall. She used the floor displays as cover to prevent being seen by anyone outside the store.

They quickly moved toward the cash wrap designed to look like the stern of a vintage fishing boat. The polished teakwood reflected the fluorescent lighting from above. Because it was well lit and positioned in a way for store employees to have a clear view of all corners of the store, Susan and Kaitlin would be exposed during their time at the register.

"Let's crawl now," suggested Susan in a voice just above a whisper. She dropped to her knees, and Kaitlin followed her lead, scrambling on all fours to keep up. Seconds later, they were wedged in between the bow and the interior cabin of the mock fishing boat.

"Okay, I can do this," Kaitlin said, willing herself to be brave. She stood on her knees and nervously fumbled at the keyboard of the computer register.

On her first try, her nervous fingers made mistakes, and the register drawer failed to open. Susan became concerned that the young woman had forgotten her password. She gently placed her hand on Kaitlin's shoulder and whispered into her ear, "Deep breath, honey. It's gonna be all right."

Kaitlin took that deep breath and tried again. Susan glanced toward the plate-glass display windows. There was movement outside the store. It wasn't the frantic activity of shoppers running for their lives. It was more disciplined.

Stalking. Searching. Seeking.

Hurry, Kaitlin! Susan shouted in her head. Frightening the young woman could result in her death. And the death of her girls.

The register drawer slid open. Kaitlin rose and grasped the key with her left hand.

"I've got it!" she exclaimed happily as she stood behind the cash wrap.

Susan pulled at the young woman's sweater, but it was too late.

Gunfire erupted outside the store. Bullets blasted through the plate glass and stitched the countertop.

Time stood still as the keys fell from Kaitlin's bullet-riddled body. Susan caught them just before the keys, and Kaitlin, hit the floor.

Susan didn't hesitate. She scrambled on all fours along the wall until she was behind a table display of sweaters. She took a chance and rose to a low crouch to run the last twenty feet toward the dressing room.

She was like a bull in the proverbial China shop as she hit the swinging door full force. The shooters were breaking out the remains of the plate-glass window to enter the store, their shouts easily heard over the screams of the stowaways in the back storeroom.

Susan pushed and shoved her way to the rear of the space. Others were trying to do the same, but they didn't have the will and determination of the protective mother who'd seen the horrors of war.

"Move!" she shouted at a man who'd planted himself directly in front of the push bar. At first he hesitated until Susan lowered her shoulder and shoved him to the side. She fumbled in the dark to insert the key. When it was engaged, she quickly turned it and pressed the panic bar.

She and the girls were the first to exit into the maintenance hallway that ran behind Sephora and other stores facing the central atrium. People were running in all directions as they poured out of the backs of the retail spaces.

Vineyard Vines was centrally located in the mall. The direction Susan chose didn't matter. The hope was to blend in with the other panicked shoppers trying to escape. In less than thirty seconds, they'd pushed their way into the Nordstrom Court, where Santa Claus had so graciously greeted them earlier.

Half a minute later, they joined throngs of people rushing through the large department store toward the main entrances facing North Gulph Road. Cold, fresh air greeted them together with sirens blaring in the distance. Susan searched in all directions, looking for any of their attackers who might've followed them out of the mall.

She finally breathed a sigh of relief. They were alone among thousands, yet safe.

CHAPTER TWENTY-TWO

12:40 p.m.
LEGO Store
King of Prussia Mall
West of Philadelphia, Pennsylvania

Abbie began to feel faint despite the excruciating cramps that had beset her midsection. She looked at the ceiling, mesmerized by the light fixtures designed as LEGO blocks. Their square and rectangular shapes contained round lights emulating the iconic children's toy. Her mind wandered momentarily as she pictured moving them around to create a shape.

"Madam Vice President." The head of her security detail tried to bring Abbie back into the present. "Abbie!"

Being called by her first name by the typically professional Secret Service agent startled her. The ploy worked. Suddenly, her mind raced. Abbie nervously looked around the store and toward the shattered glass. Then she focused on Win, whom she'd extracted the large shards of glass from moments ago. She also noticed Frank's little hands, which were bloodied by embedded pieces of glass. Despite the beating his skin took and the profuse bleeding, the youngster showed no signs of pain or fear.

"Yes, sorry. It's just that—" Her voice trailed off, and her face contorted as another wave of pain came over her belly.

Win and Frank were standing near the destroyed displays of *Star Wars* Imperial destroyers and A-wing starfighters. Abbie was helped to her feet and ushered toward the back of the store by the Secret Service agent. Her eyes were focused on the emergency exit sign located to the left of the bank of cash registers. The door was being held open by an elderly woman who'd been a greeter at the store's entrance. Her yellow apron was covered with the blood splatter from the other two members of the Secret Service detail being killed.

"Hurry, boys. This way," encouraged the woman as she held the door open with her foot and waved to the kids with both hands.

The head of the Secret Service detail positioned Abbie to scoot between the woman and the door jamb. Just as Abbie cleared the entry to the stockroom, the deafening roar of automatic weapons being fired caused everyone to shriek.

The elderly woman dropped to her knees and tried to scream, but primal fear prevented her from doing so.

Bravely, the Secret Service agent did her duty and shielded Abbie from the bullets, giving her protectee time to clear the opening. She received half a dozen bullets to her back, killing her instantly.

Abbie's adrenaline kicked in as she forced the pain into the deep recesses of her mind. Her fight-or-flight instinct had usually deferred to fight after what the Loyal Nine had experienced during the collapse. Now she was pregnant and in charge of Julia's boys. It was time to run.

And run she did. The boys were waiting for her at the rear door, amazingly calm under the circumstances. Win held open the door while young Frank waved his arm as if he were waving a runner home from third. Blood was flying off his cherublike fingers and splattering the white block wall next to him.

As she ran past, Abbie knelt down and scooped up the thirty-three-pound child. Pain shot through her again, but she fought through it. Her will to survive and the tenacity of the Sargent boys gave her all the encouragement she needed.

She raced into the shadows of the large parking structure located by the LEGO store. Win, whose sweatshirt was now soaked in his blood, followed close behind. She rushed into the parking garage, where people were frantically searching for their cars.

Those in a frenzied panic had forgotten where they'd parked, so they all came up with the same solution. Press the panic alarm button on their key fob. The air was filled with the incessant honking of horns. Commensurate with the panic alarms being pushed, impatient drivers who were attempting to flee the garage pressed on their horns to aid their escape.

Abbie's pain returned, so she was forced to set Frank down. She waved to Win and instinctively grabbed Frank's hand to pull him along, but he recoiled from her touch.

"Ouch!" he protested, more from being annoyed by it all rather than from real pain. "I can follow you."

Abbie silently cursed herself. *Get your shit together. At least as much as the three-year-old.*

Holding her belly with both hands, she ran-waddled through the cars, using a zigzagging path to lose the gunmen if they'd managed to find their way into the garage. The three of them hustled down the ramp to the ground floor of the parking garage and began moving swiftly toward the exit. The automatic arm barrier with yellow-and-black lettering demanding SAFETY FIRST had just been ripped from its hinges. Drivers weren't interested in exiting one at a time, and safety was low on the totem pole at the moment.

Out of nowhere from inside the garage, a white Chevy Tahoe jumped the curb to drive on the pedestrian sidewalk. It roared toward Abbie, who pushed the boys out of the way to let the crazed driver past. However, the car suddenly screeched to a halt.

The driver flung the door open and jumped out. "Um, is that you? Like, you know, the vice president?"

Abbie was skeptical and hesitant. Seconds ago, the woman had almost run them over. She wasn't sure how to respond, and then the worst of the sharp pains she'd experienced thus far hit her like a lightning bolt. Her knees buckled, and she dropped to the concrete.

"Aunt Abbie!" shouted Win, who rushed to her side. "Are you okay?"

"It is you," said the woman. "What's wrong? Is it the baby?"

Abbie's eyes were clenched as she fought back tears and the agony caused by the possible loss of her unborn child. She gave up the inner debate of whether to trust the woman. She needed help, so she nodded.

"Pain," Abbie replied with a wince.

"Let me take you to the hospital."

Abbie was still unsure of the woman's intentions. If this had been a sophisticated hit team sent to assassinate her, Julia or Susan, then this could be a trap of some kind.

The apparent Good Samaritan sensed Abbie's hesitancy. "Come on. Trust me. Hey, I voted for you."

Abbie finally acquiesced. "Yes. Hospital."

The woman didn't hesitate. She jumped backwards and flung open the rear passenger door. She immediately came back to help Abbie into the truck. Abbie slid into the center of the bench seat and tried to get comfortable, using her hands to rub her midsection to alleviate the pain.

"Boys, you need to give her some room. Will you sit in the back-back?"

She motioned toward the rear swing door that opened to a single bench seat facing to the back of the truck. There were several packages in the way, which she quickly snatched up and carried to the passenger seat next to her after closing the door.

Moments later, the helpful driver made her way out of the parking lot as quickly as feasible while Abbie slipped in and out of consciousness. The woman tried to talk to Abbie in an effort to keep her awake. She slapped her legs and even asked for Win's assistance to speak with Abbie.

After she bulled her way past other motorists to exit the mall, she made her way onto Interstate 76 east toward Philadelphia.

Abbie's head swayed back and forth as the woman weaved in and out of traffic, even using the shoulder of the road to pass slower traffic. Then Abbie noticed the woman speed past an exit ramp that had a street sign indicating a hospital was nearby. Despite her semiconscious state, the baby blue, square sign with the letter H in the middle was a beacon of hope in her mind. Yet the woman had ignored it.

"Hey!" Abbie said with a gasp of air being released at the same time. "There was a hospital back there."

"Oh, um, you don't want that one. There's a better one up here. Just relax. I'll get you to the right place."

Abbie was becoming agitated. She sat up in the seat and began looking around in all directions. She turned to check on the boys, and then she studied the woman who was supposedly taking them to safety. Overhead, two military helicopters raced in formation past the SUV, en route to the mall.

Abbie felt for her cell phone, but she'd apparently lost it during their escape. Now concerned for their well-being, she began to question the driver. "Which hospital are you taking us to?"

"It's a small hospital. You'll be safest there. You know, from those people trying to kill you."

Abbie furrowed her brow. *How did she know we were the subject of the attack? Logical assumption or something more?*

"I need to call my husband," insisted Abbie.

"You can as soon as we get there. It isn't much longer."

"No." Abbie became harried. "It needs to be now. Right now. Please give me your cell phone."

"Listen, Mrs. Vice President. Please try to relax; you'll be in good hands."

"Arrrrgggggh!" Abbie screamed in pain and doubled over in the back seat. Her eyes rolled up into her head before she fell unconscious.

CHAPTER TWENTY-THREE

12:40 p.m.
Pottery Barn
King of Prussia Mall
West of Philadelphia, Pennsylvania

"Julia, are you here?"

The voice was familiar, yet it wasn't. Julia's mind searched the deep recesses of her brain, in the hippocampus, where memories were created via connected neurons. The process was complex and just another wonder of the human body. These neurons were stimulated by external stimuli—a picture, a touch, or a sound, such as a familiar voice.

In a way, Julia was comforted by the woman calling out her name. Inwardly, she wanted a rescuer. She wanted to save her daughter from harm. However, something inside her screamed warning sirens.

Red alert.

Proceed with caution.

All may not be as it seems.

As gunfire erupted outside the store, she was startled back to the present. Her body tensed as she took a risk. She slowly closed the drawer of the cash wrap that had provided them cover from anyone peering over the countertop. She firmly pressed on Rose's shoulders, indicating her daughter should remain in hiding. It was the moment of truth when Julia knew she'd either live or die.

She rose to her knees, allowing only her head to be seen if the flashlight illuminated it. "I'm over here."

The light swung immediately in her direction, blinding her. She covered her eyes with her right arm until they adjusted to the brightness. Against the dark backdrop of the store's interior, she was unable to make out who'd addressed her.

Then the sound of the person's feet stepping on broken glass and shuffling through blood-soaked body parts could be heard. Julia's anxiety took hold again. Why weren't they responding?

"Oh, thank God," the woman's voice said. "I thought … Well, we have to hurry."

The woman rounded the cash wrap and placed her arm under Julia's, urging her to her feet. She seemed to hesitate when she noticed Rose by Julia's side. That seemed odd, Julia thought to herself, mistrustful of who her savior was. Wouldn't the Secret Service be aware of Rose's presence with her mother?

"Who are you?" asked Julia, recoiling slightly from the woman's grasp.

She heard the woman take a deep breath despite the melee that was continuing to unfold in the mall.

"Julia, don't be alarmed. I'll explain everything in a minute. Once we're safe. Okay?"

Julia strained her eyes to make out the woman's face or any features that would help her identify this person whose voice was so familiar. The woman continued to shine her light in Julia's face and downward toward Rose.

"No, your voice." Julia hesitated as she attempted to force the issue. The gunfire continued, and it appeared to be closer to the entrance of the store. Nonetheless, she needed an answer, so she repeated the question. "Who are you?"

"Julia, it's me. Katie. Katie O'Shea."

CHAPTER TWENTY-FOUR

12:50 p.m.
King of Prussia Mall
West of Philadelphia, Pennsylvania

"Katie? Um, you're dead." Julia's mind raced. She tried to recall how Katie had been killed. It was a covert operation gone wrong. A bombing. That was all she could remember. Sarge had told her it was purely by accident. There had never been any question or discussion regarding Katie's death. No lingering doubt as to confirmation or identification of the body. It was presumed to be true.

"No, I'm alive and here to help. Now, please, we have to go before you two get hurt."

"Show me your face."

"Jesus, Julia. Okay." Katie acted perturbed at the question. In reality, she was prepared for Julia's reaction. She shined the light on her face and then smiled. "I know. I know. It's a lot to take in at the moment. I promise to explain."

Suddenly, gunfire sprayed bullets into the store, causing Katie and Julia to drop to their knees. A heavy-footed man came rushing into the store. The tactical flashlight attached to his automatic weapon's Picatinny rail swept the store in search of targets.

Katie timed her shot just right. As the flashlight's beam illuminated the wall behind the cash wrap, she tensed her body. The second it moved along the wall toward the rear of the store, she rose and fired twice at the gunman. Her first two shots struck the man in the hip. The third lodged in his neck as he dropped to the floor. It didn't matter that the gunman was part of her team. His death served a purpose—get Julia moving.

In a brusque voice, she addressed Julia. "Listen to me. I don't wanna die trying to save you. Would you please come on so we can get out of here alive?"

Julia nodded and swept Rose up in her arms. Following Katie's lead, they moved along the walls of the store until the trio reached the storeroom. A minute later, they'd pushed through the emergency exit and raced down a concrete utility ramp before emerging in a dumpster enclosure.

"Are you guys okay?" Katie whispered with a hint of feigned compassion. She was in control of her emotions and nerves.

"Yes," responded Julia after checking on Rose, who was no longer crying. "Katie, I don't understand what's happening. And why did they tell us you were dead?"

"I know it's a lot to digest right now. Let me get you out of danger, and I'll tell you everything."

Katie glanced outside the dumpster enclosure to get her bearings. Then she pressed a button on her watch. "I have FLOTUS. Location is—" she paused to take another look "—southwest corner entrance of Nordstrom at the Green Parking Garage. Sending GPS coordinates now."

"Roger that," a man's voice responded.

Katie gently nudged Julia on the shoulder and pointed toward the service road that separated the mall from the parking garage. Cars were honking at one another as they tried to force their way out of the structure.

Suddenly, three black Chevy Suburbans approached from their

left. Their interior grilles had alternating white and blue lights, flashing incessantly to grab the attention of anyone in their path. A passenger in the first vehicle rolled down his window to identify Katie before jumping out. He raced to the second SUV and opened the rear door.

Katie gently shoved Julia towards it, looking in all directions as if a threat was imminent. The only threat was the actual Secret Service detail discovering her kidnapping the First Lady of the United States and the president's only daughter.

Julia helped Rose into the back of the reconfigured Suburban that had seating similar to a limousine only more compact. Julia's eyes darted around the interior, and then she turned her body to look forward. A glass partition divided the driver's compartment from the passenger's. The lead vehicle turned on a siren, and the three-truck caravan sped down the service road without regard to the frantic shoppers fleeing the mall.

Once she was inside the back seat, Katie exhaled. She adjusted her clothing so her sidearm was both accessible and visible. In case Julia stupidly got stubborn or tried to escape, she wanted to remind her old friend that it wouldn't end well for her or her daughter.

Nobody said a word for a minute as the three trucks drove bumper-to-bumper, using the sirens and flashing lights to force their way through the other vehicles exiting the mall. After several minutes, they were entering the on-ramp of Interstate 76 toward Philadelphia.

Julia was the first to break the silence. "Katie, I'm sorry. I thought you'd been killed."

Sell it. Katie gulped and began her rehearsed story. "As you know, I went to work for Aegis. I was part of a security detail protecting a financial bigwig in Berlin when we got caught up in an unrelated terrorist bombing. Because it was a black ops mission, I had no identification, and my history had been erased a long time ago. I was in a coma for a month, and when I came out of it, my body had healed, but my mind was fuzzy. It took a year of rehabilitation and psychiatric treatment in Berlin before I realized who I was and where I'd come from."

"I'm so glad you're alive. And, of course, thank you for being there to help us."

Katie nodded as she studied Rose, who fidgeted nervously with her new Alex and Ani bracelet. The young child looked exactly like Julia. It would be a pity to have to kill her.

"It was just part of my job, Julia."

Julia pressed Katie for answers. "But I still don't understand something. Why were you at the mall? Are you part of my Secret Service detail? What about Abbie and my boys? Where are they?"

Katie chose her words carefully. It was in her best interest to keep Julia calm until they reached their destination. "I don't know about the others right now. My job was to safely protect you from danger. I'm sure the other members of my team performed as expected."

Julia sat quietly in the vehicle for several minutes as she tried to digest what had happened. The events in the mall played back through her mind right down to the moment Katie had shot the man entering Pottery Barn. It bothered her that Katie hadn't attempted to identify the man. She'd simply shot him as if she was indifferent as to whether he was Secret Service or one of the assailants.

The trio of SUVs had taken the ramp leading southbound onto Interstate 476. Julia was not completely familiar with the area, but she was aware the airport was on the south side of Philadelphia.

"Where are we going?"

Katie hesitated before responding. "There's a safe house. It's a pre-identified rendezvous point. We'll be there in a few minutes."

"I need to call Sarge and tell him what happened. Also, I want to know about Win and Frank. And Abbie, too."

"All in due time," said Katie with a gruff.

Julia immediately picked up on Katie's evasiveness and subtle change in demeanor. Her attention had been focused on their progress along the highway and a series of text messages she'd received on her Apple watch.

Julia became more direct. Authoritative. After all, she had the power to give Katie orders, whether the former member of the Loyal Nine was dead or alive.

"Katie, may I have a cell phone, please. I'd like to call my husband."

"Not yet, it's too risky."

"Risky? Why's that? I thought we were safe."

"Your husband isn't."

Anxiety swept over Julia once again. "Why? What's happened?"

Katie exploded on her former friend. "Jesus, Julia! Do you have to ask so many damn questions? Just shut up, already."

"What?" Julia was taken aback by Katie's outburst. She pulled Rose closer and gently wrapped her arm around her child's head. She began searching the interior of the SUV, and then her eyes surveilled their whereabouts. "Katie, I want some answers!"

"Fine! Here's an answer for you!" Katie roughly pulled the .45-caliber handgun from her concealed-carry holster. She cocked the hammer and pointed at Rose's chest.

Julia immediately hugged her daughter with both arms and tried to place her body in front of Katie's weapon. "Please don't hurt us." Julia began to cry.

"I told you I wouldn't if you'd just cooperate," Katie snarled. "Now, first things first. Give me her bracelet."

In her frenzied state, Julia sincerely didn't understand what Katie was referring to. "What? What are you—"

Katie shouted at her this time. "The damn bracelet. Give it to me!"

Julia looked at Rose's wrists, which helped clear her mind. Rose was wailing now as tears soaked her face and the front of her sweater. Julia gently rubbed her daughter's chest and then spoke to her in a reassuring tone of voice. "Honey, it's okay. I'll get you another one."

"Promise, Mommy?" Rose asked through her fits of sobbing. She subconsciously rubbed the rose-colored stone with her thumb as her eyes pleaded with her mother to make the promise.

Julia smiled and nodded. She removed the Alex and Ani bracelet from Rose's wrist and tossed it at Katie. "Here, you've got what you wanted. Now leave her alone."

Katie grabbed the bracelet, pushed the button to lower the window, and flung the bracelet on the interstate, where it was crushed by multiple sets of tires.

Then she emitted a maniacal laugh. "Do you think I'm stupid? Did you think I'd allow your husband's NSA to track us?"

Julia's demeanor became stoic. Inside, she responded to her kidnapper's question.

Yes, Katie. Actually, you are stupid.

CHAPTER TWENTY-FIVE

1:30 p.m.
Penn Terminals
Delaware River
South Philadelphia, Pennsylvania

The first fifteen minutes of a kidnapping were considered to be the most volatile. The criminal's emotions and adrenaline would be at their peak, making their actions and reactions unpredictable. Julia needed Katie to calm down in order for them to stay alive.

Under Julia's questioning, Katie had shown her cards early by angrily pointing her weapon at Rose and then discarding the newly purchased Alex and Ani bracelet. For all of her planning, Katie obviously was unaware of the purchase Julia had made at the mall. It saddened her to give up Rose's new bracelet. However, it provided Katie the misplaced confidence that she'd discovered a tracking beacon embedded in the bracelet.

It also provided Julia some insight into Katie's frame of mind. Once, she had been a loyal operative for the Boston Brahmin and had been readily accepted into the Loyal Nine as Steven Sargent's girlfriend. While Katie was of a different ilk than Julia, Abbie, and

Susan, her skills had served an important purpose for the Brahmin. Not only was she polished and knowledgeable, which enabled her to gain access to the highest levels of government, but when called upon to perform the deadly tasks expected of an operative, she was unparalleled.

Julia continued to keep her questions and thoughts to herself. Katie stared out the window with the occasional glance in the direction of her hostages. Rose had calmed somewhat by clinging to her mother. Julia hugged her daughter out of love and as a security blanket, of sorts. The loving act calmed her as well, allowing her to clear her mind to formulate a plan.

She didn't want to wait too long before she began her own form of psychological operation on Katie. She drew upon what she could recall of their relationship in order to humanize herself once again to her kidnapper. However, she felt her options would decrease once they arrived at their destination.

"Katie, I guess I'll never truly understand what you've gone through, but would you just tell me why you're doing this?"

She rolled her eyes and shook her head in disbelief. It was if Katie thought the whole world should already know the reason behind her anger and resentment. Julia sensed Katie wanted to lash out in her response, so she held Rose a little tighter. Instead, her captor was eerily calm.

"You really don't get it, do you? I mean, you people robbed Steven of his life. A life with me. A life that should've given him a seat at the table alongside your husband if not in his damn chair."

Julia remembered the events surrounding Steven's death much differently than Katie did. Certainly, she and Sarge were aware Steven felt slighted by John Morgan's decision to name Sarge as his replacement at the top of the Boston Brahmin. Steven had voiced his opinions. He'd paid his dues, he thought at the time.

Later, Sarge learned that Katie had been influencing his brother to pull away from Sarge's authority. Katie had not only encouraged Steven to follow his own path during the collapse but actively poisoned his mind against Sarge. In the end, in Sarge's opinion and all the others within the Loyal Nine, Steven had become distracted and lost his edge as a result of the inner conflict. For an operator who'd spent his life killing others and trying to avoid getting killed, the lack of focus had resulted in his death.

Clearly, Katie never saw it that way, but Sarge had been faced with a dilemma—what do you do with a malcontent who was once a valued member of your inner circle? Because she'd been trusted, Katie knew things. Details of operations, logistics, and finances that could easily have been used against the Loyal Nine and the Boston Brahmin.

After careful consideration and counsel with the others, Sarge had elected to banish Katie from the Loyal Nine while keeping her close enough to maintain some semblance of control. He assigned her to head up her own team at Aegis, the Brahmin's security company. Katie's activities were closely monitored and reported to Sarge. He even touched base with her on occasion to gauge her state of mind. As time passed and the nation began to rebuild, Katie's duties increased, and any discussion of Steven seemed to dissipate.

Then Sarge received word that she'd been killed in Berlin. While he was sorry to see her die, he was somewhat relieved that this dangerous loose end had been extinguished. Or, at least he thought.

"Katie, we were all crushed by Steven's death. Especially Sarge. The loss of someone you love can be devastating. But please, help me out here. That was so many years ago. Why are you doing this now? I mean, the fact you're alive is a blessing, and we should have all joined together after your recovery from the bomb blast."

Katie let out a maniacal laugh. "Wow, Madam First Lady, you sure have mastered the art of political bullshit."

"I'm sincere, Katie. Sarge and I would've welcomed you back with open arms. We would've helped you any way we could."

"Yeah, from the outside looking in. You don't think I noticed that Sarge was kicking me out in the cold? Sure, I got a fancy new gig with Aegis. Really, he threw me in a position with a short leash. Everything I was asked to do was overseas. Hell, it was inevitable that I'd die during an op."

Julia noticed the vehicles slowing as they approached the intersection with Interstate 95. The spaghettilike system of ramps confused her as she tried to gauge the direction they intended to travel. She felt the time to make a move was waning.

"You've got it wrong, Katie. I swear. Let's end this."

"That's not up to us, Madam First Lady," said Katie, her voice reeking of snark. "That's gonna be up to the most powerful man in the world. Your husband."

"What is it you want? Money? Some kind of job with the Brahmin? What?"

Katie leaned forward and hissed at Julia, "I want your husband to pay a price for what he did to me and Steven. We need something, and he's gonna give it to us. Then maybe you'll live, or maybe you won't. All's fair in love and war, right?"

We? It dawned on Julia. This well-orchestrated attack and kidnapping was part of a bigger picture. One that transcended Katie's anger and determination to seek revenge. It required planning, training, personnel, and most importantly, financing. Julia had to know. Who is *we?* And she still didn't know the *why?*

As her mind wandered, she lost sight of the caravan's direction. The sirens had been turned off, and the vehicle behind her had disengaged its flashing lights. The trucks suddenly stopped under a bridge overpass on a desolate, narrow street. Men rushed toward the passenger doors of the SUV and flung them open.

"What's happening, Mommy?" asked Rose, who suddenly burst into tears again.

"I don't know, honey. Katie? What are you doing?"

Katie didn't respond. She slid over to one side as a man stepped half into the truck to grab Rose out of Julia's arms.

"Nooo!" shouted Julia as she fought the man for control of her daughter. Rose was flailing and crying, screaming her mother's name in utter fright.

"Sedate her!" shouted Katie, who used the butt of her pistol to slap Julia's arm away from Rose. Another man reached through the other side of the SUV and rammed a needle through Julia's pant leg into her thigh. He depressed the plunger, and within seconds, Julia's eyes rolled into the back of her head. She tilted and then fell over unconscious in the seat.

"Ma'am, what do you want us to do with the child?" one of the men asked after Rose had been whisked away to the trailing vehicle.

Katie debated within herself. On the one hand, the young child presented a complication she wasn't prepared for. On the other, what better bargaining chip was there for a president who was being forced to make a dreadful decision?

"Sedate her, as well. We'll take them both and provide them separate accommodations."

Minutes later, the three SUVs pulled alongside a massive freighter docked at Penn Terminals, one of the busiest international shipping facilities on the Atlantic seaboard. Every day, massive cargo ships arrived and departed, carrying everything from forest products to steel to consumer goods. Today, this container ship operated by Cabot Industries would sail into the Atlantic with Katie and Sarge's precious cargo.

CHAPTER TWENTY-SIX

1:30 p.m.
Monocacy Farm
South of Frederick, Maryland

The explosion caused by the rocket-propelled grenade lifted the already rickety bridge crossing the river high into the air before it splintered into thousands of pieces. Some chunks of wood flew in the direction of the hunters while the rest fell harmlessly into the river, where it was carried away by the swift current.

With Sarge and his hunting party stunned by the unexpected turn of events, their attackers immediately gained the upper hand. Bullets tore up the snow-soaked turf around their feet and sailed past them into the woods, shredding the bark off trees while embedding in others. Two bullets, however, found their mark.

Captain Morrell turned to shield the president from the gunfire. Sarge reacted as well, but it was too late for his longtime protector. The head of Sarge's Secret Service detail took bullets in the back and shoulder, slamming him forward into Sarge's legs. Both men tumbled to the muddy ground as the onslaught of bullets sailed around them.

"Help them to the trees!" shouted Drew as he stepped forward and dropped to a knee. He squeezed the trigger and laid down suppressive fire in the direction where the automatic gunfire was coming from. He couldn't see his target, but that wasn't necessary at the moment. He simply needed to force their attackers to back off until Sarge was safe. He emptied his magazine and expertly dropped it while inserting another in one continuous motion.

"Done!" shouted Brad from the woods.

Drew took a glance over his shoulder to confirm they were behind some form of cover before quickly backing up the hill. He sent several more rounds along the bank of the river where the bridge had been destroyed before disappearing behind a large white pine.

"What the hell?" asked Sarge in a loud whisper to no one in particular. His hands were covered in Morrell's blood from helping the wounded man to safety. Sarge scooted out of the way to allow J.J. to examine Morrell's bullet wounds. Brad knelt next to Morrell to lend an assist.

Drew stood with his back against the tree. More gunshots rang out, piercing the once quiet woods. The bullets whizzed past, ripping through the foliage and embedding in the ground beneath the snow. His head was on a swivel, looking to both sides as well as the slight incline that rose to the top of a hill.

"We've gotta move!" he ordered, his voice filled with apprehension and excitement. "If they fire off another RPG, we're screwed."

Sarge looked to J.J. "Can we move him?"

"I don't know. We probably shouldn't until—" J.J.'s response was cut off by Morrell, who lifted his head off the ground.

"Leave me," he said before he began to cough violently. He recovered long enough to say, "Sarge has to be protected."

Sarge ignored him. "J.J., can we move him? I'm not leaving him behind."

"We don't have a choice," Drew replied on J.J.'s behalf. "We don't leave anyone behind, but we gotta move. Now!"

He slapped J.J. on the shoulder and gestured for him to lift under Morrell's left arm. Drew did the same on the right side while keeping his weapon ready to fire. They began to drag Morrell to his feet, who managed to stumble along to help.

Sarge and Brad took up defensive positions in front of and behind the group. Sarge made his way up the hill to ferret out any attackers who might be waiting for them. Brad urged them on, reporting that he'd seen several members of their Secret Service detail gather on the other side of the river near the location where the bridge once stood. Their orange-clad vests caused them to stand out against the woodsy backdrop.

The gunfire erupted once again as the three remaining agents came under fire. They dove behind fallen trees and tried to shoot back to subdue their unknown assailants.

"They're pinned down," began Sarge. "We need to help them."

Drew dispelled the notion. "No, Sarge. We can't. If we get near that bank, they'll—"

Another explosion shook the earth, causing all of them to lose their balance on the slippery, snow-covered slope. Brad slid the farthest toward the spot where the second rocket-propelled grenade had struck. It was mere feet from where they'd stood moments ago. He feigned a scream, moaning as if he'd been hit in order to give their attackers a false sense of nailing their target. Then he scrambled back up the hill and joined the others, who were in turn rushing toward the top with a new sense of purpose.

Brad's tactic succeeded in delaying the onslaught. The return fire from the Secret Service details' weapons ceased, leaving Brad to conclude they were killed. The trees cleared as they sloshed through the snow that had accumulated at the base of a massive limestone outcropping. All of them were breathing heavily from the moist air and their scramble up the hill while carrying Morrell.

Drew took charge. "Sarge, Brad, take up positions behind those rocks. J.J., help me with Morrell. I need his comms and cell phone."

He and J.J. lifted Morrell to a flat rock at the base of the large boulders. Drew cleared the rock of snow and debris so they could place Morrell on the table-like outcropping. Morrell regained consciousness just as Drew was about to remove his hearing device and microphone.

"Let me call it out," he said with a groan. "We need to convince them that Sarge is dead."

"What?" asked J.J., his eyes darting between the injured man and his longtime friend. "Are you sure?"

Morrell gave him an imperceptible nod. "If they think their target is eliminated, they might give up the chase."

"The river is between us and them," said J.J.

Drew understood the implication. "They're equipped with RPGs. I guarantee they've got operatives on this side of the river. Morrell, make the call—POTUS is down."

While Morrell tried to reach out to his team and provide the notification that Sarge had been killed, Drew attempted to call for help. Unfortunately, this remote part of the woods and surrounding ridges did not have cellular service. He looked up at the rock outcropping and knew that was his best option to make a call.

"Guys, eyes wide open." Everyone turned toward Drew. He studied their faces. There wasn't fear in any of them, including Morrell, whose blood had soaked the once snow-covered rock. "I'm gonna find my way up there to call help and hail a chopper."

Brad agreed. "Do it. Go. We've got this." He and Sarge made eye contact. The two men had fought side by side in the early days of the collapse when the former president had sent operatives into Quabbin Reservoir to assassinate Sarge and all the Boston Brahmin. When that effort had been turned away by the Mechanics, the future president of the Pacific States called in a drone attack to bomb the Brahmin's facility on Prescott Peninsula. That, too, had been thwarted.

After patting Donald on the back and providing the former accountant a thumbs-up, Drew hustled around the rock outcropping and disappeared from sight. Sarge and Brad made their way back to the fallen rocks that allowed them a clear view of anyone approaching from the river. After a moment, Brad spoke to Sarge in a hushed voice.

"This is all kinds of FUBAR."

"Yeah, no kidding. I got a list of suspects."

"Does it start with Gardner Lowell?"

"You bet, or his mother," replied Sarge. "Either way, he was pissed enough to come at me hard."

"I'll kill the puny bastard myself," grumbled Brad as he returned his attention to the tracks in the snow made by dragging Morrell up the hill. He realized they'd have difficulty hiding from their attackers with the disturbed turf betraying their footsteps.

Sarge didn't reply to Brad. He only thought to himself that he should've dealt with Gardner already. Sarge suspected Gardner perceived him as weak for not fighting back on his level. In the gutter where the Brahmin often went to accomplish their purposes.

He glanced back at his friend who'd saved his life by taking a bullet. Morrell was writhing in pain as J.J. did his best to administer first aid. He vowed to make Lowell, and his mother, pay for what they'd done. But first, they had to survive.

CHAPTER TWENTY-SEVEN

1:35 p.m.
Monocacy Farm
South of Frederick, Maryland

Drew was in his element. Having grown up on the Cumberland Plateau, he was used to scaling rocky terrain and dense woodlands. While it didn't snow all that often in the geographically unique region of Tennessee located equidistant between Knoxville and Nashville, the two-thousand-foot elevation often created slick, icy conditions. In a way, the fresh, wet snow underfoot gave him more traction than what he was used to.

Nonetheless, he chose his footing and grips carefully as he moved from one limestone rock formation to another to reach the top of the ridge. Despite his desire for safety, his sense of urgency forced him upward at a quick pace.

Like the others, his mind processed what was happening, and not surprisingly, Drew also tried to determine who his attackers were. In addition to Brad, Drew knew the special ops forces of the U.S. government as well as anyone, having been trained and deployed as such. This had all the earmarks of a covert kill mission with the intention of assassinating the President of the United States. What shocked him was their use of RPGs.

The tremendous explosions would've been heard for many miles across the quiet woods and surrounding farms. To be sure, the security detail protecting the Marine One squadron would've come to their aid after the first grenade destroyed the bridge across the river. If that didn't raise alarms, the staccato gunfire should have.

Yet their cavalry wasn't coming. Over his heavy breath and the crunching snow, Drew listened intently for the sound of the choppers. He expected to hear sirens in the distance. Instead, there was the calm and serenity of the woods on a snowy day. However, his sixth sense told him danger lurked all around.

Drew tried to put himself in the shoes of their attackers. Destroying the pedestrian bridge served a twofold purpose. Any Secret Service agents who hadn't been quietly killed in the woods were now cut off from the president. Second, the hunting group's means of escape or a route back to Marine One was eliminated.

He silently cursed himself for not spending more time studying the geography of Monocacy Farm and the surrounding areas. This was unfamiliar territory for Drew, and he should've done his homework. He refused to allow himself the excuse that he'd arrived home from Taiwan after a twenty-hour flight that allowed him less sleep than he'd told Abbie. If the truth were told, Drew would've opted out of the all-day hunting trip if he had been asked by anyone else besides his friend Sarge.

Drew reached the summit of the ridge and looked toward the south. In a way, he'd hoped to see plumes of smoke rising into the sky, indicating Marine One and its accompanying helicopters had been destroyed. They had not been blown up, anyway. Most certainly, they remained grounded.

His mind raced as he tried to recall the weaponry available to the HMX-1 squadron. He was only aware of the standard military anti-missile countermeasures such as flares to defend against heat-seeking missiles and chaff to counter radar-guided missiles.

Because of the ease with which their attackers had eliminated

Morrell's team on the ground, he had to consider the possibility that some members of the Secret Service detail had been compromised. He was aware that Sarge had been through a difficult week related to the Pacific Statehood Act. It was possible one of his political adversaries had arranged his assassination because of his position on the vote. If that was the case, they couldn't trust anyone within the protection detail. They were on their own.

Drew checked the phone display to determine if he had coverage. "One freakin' bar. Gee, thanks, Verizon."

He paced back and forth. His first instinct was to call in his own people. However, King and the others were on leave following their heroic efforts in Taiwan. It wasn't that they wouldn't come to his aid. The problem was logistics. It would take hours for them to arrive. He and the others would be dead by then.

He dialed Abbie. Her phone rang and rang, but she never answered. He left her a message and then repeated it with a text. He provided her their GPS coordinates, immediately realizing he needed to get everyone moving again to avoid a second wave of attackers.

Initially, Drew didn't want to get the local law enforcement involved, but he felt he had no choice. If the woods were full of operatives closing on their position, their only hope was to flood the area with police on four-wheelers accompanied by hunting dogs.

"Nine-one-one. What is your emergency?"

"My name is Drew Jackson, and I am part of the hunting party accompanying the President of the United States. We are under attack at Monocacy Farm south of Frederick, Maryland. We need all available law enforcement units dispatched to my location immediately."

"Sir, one moment, please."

"What?" asked Drew incredulously. The line went silent for a moment.

"Sir, this is Sergeant Robinson. I am the dispatch supervisor. What is your emergency?"

"I told the other lady. I am with the president's hunting party on Monocacy Farm on the north side of the river. We have been attacked by unknown assailants. We have one man shot, and there are probably several Secret Service agents killed on the other side of the river. We need all hands on deck here!"

"Sir, what is your name?"

"Drew Jackson. My wife is the damn vice president!"

"Abbie Morgan?"

"Yes!"

Automatic gunfire broke out from Drew's rear. He dropped to the ground as the bullets ripped through the pines and ricocheted off the rock formation.

"Sir? Sir?"

Drew could hear the 9-1-1 operator's voice, but he couldn't find his phone. As he hit the ground, it had fallen out of his hand and dropped into the snow between the rocks.

"Dammit! Send help!"

"Sir? Where are you?" The sergeant was shouting back.

"On a ridge above the river!"

More gunfire strafed the ground around him. Drew was an easy target with no cover. And worse, their assassins had now confirmed their targets' location. He abandoned any notion of finding the phone to speak with the local law enforcement. If they could hear, he'd allow the gunfire to speak for itself.

As he slid off the side of the ridge, following the same path he'd used to climb up, Drew was fully aware they were about to be engulfed by a shitstorm.

CHAPTER TWENTY-EIGHT

2:00 p.m.
Monocacy Farm
South of Frederick, Maryland

"We have to move him!" J.J. shouted to Brad and Donald. J.J. closely monitored Morrell for signs he might be going into shock. He'd loosened Morrell's belt and cut the collar, which was tight around his neck. He removed his jacket and covered Morrell with it to keep him warm. The most difficult task, in addition to stopping the bleeding, was keeping his patient still.

J.J. admonished himself for not bringing at least basic first aid treatments like gauze, tape, and Neosporin. He'd gotten soft, he thought to himself. After years of being a battlefield trauma surgeon followed by those many months as the Armageddon doctor for the Boston Brahmin at Prescott Peninsula, he'd settled into an administrative job at the Veteran's Administration.

To be sure, J.J. had been credited for a remarkable turnaround at the VA. As a soldier and physician, he understood the needs of his fellow veterans, especially those with mental issues. He was roundly praised by everyone within the agency and the top brass in the U.S. Armed Forces.

However, he was angry that he'd lost that edge required to save lives on the battlefield. Despite the fact they were hunting with a Secret Service detail supposedly protecting them, J.J. was angry with himself for not preparing for the possibility of an accident.

Once Morrell had been positioned on the flat rock, with the assistance of Donald, J.J. was able to better examine his gunshot wounds. One bullet had entered Morrell's upper back, fortunately missing his internal organs. His breathing was steady and not labored, indicating to J.J. that miraculously, the bullet had not punctured his lung. Most likely, it was embedded in his back muscle. The second had done significant damage to Morrell's rotator cuff, the four muscles that kept the upper arm in the shoulder socket. This was causing him the most pain.

That was the good news. The bad news was these foreign objects, gunpowder-covered projectiles, were inside his body and potentially causing an infection.

The first thing J.J. had to do was stop the loss of blood flowing from the bullet holes. He removed his own thermal undershirt and applied pressure to Morrell's wounds to stem the blood loss. However, in the cold conditions exacerbated by their being in the shadow of the large rock formation, Morrell began to shiver uncontrollably.

He had to find an alternative way to stem the bleeding. J.J. drew upon his experiences on the field of battle. There were times when soldiers suffered bullet wounds and a medic was not readily available. He'd learned that one of the most abundant materials on Earth, its soil, could be used to clot the blood.

There was a high risk of infection using this method, and it was only recommended in extreme circumstances coupled with a realistic possibility of getting medical attention within hours. Dirt contained soil silicates that acted as a clotting agent by activating a blood protein referred to as coagulation factor XII.

Once activated, the protein starts a chain reaction leading to the formation of a plug, which seals the wound and limits blood loss. When there were no better options, the soil could trigger clotting, thus helping manage the bleeding. Since half of all trauma patients die from excessive bleeding, it was worth the gamble in Morrell's case.

After packing the wounds with dry soil he located underneath a rock outcropping devoid of snow, J.J. wrapped the arms of his thermal undershirt around Morrell's body. He then dressed him and covered him with the jackets to keep him warm. Thus far, his Armageddon doctor skills were paying off, until the gunshots directed at Drew were a reminder they were still in grave danger.

Sarge and Brad retreated up the hill to join J.J. They rushed along the base of the ridge in search of cover. Sarge was the first to locate a suitable option.

"There's a cave over here!" he shouted from fifty feet away. He began trudging through the snow to return to J.J. and Morell. "I mean, it's not much of a cave, but it's enough for us to lay him flat and out of the snow."

Brad returned at the same time. "There's nothing my way. Let's move him."

Sarge, Donald and Brad worked together to carry Morrell to safety within the overhang of the limestone rock formation. J.J. was careful to apply pressure to his wounds while Sarge and Brad slowly lowered him onto the ground. Within seconds of Morrell being secured, Drew arrived by their side. He was breathing heavily, not from being out of shape but from the surge of adrenaline coursing through his body.

"They're coming," he began, pointing over his head. "They're gonna have the high ground."

"Did you get through to anyone?"

"Local law enforcement only," he replied solemnly as he studied Morrell. "Guys, I don't know if we can trust the Secret Service. Either these operators have a helluva large force, or our people were in on it. If I can't answer one way or the other, then we've gotta play it a different way."

"Deputy Dawg and the mounted police on their four-wheelers?" asked Donald sarcastically.

"They wouldn't be part of a hit squad to kill the president," replied Drew. "Plus, they're warm, enthusiastic bodies flooding the kill zone. My guess is that whoever is after us doesn't want to be caught and interrogated."

"Agreed," said Sarge. "If I'm right and Lowell is behind all of this, he's instigated a war within the Brahmin. He'll not want to leave any loose ends."

"He'd be out of his mind," added Donald.

Drew turned to Brad. "Would Marine One be equipped with RPGs?"

"Doubtful, or at least not to my knowledge."

Drew nodded and surveilled his surroundings. "Then they might be outsiders. It's hard to say for sure."

"They'll be coming for us," said Sarge. "What do you guys suggest?"

"Protect the king," Donald responded.

J.J. joined them. "Sarge, can you stay with Morrell and monitor his condition? The rest of us will find a way to defend our position until help arrives."

Drew addressed Brad. "If they're coming from the north, the high ground, as I suspect, they're not gonna fire off another RPG. They'd never get the angle to take the shot."

"You're right. They'll hit us from the sides or from the river."

"Okay, let's do this," Drew started. He was outranked on all sides, but he was the most seasoned operative of the group. Brad had been a battlefield general and was rarely involved with field operatives. "I'm gonna take up a position down the hill with a clear shot to the top of the ridge. I can protect us from anyone approaching from the river and prevent them from firing upon us from above. You guys split up and protect our flanks. Don't expose yourself to those above us and focus on picking them off if they descend the ridge. The longer we can fight 'em off, the better are chances are of getting out of this alive."

Drew's final words hung in the air, a reminder to them all that this might be their last day on Earth.

CHAPTER TWENTY-NINE

2:10 p.m.
Monocacy Farm
South of Frederick, Maryland

Drew scrambled into place after locating a fallen tree that had broken in half over an eight-foot-wide rock. He resisted the urge to dart the hundred yards to the riverbank to determine if any hostiles were approaching from below them. He'd resigned himself to holding his position and using the eyes in the back of his head, so to speak, to watch his six.

He dropped to his knees and knelt in silence for an eternity, it seemed. Waiting. Straining his ears to hear something. Heavy feet crunching through the snow. A broken branch inadvertently stepped on. The faint sound of a chopper in the distance, responding to his call for assistance. Gunshots. Anything to indicate what would happen next.

Despite his heightened sense of awareness, he received nothing in return. Only silence and the sound of the river passing by. He remained on edge. Rarely blinking. Scouring the landscape in search of any form of movement. A gust of cold wind swept over him, instinctively causing him to hunch his shoulders.

Inside him, he felt a cold fist squeeze his nerves, forcing him to attention. He tensed as he could feel the gunmen approaching. From all sides. Multiple hostiles. Drew took a deep breath and wondered how they'd survive the onslaught. He was the only one battle tested and armed with an automatic weapon. He was limited to three magazines now, having spent one as they'd fled the river's bank. He'd have to be judicious with his shots.

Also, he was keenly aware that the others were defending themselves with hunting rifles. They'd never trained on the rapid fire and reloading of a rifle. Their attackers would have a decided advantage.

He'd just taken a deep breath and began to surveil the higher ground when the first rounds of gunfire invaded the silence of the woods. The rounds cracked loudly, echoing off the rock formation. Their quick burst clearly came from the operatives who'd stalked them to this spot.

Drew immediately noted that none of the others returned fire. They'd abided by his warning to maintain ammunition discipline. The attackers' first shots were most likely designed to draw return fire in an attempt to identify their targets' location. Brad and J.J. held their fire, waiting on a clear shot, as they'd discussed.

A burst of gunfire, sounding like the pops of a large firecracker, was heard to his right. It was followed by more coming from atop the boulder. Apparently, the operatives were convinced of the hunters' location and were ready to engage.

Drew took a brief moment to search his rear for movement. Thus far, all of the activity was up the hill. After settling into a prone position behind the fallen tree, he rested his rifle on a spot between the trunk and a broken branch. Then he used his scope to scan the top of the ridge for logical places where the attackers might reveal themselves.

He laughed to himself. What he was doing in search of a target was no different than what he did as a hunter. Identify likely places for a target to appear. Settle in and be patient. Take a deep breath and prepare to fire. Only, he was using a high-powered assault weapon. A tool that was every bit as useful to a hunter as a Remington 700 bolt action.

"I'll show you how to hunt," he mumbled to himself as he prepared to fire.

CHAPTER THIRTY

2:22 p.m.
Monocacy Farm
South of Frederick, Maryland

Sarge spoke softly to Morrell, who was managing to hold onto consciousness. "Dave, they're coming for us. I've got to provide backup to Brad and J.J."

"Go," he said, and it could have easily been mistaken for a moan. "I'll be fine. But, Sarge, this country needs you. Don't get your ass shot like I did."

Sarge chuckled. He gently placed his hand on his friend's forehead to feel for fever as well as a gesture of friendship. "You saved my life. Again. We're gonna get through this and get you fixed up. Then you're gonna retire to that cabin on the Hudson."

"Screw you," said Morrell, who managed a smile despite his pain. "We're a team, remember? I've endured this bullshit for eight years, waiting for you to be a private citizen again so we can go to Hooters together."

Sarge stifled a laugh. "You'd better clear this with my missus."

"She can come, too," Morrell said with a laugh. He began to cough, prompting Sarge to place his hand on his chest.

"Easy, Dave. You plan our day to Hooters, and I'll make sure we're alive to get there."

"Roger that, boss."

There was another crack of gunfire, and a shower of limestone chips cascaded down the ridge on top of Sarge's back. He inched forward until the deluge had passed and immediately turned to look down the hill toward Drew's position.

Sarge set his jaw and gently patted Morrell on the arm. "Today is not our day to die."

He and Donald exchanged a few words. Donald agreed to watch over their patient while Sarge helped defend their position. Sarge hustled along the rock formation until he found cover equidistant between J.J. and Brad.

There was a sustained, almost rhythmic barrage of gunfire that sounded closer to him than he'd expected. From above, several shots rang out. Sarge didn't know whether to look up or down. Drew was returning fire, engaging the enemy with short, quick bursts of just a few rounds with each squeeze of the trigger. His AR-10 sounded like cannon fire compared to their attackers'. Sarge held firm until the fight was brought to him. Sort of.

A body came careening down the face of the limestone outcropping, snapping and breaking as it hit every jagged rock. If he wasn't killed by Drew's bullets on impact, he certainly would not have survived the sixty-foot drop. The gunman landed on his back; the sound of his spine being cracked apart was heard by Sarge, who was only feet away.

Sarge tensed his muscles and gripped his rifle. As had always been the case when he left the friendly confines of the White House, Sarge was also carrying a sidearm. While there have been presidents who frequently used weapons while hunting, not since Andrew Jackson's derringer and the rumored pistol kept in Ronald Reagan's Oval Office had a president carried a concealed weapon. Sarge had insisted upon it.

Now Brad and J.J. were engaged with the gunmen. A long *braaap* from the operatives' automatic weapons tore through the trees and rocks around them. The two men in their late sixties fired back in an effort to hold off any advance by the gunmen.

Sarge was frustrated. He felt like he'd been sidelined because he was more important than his friends in the Loyal Nine. He saw it differently. It hearkened back to those days during the collapse when he'd fought side by side with the Mechanics as they took the battle to the UN occupying forces in Boston.

This was no different. Freedom was worth fighting for then, and the attackers today were trying to force him to subject himself to someone else's will. He refused to live on his knees, so he broke cover and raced to an outcropping farther down the slope where he could get a better vantage point.

His footsteps were chased by bullets tearing up the snowy turf and ripping through the pine trees he used for cover. Sarge evaded death, that time, and slid to a stop behind a rock just in front of Drew, who immediately unleashed a stream of expletives.

Drew was pissed, but all Sarge could do was manage a smile. He was now part of the action.

CHAPTER THIRTY-ONE

2:30 p.m.
Monocacy Farm
South of Frederick, Maryland

For twenty minutes gunfire was exchanged between the operatives and the hunters-turned-hunted. Drew had been deadly accurate in picking off the unsuspecting attackers from the top of the ridge. For a while, they stopped trying to fire from the high ground, and Drew sensed they were flanking his position.

He'd been caught up in the firefight, trying to pick off targets as they appeared while monitoring the battle between his guys, who were pinned down against the ridge. Drew became hyperaware of his surroundings. He considered breaking cover and joining Sarge, who was barely thirty feet up the hill from his position.

Then he heard the crunch of a foot through some crystalized snow. Drew shouldered his weapon and eased backwards to a twin-trunked tree. He remained still, controlling his breathing to focus on the sound of the approaching assailant.

He reached down and pulled his Garberg BlackBlade knife made by MoraKniv from his ankle sheath. The four-inch carbon-steel blade was coated in black, ideal for Drew's profession. He slowed his breathing and waited for the man to approach. He was well trained, walking softly in the snow. Heel to toe. However, it was not quiet enough.

As he revealed himself to Drew's left, the swishing sound of the knife caught him off guard. The sharp tip embedded in the man's neck. He tried in vain to dislodge it, and in a split second, the agile Drew pounced on him.

Drew covered the man's mouth with a death grip to keep him quiet before he twisted the Garberg. The sharp blade easily severed the man's carotid artery, bringing his life to a quick, bloody end.

Drew paused for a moment in a low crouch, disregarding the blood spurting from the man's neck and the immediate acrid smell of his bowels releasing into his pants. Confident nobody else was coming for him, he searched the man for identification. There wasn't any, but the man was equipped with communications to stay in touch with his team. Drew hurriedly removed it from the dead man and inserted the earpiece to listen to their communications. He gritted his teeth and shook his head once out of disappointment. They were maintaining radio discipline. No chatter whatsoever.

Still, this was a potential force multiplier for Drew, as it enabled him to relay instructions to the others. Now he had to deal with Sarge, who had no business engaging in a firefight. He ran through the snow and ducked behind a rock near Sarge's position.

"What the hell, Mr. President?" he asked sarcastically.

Sarge didn't look in Drew's direction as he continued to scan the landscape for a target. "Don't call me that. You only do that when you're pissed."

"I am pissed," Drew shot back. "You're still the dang president, and you've got a family."

"I know. I know," said Sarge before changing the subject. "Listen, they're gonna overwhelm Brad and J.J. if we don't give them a hand. What should we do?"

"*We* should do nothing," responded Drew harshly. "You stay here and watch your back. I just took one guy out, and there may be more."

"You did? I didn't hear—"

Drew slid closer to his friend. "Dammit. Watch your six. I'll help the guys." He paused and tapped his ear. "Plus, I've got their comms."

More automatic gunfire rang out against the hillside, followed by two quick shots in succession from Brad's rifle. His bullets must have found their mark, as bloodcurdling cries of agony echoed weirdly off the limestone bluff.

Drew advanced up the hill while the gunmen were preoccupied with Brad. One of the shooters raced around a boulder to get a better position. He never saw Drew.

He squeezed the trigger and let out three rounds. The bullets slammed into the approaching operative, punching holes in his body. The man spun around and crashed into a rock. Startled by the sudden gunfire from below, another assailant appeared in the open and fired wildly in Drew's direction. He, too, was dispatched with a quick burst from Drew's rifle.

There was a brief respite during which time neither side fired. Faintly, but loud enough to be heard by all the combatants, the *whomp-whomp-whomp* of a helicopter's rotors approached from the east. In the distance, the rumble of four-wheelers could be heard slowing and accelerating as they traveled through the woodsy landscape toward the field of battle. And then the first to arrive on the scene were hunting dogs that were used by the locals to track the operatives.

For the first time, Drew was beginning to feel relief. And then Sarge shouted at the top of his lungs.

"Incoming!"

CHAPTER THIRTY-TWO

2:35 p.m.
Monocacy Farm
South of Frederick, Maryland

The RPG-7 was a forty-millimeter warhead designed to send a kinetic shockwave through anything it hit. Its main military function was to destroy tanks and armored personnel carriers. Once fired, the RPG would receive a signal that initiated a propeller, causing the grenade to race away from the launcher. The metallic fins that sprouted during this process gave it stability in flight. It also generated a distinctive whistling sound.

It was fired just below Sarge's position. If they were trying to hit him, they missed high and to the left. If their target had been the largest boulder comprising the ridge's outcropping, then they scored a direct hit.

Although relatively soft compared to granite, dense limestone was capable of having a crushing strength that could withstand most anything nature threw at it. This massive rock, however, could not absorb the impact of the rocket-propelled grenade. It slammed into the face of the rock, causing the entire ridge to shake. Rocks all around the outcropping became dislodged or broken, instantaneously raining stones large enough to crush those below it.

Brad and J.J. shouted to one another to take cover while Sarge, throwing caution to the wind, rushed up the hill to help them.

Drew, on the other hand, ran after the operator of the device to ensure he didn't get off a second shot. Darting from tree to tree, he found the man's hiding spot. He was in the process of locking another warhead into its firing tube. Drew heard the clunk, a sound he was familiar with, as it was secured in place. The operator, however, would never get the opportunity to fire.

Drew unleashed a fusillade of NATO 7.62-millimeter ammunition into the man's body, knocking him backwards until he crashed into a tree. The launcher fell into a snowdrift and became buried underneath it at the feet of the dead man.

Without hesitation, Drew ran up the hill, trudging through the snow with his weary legs. There was no gunfire, but chaos reigned, nonetheless.

"Rapido! Rapido!"

"Extraer! Andale!"

Drew pressed the earpiece deeper into his ear canal as if having less ambient noise enter his mind might change the language of their attackers.

He reached the base of the ridge where Donald was helping Brad remove fallen rock from J.J.'s legs. His head was bleeding, and he complained that his right leg might be broken. Drew saw his disfigured leg the moment he stood over J.J. *Might be broken* were not the words he would've used for the hideous compound fracture.

Multiple dogs were barking all around them. They came rushing around the side with uniformed deputies from the Frederick County Sheriff's Department close behind. All had their weapons drawn and were pointing them menacingly toward the hunting party.

Confident their attackers had fled the scene, Sarge approached them with his hands raised high. "Easy, everyone. We're the good guys."

The exhilarated deputies slowed their pace and used verbal commands to calm the K-9 unit that had led the way. One of the deputies immediately recognized Sarge despite his unusual attire.

"Mr. President, are you okay? We got a call. Um, dispatch wasn't certain it was genuine."

"I'm fine, but we need help. I've got one man with gunshot wounds and another with a broken leg."

"We've already requested a chopper from the Johns Hopkins trauma unit in Baltimore. They're hovering just to our north, awaiting the all clear." The deputy holstered his weapon and reached for his radio from his utility belt. The other deputy looked upward to the boulder that had just been split by the warhead.

"Do you think they can still land up top?" Sarge asked Drew, pointing up to the outcropping.

"I'll check," he responded. He turned to Sarge and tilted his head toward the trail he'd used earlier. "Up for a quick hike?"

Sarge asked the deputies to help with J.J. and Morrell. They readily agreed, and just as the guys began the trek up the hill, the four-wheelers were making their way to the injured.

"Everything okay?" asked Sarge as he followed in Drew's footsteps.

"I think we're safe, for now. I heard something after the RPG was fired."

"Yeah, it was the sound of a rock splitting in half."

"No. I'm talking about through their comms. Sarge, they were speaking Spanish."

"What? Really?" Sarge was confounded.

"No doubt. Of course, we'll have the FBI run prints and all that on the dead bodies. However, they might be a foreign hit squad. Most likely Colombian or Mexican cartels. Those guys were well trained."

"Yeah, by us, right?" asked Sarge facetiously.

Drew grimaced and nodded. He replied as they made their way up the ridge, "Not your administration but the prior one. In 2013, the Mexican cartels went on a hiring spree of our former military and set up a training camp in Jalisco outside Guadalajara. Previously, Los Zetas had been very successful in 2010 recruiting some of our soldiers who trained at Fort Bragg."

The two men reached the top of the limestone rock outcropping. It was large enough to land a chopper, but gingerly. Drew studied the woods again, keeping his body between the trees and Sarge. He didn't want to fall into a false sense of security. Somehow, he thought, this might not be over.

CHAPTER THIRTY-THREE

3:00 p.m.
Monocacy Farm
South of Frederick, Maryland

After the LifeFlight helicopter from Johns Hopkins lifted off with J.J. and Morrell, Sarge, Brad, Donald, and Drew were taken by four-wheelers to an adjacent farm where a new Secret Service detail awaited. The White House physician had also been summoned to provide Sarge a quick medical exam. He looked over the others, and the hunting party was secured inside a caravan of vehicles that quickly pulled away from the vicinity of the attack.

Sarge insisted they be taken to Camp David, which was the closest secure facility. After they had traveled several miles away from Monocacy Farm to the north side of Frederick, the four-truck motorcade pulled over on a rural section of Catoctin Hollow Road. The security detail poured out of their vehicles and fanned out to secure the perimeter.

"I don't like this," mumbled Drew as he reached for his rifle.

Sarge pressed the communications button on the console above his head to address their driver. "Why are we stopping here?"

"Sorry for the delay, Mr. President. We're being greeted by the deputy director of Homeland Security, who has been awaiting your arrival at Camp David."

"Well, from my recollection, we're only a few miles away," said Sarge.

"Yes, sir. He's asked that we hold you here until he speaks with you. Oh, they are pulling up now, sir."

Three vehicles led by a sheriff's deputy car with its bar of emergency lights turned on approached at a fast rate of speed. The vehicles slowed to a stop, and the administrator rushed out of the car without waiting for his security team to check the surroundings. He ran toward the middle SUV, which held Sarge and the others.

Sarge flung his door open and exited the SUV, immediately causing his new security detail to scramble to surround him.

"What's going on?"

Miguel Ruiz, a DHS assistant secretary, eased up to Sarge and spoke in hushed tones. The man's voice was comforting yet disconcerting. Sarge searched his eyes, wondering if this was some kind of cruel hoax. Was there more to the story than what Ruiz was letting on?

Sarge tried to restrain his emotions. There was a time to remain strong and presidential. And then there was a time for a husband and father to lose it. Tears streamed from his eyes as he returned to the safe confines of the SUV. Seconds later, the others knew the grave danger their loved ones were in.

PART V

The Assassins
Black Friday, November 2024, late afternoon

CHAPTER THIRTY-FOUR

Late Afternoon
Penn Terminals
Delaware River
South Philadelphia, Pennsylvania

Katie supervised the surreptitious removal of her unconscious captives from the vehicle. The child was easy, as she was able to be stuffed into a large seaman's duffel. Her team summoned one of the many dockworkers who'd been handsomely bribed to assist as she loaded the unusual cargo aboard the freighter. He easily hoisted the duffel containing Rose onto his shoulder, carrying her aboard as if she were the gear belonging to another member of the oceangoing freighter's crew.

Bringing Julia on board was different. She had to be carried aboard, so two members of her team slung her arms over their shoulders and dragged her dangling legs up the gangway as if she were a semiconscious member of the crew. They'd disguised her with an olive drab green windbreaker and a cap bearing the Philadelphia Eagles logo.

These were just two of the many actions Katie orchestrated to help avoid discovery. She expected Sarge would use all the resources available to him in America's vast intelligence network to locate his wife and daughter.

While obscured from the view of any National Security Agency satellites, three more vehicles had arrived on the scene. The SUVs had been dispatched in different directions, and unmarked vans had been used to bring the First Family to the docks.

"Has the captain been cleared to leave port?" Katie asked as she reached the top of the gangway. She stared upward to the wheelhouse located near the top of the massive bridge that rose seven stories above the container ship's deck.

"Yes, ma'am," the man replied with a heavy Hispanic accent. "Your cargo has also been secured as you requested."

Katie's eyes grew wide as she took in the rows upon rows of steel shipping containers stacked three high atop the deck. Most of the containers were forty feet long, but many on the deck level were only twenty-footers.

"Where are they?" she asked, and then she suddenly decided she didn't want to know. She abruptly raised her hands and stopped the man before he answered. "I don't need to know until we reach our destination."

"Yes, ma'am. Understood."

She turned to the man and jabbed her finger into his chest. "Those two are worthless to me if they die. Keep them alive."

He nodded. "We have a schedule to feed them, provide water, and comfort. It will become cold at sea, and they will need blankets."

"Whatever it takes. I don't give a damn if they're miserable. When it comes time to show proof of life, let them wail about their horrible treatment and conditions. That will bring this to an end much sooner."

"Yes, ma'am," the man said in conclusion as he gestured for Katie to step away from the gangway.

She took a deep breath of the diesel-filled air that floated like a haze over the Penn Terminals. The facility was one of the largest privately operated marine terminals on the East Coast. It was also owned by a prominent member of the Boston Brahmin—Walter Cabot. In fact, the container ship that was now pulling away from the dock was part of Cabot Industries' vast holdings. The *Crowley*, also owned by Cabot's shipping conglomerate, had logged many miles sailing from the U.S. East Coast, through the Panama Canal, toward destinations in the Pacific. They would embark on a similar route.

The *Crowley* would be at sea for five days before entering the Panama Canal. Including the travel time through the canal to their final destination, the freighter would be carrying the special cargo for a total of fifteen days. That would be a long time for anyone to live inside a steel container. It would be an unbearable amount of time for a child. Katie made a mental note to point out that fact to Sarge if he refused to cooperate.

She smirked as the Philadelphia skyline shrank on the horizon. Katie, and her employers, held all the cards now. It was nice, for a change.

CHAPTER THIRTY-FIVE

Late Afternoon
Camp David
North of Frederick, Maryland

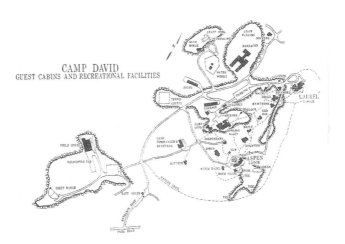

CAMP DAVID
GUEST CABINS AND RECREATIONAL FACILITIES

The group of seven vehicles raced through rural Maryland toward the entrance to Camp David. The local law enforcement vehicles that acted as escorts remained outside the entrance off Park Central

Boulevard while the Secret Service SUVs roared down the tree-lined driveway, kicking up fallen leaves in hues of red, orange, and brown.

Out of an abundance of precaution, all the vehicles in Sarge's caravan were swept and inspected by bomb-sniffing dogs. Because there was still doubt between the Secretary of Homeland Security and the Secret Service as to whether their own personnel might have been involved in the ambush, everyone's credentials were checked and rechecked before they were granted entry onto the Camp David grounds.

Sarge's vehicle was embedded within the group of three decoy vehicles used by Homeland Security under these unusual circumstances. As a result, he was fourth in line to be inspected at the gatehouse.

At the moment, Sarge was not a patient man. It had taken over five minutes to clear the first vehicle. That was five minutes too long for Sarge.

"The hell with this!" he exclaimed, startling the rest of the group. "They can clear us in seconds if we're walking. Come on!"

"Sarge! Not a good idea!" yelled Drew, but his suggestion fell on deaf ears.

Sarge flung the door open and stepped out into the cold mountain air. Donald, who sat to his left, threw his door open as well and began walking briskly past the astonished Secret Service agents, who were scrambling amidst the confusion. Seconds later, all four men were half-jogging toward the armed guards at the gate. Surprised by the sudden appearance of the men in camouflage clothing, they instinctively raised their weapons to stop the group's progress.

"Lower your weapons," Drew shouted as he ran in front of Sarge. "Can't you see this is the damn president?"

The contingent was suddenly swarmed by Secret Service personnel facing the woods in search of threats. Determined, Sarge strutted toward the gatehouse. "Do you recognize me? Am I clear?"

"Um, yes, Mr. President," replied the shocked lieutenant colonel who supervised the gate when the president or any dignitaries were in residence. "Sir, may we get you a car?"

"No time," said Sarge with a gruff, who was far from his usual amiable self with his security team. "They're all with me." He pointed his thumb over his shoulder at Donald, Brad, and Drew.

Seconds later, the four of them were running past the nature trail into the clearing near the Camp Commander's Quarters. Drew led the way, followed by Sarge. Both Brad and Donald were lagging well behind because neither had spent much time on a treadmill while in Washington, much less jogging like Sarge and Drew did regularly.

Nobody spoke as they made their way across the clearing. The Secret Service detail hustled to keep up, alternating between maintaining their footing and studying the dense forest that surrounded Camp David.

Formally known as Naval Support Facility Thurmont, the facility was located in the Catoctin Mountain Park in Northern Frederick County. It had been built during the Franklin Roosevelt administration. In 1943, the first high-level meeting between world leaders was held between Roosevelt and Prime Minister Winston Churchill of Great Britain.

This weekend, it was supposed to be used as a place to gather with friends, enjoy good food, and reminisce about good times. While there, the Loyal Nine and their families had planned to talk about the future when they returned to Boston to start a new chapter in their lives.

Then tragedy struck. All presidents have nightmares about the worst-case scenarios that could befall the nation they represented. However, in the back of their minds, their night terrors included threats resulting in harm coming to their families or the ones they loved.

Today, Sarge learned the threat was real.

CHAPTER THIRTY-SIX

Late Afternoon
Undisclosed Location

Rikki had remained high up in the white pine tree, swaying with the occasional gust of cold wind, listening to the contemporary beach music that mentally kept her warm. Her rifle had been trained on the circular drive at the front of the building where she expected her target to emerge from his car. Then the plan changed, so she was forced to adapt. Quickly.

She'd expected her target to drive straight up to the door. Inexplicably, he'd appeared farther down the winding driveway. She didn't have time to process what might have changed his means of arrival other than the aftereffects of the prior attack. Fortunately, she now had a closer, better means to make an accurate shot.

She remained focused as she took a deep breath. A missed shot would be worse than taking no shot at all, her employer had explained. There would be other opportunities, although he stressed the timing of her attempt would be most advantageous for his purposes.

She replayed the steps necessary for a successful long-range shot. She'd made the necessary adjustments on her scope throughout the day as conditions warranted. She'd picked a spot where her target would hopefully cross that would produce the desired result. She expertly adjusted to the change of location, her professional skills learned in the desert easily translated to the cold, woodsy environment today.

Remember, she thought to herself. *Relax. Breathe. Aim. Gently squeeze.*

Her target was not alone. That was not necessarily unexpected although it would complicate the shot if her target was partially obscured. Complicate, but not prevent her from doing her job.

Her finger gently caressed her rifle's trigger. *Relax.* She could feel the adrenaline flowing through her body, her heart beating faster despite her controlled breathing.

The target was approaching a stand of trees. There he was. Unknowingly ready to die.

Aim.

Squeeze.

The report of her rifle reverberated across the forest and echoed off the surrounding mountains. The butt of her gun slammed into her shoulder and caused loose snow to fall off the pine needles from above. Yet despite the distractions, Rikki operated the bolt action on her rifle and chambered another round.

She studied her target through the scope, his lifeless body lying on the ground. Others were rushing to his side, so Rikki didn't hesitate to provide one last bit of confirmation as required by her employer. It was unnecessary, but she'd agreed to the condition.

She sent another round from her long rifle, the bullet piercing the skull of the target, splattering blood all over the snow and his companions.

Before she retreated from her hide, she prepared a simple text message to her employer. In a way, it was impudent, but someone of her skill needed to issue reminders from time to time. The head shot was unnecessary. The first bullet through the target's heart had done the trick. She pushed send.

1S1K.

One shot. One kill. The sniper's motto.

CHAPTER THIRTY-SEVEN

Late Afternoon
Aboard the Container Vessel *Crowley*
Atlantic Ocean

The *Crowley* had steamed down the Delaware River, passing the shorelines of both New Jersey and Delaware until it reached the Atlantic Ocean. Everyone on board was settling in for the days-long trip to the Panama Canal in Central America except for Julia and Rose, who were beyond distraught.

The two were placed in containers centrally located on the ship's deck. They were adjacent to one another, and unbeknownst to them, the containers were monitored by an armed guard around the clock.

Julia sat wrapped in a wool blanket, her knees pulled up to her chest with her arms tucked tightly around her. Overcome with worry, sadness, and stress, Julia curled up in a fetal position and bawled continuously as she rocked back and forth. She'd never experienced this much emotional agony in her life. She felt so helpless and frightened.

"Mommy!" Rose wailed in between crying fits. She began pounding on the side of the steel container where she was held, slowly losing her ability to cope with the separation from her mother.

Julia caught her breath and called back, "I'm here, Rose. Um, I think I'm right next to you. Can you hear me?"

"I hear you! Mommy, I wanna go home. I don't like this. Please come get me!" Rose began crying again, her last words barely discernible to a stranger but clearly understood by her mother.

"I know. I know, honey. We will take care of this soon. Please try to calm down so you don't work yourself up. Okay?"

"Mommy! It's dark and cold. And I'm hungry."

The simple conversation between the two, however distraught they were, had the effect of calming both mother and daughter. While there was nothing Julia could do to help Rose, she was determined to keep her daughter calm through the conversation. It helped her take her mind off their predicament as well.

Julia was consumed by so many emotions, which resulted in waves of anger and fear sweeping over her as she tried to maintain contact with Rose. She was mad at herself for trusting Katie. She'd warned Sarge about her years before, especially when Julia had observed Katie's behavior concerning Steven.

"Why in the hell did I trust her?" she whispered to herself as she gently banged the back of her head against the steel wall of the container. "I knew it the moment she killed that man in the store without confirming who he was." Julia shook her head in disappointment.

Then incredulity took over. She desperately wanted to pound on the doors and curse at anyone who could hear her. She wanted to grab Katie by the throat and choke the living shit out of her. At one point, when the anger within her boiled over, she jumped to her feet and stomped toward the door. She had every intention of whaling on it until someone opened up. Then, like a madman, she planned on pummeling her captors.

However, she stopped herself as she realized her angry ploy wouldn't work and most likely would result in her death. And Rose's. As reality set in, Julia began to accept their captivity although she refused to accept their fate. Her goal had become to keep her daughter calm and somewhat comforted even though there was little chance of them being held together if she requested it.

Katie had learned psyops from the best—Steven Sargent. He was a renowned operative who was capable of extracting information from anyone and executing a kill order under the most difficult of circumstances. Katie would know that Julia's most fervent request would be to reunite with her daughter. If Julia played it cool, she might be able to play on the sympathies of a guard or somebody else aboard the container ship.

After she'd slowly regained consciousness, she felt the vessel pull away from the dock. She had no idea if she was in Philadelphia or another Atlantic seaboard port. She didn't know if the ship was large or small. She presumed Katie would want to get away from the mainland as soon as possible, so Julia used Philadelphia as her departure location.

Julia was certain once the ship pulled away from the dock and set sail, it had picked up speed as it entered the open waters of the Atlantic. She tried to analyze the ship's course based upon her recollection of the coastline. As best she could tell, it was continuing in a southerly direction, as there had been no abrupt left turn northward.

Julia wasn't sure any of this mattered except she needed to do something that might help her escape or get rescued. She played the events of the afternoon over and over again in her mind. Every step she took. Where everyone had probably been located when the bomb blast rocked the entry to the Pottery Barn store.

She considered the fact that Abbie, by virtue of her status as vice president, was the most protected of the group that afternoon. This comforted her, as she worried for Win and Frank. The boys were probably safer with Abbie than with their mother. Plus, if she could be believed, Katie had made it very clear Julia was the target. Again, another reason to give her hope that her sons were safe.

Her thoughts focused on Sarge. How distraught he'd be. And angry. He would go out of his mind, demanding information or results from the NSA or FBI as to what had happened. Drew and Donald would be right there with him as they worried for their families.

She tried to think about what time it was. The oceangoing containers were sealed to prevent sea spray or rain entering them. There was not even a pinhole of light peeking through that might give her an idea of whether nightfall had descended over them.

So Julia continued to talk with Rose. They dreamed of their time together back in Boston. Rose asked about the schools she would be attending. They talked about the last Christmas in the White House. They joked about Frank rummaging through the closets of the Executive Residence in search of presents.

Eventually, they got settled in for the ride, and their conversation turned to exhaustive sleep. Rose told her mother she was gonna curl up with the blankets and pillows she'd been provided, and then she asked a question.

"Mommy? Should I ask God to help us?"

Julia couldn't fight back the tears that streamed down her cheeks. "Yes, honey. I think we should. Do you still have your cross necklace that matches mine?"

"Yes. I always hold it when I pray at night."

Julia smiled. She reached into her sweater and pulled out the matching religious symbol of faith that Sarge had given her when Rose was born. She gently stroked the beautiful diamond mounted in the center. Rose had a smaller version of the same cross only it was made out of rose gold. It, too, had a solitary diamond in the center of the cross. The tears began to flow in earnest as Julia recalled Sarge's words when he'd presented it to her the day she returned to the White House with their baby girl.

"God will always protect you both with this cross. It's a symbol of both hope and life that connects the two of you together, and to me." He showed her the cross necklaces created for him and, at the time, Win. Frank would receive his later. The couple had a tender moment as he lovingly placed it around her neck, and then, despite her tender age, he did the same for Rose.

It wasn't until this day did Julia realize how powerful their cross necklaces could be.

CHAPTER THIRTY-EIGHT

Late Afternoon
The Aspen Lodge
Camp David
North of Frederick, Maryland

Assistant Secretary for Homeland Security Miguel Ruiz bolted out of his car with two armed guards hot on his heels. They ran to catch up with Sarge and the others.

"Mr. President, there has been another development! Would you please allow the security detail to envelop you, sir?" Ruiz implored Sarge to comply with their enhanced security protocols.

Sarge stopped and took in his surroundings. He'd never seen Camp David so beautiful. There was just enough snow to bury the last fallen leaves of autumn. In the quiet, beyond the woods, he could hear the streams running along the spectacular bluffs. The serenity was not unlike the woods along the Monocacy River. Until it wasn't.

"What is it now, Ruiz?"

"Sir, the House Minority Leader, Congressman Herman, has been assassinated."

"What? When?"

"Sir, we're just now receiving word. He'd attended a local function in Woodstock and was returning to his home nearby. From preliminary reports, a lone gunman, a sniper, shot him from long range, sir."

Ruiz instinctively looked at the treetops surrounding Camp David. Because of the density of the woods, it would've been difficult if not impossible for a sniper to get a clear shot at any occupant on the grounds located in the center of the compound.

"This can't be coincidental, right?" asked Donald, whose eyes darted all around the woods. "Can we get our asses inside before somebody takes another shot at us?"

The entire party jogged the last hundred yards surrounded by golf carts, the preferred method of transportation within Camp David. They reached Aspen Lodge, the name designated for the presidential cabin, which was more estate home than it was a cabin. It was the most secure structure within the compound and was designed to be a working office for the president when he was in residence.

The staff had started a fire in each of the fireplaces, using a combination of oak and hickory logs. It was warm and inviting, as the staff had expected the First Family, the vice president, and their guests to be enjoying a weekend of relaxation. Instead, they'd be assisting the president through a national as well as personal crisis.

The security detail surrounded Aspen Lodge while Ruiz and a single aide provided Sarge a summary of what they knew so far.

"We had no active threats issued on the Minority Leader's life, sir. His two-man security team assigned to protect him was standard protocol for his public events. At his farm located at the base of Suicide Six, the local ski resort, he had private security at his disposal. However, he'd given them the weekend off."

Sarge paced the floor and studied the faces of his friends. Donald appeared the most distraught concerning the safety of Susan and the girls. He quizzed Ruiz about them first.

"Before we get into the details of how this obviously coordinated attack unfolded, let's talk about our families. Where are Susan Quinn and the girls?"

"Mr. President, they've been safely recovered and are being protected at the FBI field office on Arch Street in Philadelphia," replied Ruiz. He turned to Donald. "Sir, they are unharmed and relieved. They are unaware of what has happened to the hunting party, as we've put a lid on the media. For now, anyway."

Donald broke down in tears and collapsed into a leather recliner near the windows overlooking the upper terrace. The snow had been removed, and tables were arranged for the planned barbecue cookout that evening. Just beyond, a steamy haze hovered over the heated swimming pool.

Brad patted Donald on the back to comfort his friend. He noticed how tense Drew was, who, like Sarge, was a floor-pacer. "What about the vice president?" he asked Ruiz.

The DHS official gulped as he turned to Drew. "Sir, while we were rushing to Aspen Lodge, I received word that your wife is at Roxborough Hospital east of the King of Prussia Mall. She was taken there by a Good Samaritan who found the vice president and the president's sons in a parking garage."

Drew was remarkably calm although his tone of voice spoke volumes. The man was seething with anger. "What about our baby?"

Once again, Ruiz hesitated as he chose his words carefully. "Sir, your wife was unconscious on arrival and was having some difficulty with her pregnancy. However, I'm told this facility has an excellent obstetrics department."

"And the boys?" asked Sarge hopefully.

Ruiz stood a little taller and looked the president in the eye. "They are being treated for wounds sustained in the attack. Namely, glass breakage."

"How serious?"

"Your youngest received superficial cuts and abrasions to his hands. Otherwise, he is fine and in remarkably good spirits, I'm told."

"Win?" Sarge sensed Ruiz was preparing him for the worst.

"Sir, your son is a hero. According to the doctors who provided me their status, your son Frank bragged about Win protecting the vice president. He shielded her and Frank from flying glass. As a result, he was struck by several large shards that embedded in his back. He suffered extensive wounds and lost a lot of blood. That said, the doctor assured me that there is nothing life threatening, and other than scars that will be addressed by the plastic surgeon on staff, he'll pull through just fine."

Sarge closed his eyes and muttered the words, "Oh, thank God." The room fell silent for a moment to allow him to gather his thoughts.

"Sarge, why don't you sit down?" Brad suggested as he took his friend by the arm.

Sarge shook his head side to side. "No, um, thanks, Brad. I'm fine." Sarge took a deep breath. "Do you have any idea where my wife and daughter are?"

Ruiz hesitated. His eyes darted around the living room at the president's inner circle. "Not yet, sir. We have all available intelligence assets redirected to scouring video and satellite reconnaissance of the area to locate them."

Sarge touched his chest before he and Donald exchanged knowing looks. Donald had suggested the tracking beacons for their cross necklaces. His friend was always considering every possible threat scenario and prepared accordingly.

"We have a way to track them," said Sarge. "Donald can provide you the details."

Drew motioned for the aide to join him. "I need your phone."

As Sarge revealed his cross with the diamond stone sparkling from the glow of the fire, Drew placed a call to Master Sergeant Johnson King Dawkins, his friend and right arm within the Elite Eight. He led Drew's handpicked team of operatives, who were capable of accomplishing the impossible.

"Who is this?" King's deep voice barked into the phone.

"It's Slash. Gather the team. It's time to saddle up."

"Where to?"

"Meet me at Roxborough Hospital in North Philly. We'll stage there."

"What's the op?" King asked unemotionally.

"Julia and Rose have been kidnapped."

"Jesus. On our way."

Drew disconnected the call and made eye contact with Sarge. He nodded to his friend, offering him unspoken reassurance they'd get his wife and daughter back. And he'd determine who was behind this heinous attack.

CHAPTER THIRTY-NINE

Late Afternoon
Camp David
North of Frederick, Maryland

Drew left on a helicopter maintained by the Navy at Camp David to ferry dignitaries back and forth to Washington. He promised to provide Sarge a full report on his sons and the opportunity to speak with them by phone. Then, if Abbie's health permitted, Drew and his team would rescue the rest of Sarge's family.

"Mr. President," said Ruiz, "I strongly urge you to return to Washington and the safety of the White House. Secret Service can better protect you there."

Sarge was torn. He wanted desperately to see his boys. He also wanted to race to Philadelphia and kick down doors in search of Julia. He was pulled in many directions, but he was keenly aware that he was still the leader of the free world, and America's adversaries might use the crisis to their advantage.

He managed a smile as he addressed Ruiz. "I assume Marine One is en route, right?"

"Yes, sir. We've dispatched another squadron from Quantico. Those on Monocacy Farm were rendered inoperable."

Sarge felt remiss for not asking about his security detail. "Have you located all our personnel?"

Ruiz grimaced. "KIA, sir."

"All of them?" asked Brad.

"Yes, General. The hit team inserted into the woods appeared to have been tracking them from the moment you touched down. Their preparation was impeccable, sadly."

Sarge rolled his eyes. While the words Ruiz spoke were accurate, they were somewhat insensitive. Sarge had been guilty of being inappropriately frank in the past, such as after the attacks on the Twin Towers and the Pentagon on 9/11. He'd stated that it was the most successful attack on American soil in history. At the moment he uttered those words, the nation was reeling in grief. Nobody wanted to voice kudos to the radical Islamists who orchestrated the horrific act. He regretted the statement despite its accuracy.

"Okay. Ruiz, give us a moment, please," instructed Sarge. Ruiz quickly exited Aspen Lodge with his aide in tow. Brad wandered behind them and ensured the door was closed. Then he glanced into the kitchen to confirm there weren't any members of Camp David's staff eavesdropping.

"We're alone," Brad announced as he returned to the living room. Sarge and Donald waited patiently for his return.

Sarge dangled his cross necklace in front of Brad. "Julia and Rose are chipped. We can track them right down to the precise place they're sitting at the moment."

"Infallible?" asked Brad, a logical question.

"There are some limitations," replied Donald. "Like any broadcasting beacon, they require line of sight with the satellite designated to track them. If, for example, they are held deep underground or in any facility surrounded by lead or lots of steel, the beacon will transmit although it might not be picked up by our satellites."

"We also have to hope the kidnappers didn't remove the necklaces."

"Let's break this down for a moment," Brad said as he grabbed a bottle of water. "Ruiz seems certain they were missing but then went on to reach the conclusion they'd been kidnapped. Do we trust his theory?"

"It's all we've got, and unfortunately it's the worst case," Sarge began in response. "Well, not the worst case, God forbid. I hope. Ruiz said video testimony, as confirmed by witnesses, shows three black SUVs pushing their way out of the mall toward the interstate. From there, the locals lost sight of them."

"Well, that sounds like Secret Service," opined Brad.

"Yeah, just like the Secret Service that surrounded us in the woods?" asked Donald sarcastically.

Brad furrowed his brow and nodded. "I understand, Donald. I'm just trying to consider all the angles."

Sarge continued to analyze the facts. "Well, there's also the time factor. It's been hours since the attack on the mall. Susan and Abbie have surfaced with the kids. According to Ruiz, there is no evidence that Julia or Rose were killed in the last store where they were seen. The SUVs departed from the back of that same store. The Secret Service has no knowledge of any additional personnel being assigned to the security detail accompanying them."

"They used Secret Service tactics as cover," mumbled Donald as he walked to the fire to warm his backside.

"I'm thinking the same thing," added Sarge.

Brad looked at the growing shadows on the snow behind Aspen Lodge. A feeling of dread came over him as he tried to offer unemotional advice to the two men whose families were imperiled.

"We can approach this two ways," he began. "One is to use the technology to locate Julia and Rose. Drew's team is more than capable of rescuing them from their captors."

"We don't even know what they want." Sarge threw his arms up in frustration and walked away from Brad into the middle of the living room. "What the hell do they expect will happen when you try to kill a sitting president and his family? I mean, Brad, what if this isn't a kidnapping? What if Julia and Rose are already—?"

Donald got forceful with his friend. "Don't say it, Sarge! If that was their goal, we'd know it already. There's something more to this."

"Like what?" asked Sarge as he tried to suppress his emotions.

Brad didn't have an answer; however, he led the conversation in that direction. "We need to think who would have a motive to go to these lengths, and great risks, to take you out."

"And to kidnap Julia," added Donald.

Sarge shoved his hands in the pockets of his camouflage pants. Morrell's sticky blood had dried over the front of Sarge's thighs.

"Trust me, I thought of this while we were still in the woods fighting for our lives. Lowell is the first, and only, person to come to mind."

"I agree," added Donald.

"Drew mentioned the hit team was speaking Spanish," interjected Brad. "We know the Chinese have made inroads into Venezuela and other parts of South America. They might have trained special ops personnel for this mission."

Sarge wasn't so sure. "Listen, I know I pissed the Chinese off by standing between them and Taiwan. They shouldn't have been surprised by that especially since they tried to take out our ambassador."

"Listen, I'm no expert," began Donald, "but this operation required planning and logistics. I can't imagine Beijing could've pulled it together this quickly even if that was their motive. Guys, sadly, I think this was orchestrated by someone closer to home."

"What about Briscoe, our gracious host?" asked Brad.

"I thought about him as well," replied Sarge. "The problem is he and I are one hundred percent on the same page. I mean, between Briscoe, Trowbridge and their pals—the Bonesmen–there's not one iota of ideological differences."

"Maybe they're making a power move against the Brahmin,"

suggested Donald. "There are those who don't believe you're capable of filling Mr. Morgan's shoes."

Sarge shook his head in disbelief. "Well, I suppose. If so, they've screwed with the wrong Marines, right, Brad?"

"Damn straight!" he exclaimed in response.

Then all hell broke loose. Again.

CHAPTER FORTY

Late Afternoon
Camp David
North of Frederick, Maryland

Katie O'Shea knew her prey. She'd worked alongside them and watched as they stood up to the UN occupying force that had spread its blanket of tyranny over Boston. She'd anticipated Sarge and her former friends might escape the woods despite her careful planning. There was always more than one way to skin the proverbial cat.

Patiently waiting along the hillside of the mountains bordering Camp David was her second team of operatives. Neither Alpha Squad, who'd failed in their mission at Monocacy Farm, nor Beta Squad, who'd taken up positions around the perimeter of the presidential retreat, was considered superior to the other. Each had their own special set of skills.

While Alpha Squad was comprised of hunters, Beta Squad had been handpicked because each of the operatives were considered attack dogs—seasoned mercenaries who'd die for the high price they were being paid just to set up their families for life. Or because they fought for a cause worthy of giving up their lives.

The hardened professionals watched and waited for their opportunity. Many of them had trained in Tiera del Fuego, the extreme southern tip of South America, where temperatures hovered near freezing in July, the coldest month of the year.

Their clothing and weaponry were state of the art. Their winter camouflage was lightweight yet insulating. Their Heckler & Koch MP5 submachine guns were versatile and packed a healthy punch. Several carried Colt carbine assault rifles equipped with under-barrel forty-millimeter grenade launchers.

Then there were the explosives specialists. They were equipped with a variety of fragmentation and thermite grenades, as well as the RPGs used against the hunting party in the woods.

Katie's personal goal was still to kill Sarge. She wanted to inflict maximum pain on him and those who blindly followed him. However, she'd settle for instilling the fear of God in the man. Bring him to the point of begging for Julia and the kid's return. Force him to his knees to capitulate to the will of her employer. It was the only way to achieve their stated goal.

Beta Squad moved carefully through the woods as darkness set in. Their night-vision goggles provided them the ability to avoid spooking the abundant wildlife that traversed the hills bordering Camp David. Their stealthy maneuvers also avoided setting off the vibration sensors spread throughout the grounds of Camp David.

Once they learned that the president had escaped the first assault, they began moving closer to the perimeter. Methodical. Silent. Ghostlike.

The squad leader, Juan Pablo Garcia, was an expert in guerilla warfare. He'd trained the soldiers of Sinaloa Cartel, the Colombian-based drug cartel considered one of the largest in the world. With the permission of El Mayo Zambada, the cartel's leader, her employer had recruited Garcia to head up the operation. Accommodations and promises were made to Zambada in exchange for using his top general.

Garcia sensed the apprehension of his men, all of whom had been handpicked by him. He'd warned Katie that the first attack was full of holes and was destined to fail. He was right. Beta Team had traveled over several miles of rocky terrain, knee-deep in snow. It had been slow and grueling, but the hardened mercenaries were up to the task.

As darkness came, the wind died down, leaving the hills eerily still. Deathly quiet. The calm before the storm.

They continued to approach until they were in position, confirming their state of readiness into their communications devices. It was time.

CHAPTER FORTY-ONE

Late Afternoon
Camp David
North of Frederick, Maryland

Camp David was one of the most secure facilities in America, yet there had been security holes in the past. During the week of July 4 in 2011, US Air Force F-15 fighters were scrambled to intercept three separate civilian aircraft that had flown into the restricted airspace over the presidential retreat. From time to time, supposedly innocent hikers who'd roamed through the adjacent Catoctin Mountain Park found themselves on the wrong end of a barrel. Most pleaded ignorance, claiming to have wandered off the trail by accident or that they were unaware of their proximity to Camp David. A few tried that excuse only to be searched, which revealed their press credentials, cameras, and long-range microphones in their backpacks.

When hired, Garcia had studied all the materials given to him by Katie of these incidents. He absorbed the protocols used by the Navy and Marine contingent guarding Camp David. There was an obstacle that stood in his way, one that provided those within it a false sense of security.

Humans believed walls and fences were the solution to keeping bad people out, or in, as the case may be. Maximum-security prisons were built with multiple layers of protection. Oddly, the lowest security facilities contained fences to keep others out.

Some national borders were constructed with enormous structures to deter the marauding hordes, like the Great Wall of China. Other nations sought a means to prevent illegal aliens from entering their lands.

One man might install a fence around his home to stop a burglar, while another might build a fence to keep his dog from roaming the neighborhood. Another might simply enjoy the look of a white picket fence that also prevented people from tracking up his lawn.

At Camp David, the high-voltage fence crowned with a double roll of razor wire had a singular message. *Stay the hell out!* Within the protective barrier, security personnel roamed the grounds so the honored guests might enjoy a cocktail or a swim in the pool.

Regardless, all had a comfort level because they knew that mighty fence was going to prevent evil from knocking on their door.

They were wrong.

Garcia gave the order to his explosive experts, who were twenty yards to his right. Seconds later, a light flashed, followed by a sizzling sound as the operatives lit the detonating cord. The det cord was a very thin, flexible plastic tube filled with explosives capable of burning at thousands of feet per second. Thus, the results were near instantaneous.

With unfathomable speed, the PETN within the tubing flashed along the fence row where Garcia's operatives lay in wait. Near simulataneously, the linked charges attached along the chain-link fence began to detonate. The enormous heat generated by the explosive compound melted through the chain-link fence like a huge zipper being opened.

Not only did the chain reaction provide an opening in the fence, but it also interrupted the electrified circuit. It was no longer charged although it would trigger an alarm within the Camp Commander's Quarters and at the two gatehouses located at both ends of the retreat.

Any patrolling guards who didn't personally observe the quick, brilliant flash of light caused by the det cord would be advised to immediately patrol the perimeter to search for a breach. Ordinarily, panic would not invade their minds. In the winter, especially when the ground was wet with snow and the wind had been blowing, it was not uncommon for tall trees to fall onto the fencing. Sometimes, an unsuspecting buck tried to rub his antlers on the fence posts, much to his consternation. This had caused failures in the past.

Nonetheless, Garcia and his squad were prepared for a security force who were operating under the highest level of awareness. They expected to be under intense scrutiny within minutes. Their goal was to move into position faster than their counterparts within Camp David could find them.

CHAPTER FORTY-TWO

Evening
Camp David
North of Frederick, Maryland

"What's going on?" asked a skittish Sarge. An alarm began to sound throughout Aspen Lodge. Its persistent, muted ding was accompanied by blinking amber lights, not dissimilar to the activation of a fire alarm in an office building.

The lights were suddenly dimmed as the building was flooded with agents, their weapons drawn. Within a minute, every curtain in the house had been pulled shut, and all the blinds had been lowered. Sarge, Donald, and Brad had been physically placed into the center of the living room while another agent separated the logs to douse the fire.

"We have a breach, Mr. President," replied James Tankersly, whose last name was befitting. The former Penn State University linebacker stood six five and was a stout two-forty pounds. Tankersly filled the room and towered over the others. He spoke into his walkie-talkie. "Professor is secure."

"Armed intrusion?" asked Brad.

Tankersly's eyes darted around the room to confirm his team had done their jobs. "Unknown at this time, General. The electrified fence has failed along the eastern perimeter. We've sent a team to investigate."

"What is the status of Marine One?" asked Donald.

"Forty minutes out, sir," the lead agent replied. "As part of our protocols under these circumstances, we've notified the FAA to clear the airspace between here and the White House. Marine One is being escorted by several fighter jets. However, we have to ensure your safety to the chopper and be confident that you won't be targeted when leaving."

"Understandable," said Sarge.

"Mr. President, we'd like you to enter Orange One," suggested Tankersly. Orange One was a fortified bunker built underground in the backyard of Aspen Lodge during the Eisenhower administration. When President Richard Nixon added the swimming pool, it was built above Orange One, which allowed for additional fortification from a bombing raid.

"Lead the way," Sarge said without argument.

The agents crowded around their three protectees, eyes roaming the darkness in search of hostiles. Outside, uniformed military personnel surrounded Aspen Lodge with their weapons trained on the tall pine trees and the cleared ground below it. All underbrush was routinely removed to prevent any intruder using it as cover.

Within seconds of exiting through the sunroom, they were attacked.

The protective detail's radios erupted in chatter. There were reports of gunfire that preceded the unmistakable whooshing sound of an RPG sailing over the top of Aspen Lodge.

The first rocket-propelled grenade missed its intended target but obliterated tiny Birch Cabin nearby, a recently renovated cabin best known for housing Gerald Ford when he'd visited Camp David as Richard Nixon's vice president.

The explosion shook the ground, causing Sarge and the others to lose their footing. The Secret Service personnel scrambled to help the three men to their feet.

"Tank!" shouted one of the agents. "We have reports of the fence being breached on the northeast perimeter. We believe the RPG was fired from atop the water tower."

"What? How did they—?" Tankersley never finished his question.

A woman's voice in the distance shouted the dreaded word —"Incoming!"

"Stay down!" ordered Tankersley, who immediately crawled on top of Sarge, his hefty weight causing Sarge difficulty breathing.

The RPG hit the swimming pool forty yards to their right, impacting into the marcite-coated concrete below the surface. The water rose into the air like a geyser before the pool shell blew outward. Over thirty thousand gallons of water rushed over what remained of the pool's sides and down the hill before lapping over the group.

"Check the entry to the bunker!" shouted Tankersley.

"Roger!"

Seconds later, the man provided an update. "Blocked, sir!"

A gun battle ensued across the western side of Camp David. Excited voices could be heard between screams of agony. Automatic weapons ripped into bodies. Shotgun blasts tore through foliage. And Sarge braced for the impact of yet another RPG soaring toward them.

CHAPTER FORTY-THREE

Evening
Camp David
North of Frederick, Maryland

"Dammit! I am not gonna die here lying in the snow and mud!" Sarge was incensed. He forced his body upward to push Tankersley off him.

"Sir, we need to get you to safety," Tankersley insisted as he leapt to his feet. He helped Sarge up as well but forcibly pushed the president into a hunched-over position. "Stay down."

"Which way to the helipad?" asked Brad, who had not spent that much time at Camp David and was unsure of the layout.

"Near the Field House and skeet range," Tankersley replied before adding, "Southwest of our position."

"Good," said Sarge. "It's the exact opposite of where they're coming from. Lead the way, Tankersley."

Tankersley's radio sprang to life. "Sir, we're fully engaged with the hostiles. All three platoons are sweeping the grounds."

Tankersley smiled, feeling somewhat relieved. The hit team had taken their shot, and now they would suffer the full wrath of

Marine Security Company Camp David. Consisting of a single forty-three-member platoon when the president was not in residence, it was bolstered with two more platoons, bringing the security contingent to company strength when the president and other guests were present.

"It sounds like a war zone," muttered Donald as he ran alongside Sarge and Brad.

"It does," said Brad. "They'll hunt the bastards down."

"Well," Sarge began as the sound of gunfire began to fade in the distance, "whatever the attackers had in mind, and whoever sent them, there's no doubt in my mind about one thing. They came with the intention of killing us. Finishing what they started at Monocacy Farm. Their motivation must be something worth dying for because I'll kill them myself once I confirm who's behind this."

Five minutes later, the group, surrounded by Secret Service personnel and now several heavily armed Marines, reached the pristine, snow-covered grounds of the skeet range. Men on four-wheelers with plow attachments had cleared landing spots for the three identical versions of Marine One.

Donald inquired about Susan and the girls. He was told that they would be en route to Washington shortly, so there was no need for him to travel to downtown Philadelphia. Sarge intervened and instructed the Secret Service to bring the Quinn family directly to the White House.

"We need to hunker down and figure this thing out," said Sarge.

"Where do we start?" asked Donald as the uniformed Secret Service agents waved to Tankersly to give him the all clear. Ordinarily, the choppers would shut off their rotors to avoid the president being pelted with debris. Not under these circumstances, however. They wanted to get the hell out of Dodge.

"We'll talk in the chopper," Sarge shouted as they ran alongside one another. "I want to see where the NSA and FBI are on locating Julia. Then I want to drag Lowell and Briscoe in for questioning."

"Shouldn't we let the FBI do that?" asked Donald.

"Nobody knows those two better than I do. I wanna look them

in the eye. And you know what? Let's bring in Walter Cabot as well. He was a little too cozy with Gardner yesterday. I need to see where his true loyalties lie."

The three men piled into the helicopter. Less than a minute later, the squadron was en route to the White House, flanked on all sides by MV-22 Osprey tilt-rotor aircrafts with several F-35s patrolling the airspace above and below them. It was the most firepower assigned to the president's helicopter in the history of HMX-1.

CHAPTER FORTY-FOUR

Evening
Roxborough Memorial Hospital
Philadelphia, Pennsylvania

Drew exited the UH-1Y Venom chopper that came to an abrupt landing atop the emergency heliport located at Roxborough Memorial Hospital. He was immediately greeted by two Secret Service agents as well as two heavily armed Marines.

The twin-engine helicopter had been dispatched from the U.S. Army War College at Carlisle Barracks in South Central Pennsylvania. Although Carlisle Barracks was not a full-fledged military installation, there was still a contingent of soldiers prepared to deploy in the event the National Guard was deployed. For now, the fifty-eight-foot-long utility chopper and its two-person crew was all his.

As he jogged under the slowing rotors, he glanced back at the chopper's armaments. Two Hydra seventy-millimeter rockets were affixed to their external stations as well as two M240D machine guns. Drew chuckled to himself before addressing the welcoming committee. He wondered why the heavy artillery was in use for a chopper that spent most of its time waiting for the rare National Guard deployment.

Regardless, he turned his attention back to his wife. After the lead Secret Service agent introduced himself, Drew asked to be taken directly to Abbie and for her attending physician to be summoned.

They rushed into the hospital, using the stairs that had been closed off to all personnel and visitors. Roxborough Memorial was a small, one-hundred-thirty-one-bed community hospital that was certainly not equipped to deal with the complications surrounding a high-profile patient like the Vice President of the United States.

In a way, the relatively small number of beds worked in Abbie's favor. The hospital quickly cleared the fourth floor's east wing of the facility so that Abbie and the boys would not be disturbed. Security personnel were positioned throughout the facility and were especially prevalent on Abbie's floor.

When he exited the stairwell door, he was greeted by Dr. Allison Myers, the head of Obstetrics. She'd been educated at Jefferson Medical College and performed her residency at Thomas Jefferson Hospital in Philadelphia. When she greeted Drew, he was immediately put at ease.

"You must be the proud dad-to-be. I'm Dr. Myers." Her friendly smile was both infectious and comforting. Drew couldn't help but provide her a smile in return despite the tension and worry that coursed through his body.

"Please tell me Abbie is okay," he said in a pleading matter, something totally out of character for the man who was trained to kill.

"She's just fine, sir. It was touch and go for a while, but your wife is one heckuva fighter. She followed our instructions and forced herself to rest despite the many external factors that worried her."

"Is she awake? May I see her?"

"Yes, sir. However, I met you in the hallway to provide you a couple of ground rules. Um, suggestions, really."

"Okay," said Drew hesitantly.

"Sir, I have been advised, and the news media is obviously reporting, that you've been through some drama of your own today."

Drew nodded. "Yes, drama."

"I understand, Mr. Jackson. There is no need to explain. May I suggest saving the discussion of what you've been through for later? Much later, actually."

"Of course," Drew replied. "How much does Abbie know already?"

"Well, not that much. The Secret Service team that arrived immediately made several phone calls per their protocols. One of those was to your wife's chief of staff. I had to provide him a similar admonition. Let's just say, um, your wife is very intuitive and insistent upon getting answers to her questions."

Drew chuckled. He was feeling better because Abbie was obviously acting like her usual self. "This is why I would never consider lying to her. She'd never buy it in the first place, and she'd pry the truth out in short order."

Dr. Myers pointed toward Abbie's door. "Well, I need you to do your best to lie by omission, then. Your wife needs to avoid stress from now until she reaches the full term of her pregnancy. Okay?"

"Sure," replied Drew. He looked around the spotless, well-lit corridor. "Where are Win and Frank?"

Dr. Myers smiled. "The boys are excellent patients. They've both been treated and are supposed to be resting. To distract them from worrying about their mother and father, their team of doctors approved a PlayStation to be installed in their room."

"That's nice of them."

"Well, the difficulty came when young Francis wished to play a game that his doctors considered to be too violent for his tender age. However, Win advised the medical staff it was not unusual for Frank to play games designed for older kids. After what the boys had been through, the medical team acquiesced."

"Good choice," muttered Drew.

"Anyway, after you've spoken with your wife, I'll have the nurse take you to them."

Drew broke away from the doctor and eased into Abbie's room, which was dark except for the faint glow of the lights of nearby downtown Philadelphia peeking through a crack in the window and the usual compliment of bright-colored lights associated with her monitoring equipment.

Abbie's eyes were closed, and he didn't want to wake her. He eased up to the side of her bed and gently grasped her hand. She surprised him when she suddenly spoke.

"Oh, Dr. McDreamy," she purred. "I didn't expect you back so soon."

"Huh? Abbie, it's me."

"Oh no. Dr. McDreamy, my husband has discovered our tryst. Quick, hide in the broom closet."

Drew almost turned around to get Dr. Myers when Abbie let out a hearty laugh, followed by tears flowing down her cheeks. She squeezed Drew's hand and gently tugged him closer.

"Thank God you're alive."

Drew leaned down and kissed her on the cheek. "Of course I am. Why wouldn't I be?"

She let go of his hand and ran her fingers across the chest and arms of his camouflage shirt. "Now's not the time to lie to me, Drew Jackson."

"It's not a lie, Abbie. We have a deal, remember?" Drew knew he'd never win this fight.

"First of all, you smell gamey as in get-in-the-shower-before-you-see-your-wife kinda stinky."

Drew fumbled his words. "Um, there really wasn't time to—" he began in a feeble effort to counter her statement before she cut him off.

"Listen, mister. I already know that you guys came under attack. Whose blood is this? And if you say it's from a deer, God pity your soul."

"Okay, fine. But quid pro quo, Madam Vice President. I have questions, too."

"Fine."

"But, Abbie, Dr. Myers said you need rest, and you don't need any stress." Drew was trying to dissuade his wife from prying into the details.

She took a deep breath and nodded. "Just give me the highlights, okay. Let's start with the blood."

"It's Captain Morrell's. He was shot protecting Sarge, and I helped carry him to safety. The only other injury was incurred by J.J. when he fell near some rocks and they rolled down onto him. He has a broken leg."

"That's it? What about Sarge?"

"He's good. We were taken to Camp David. Donald and Brad are there, too. I'm not a hundred percent sure where Morrell and J.J. were flown to. I believe it was Johns Hopkins."

Abbie reached up and touched his arm again. Her eyes lowered as she tried to peek into his soul. "You promise you weren't in any danger."

Drew leaned in and whispered, "I have always come back to you, right? That will never change regardless of what's thrown my way."

Abbie shed a few more tears, and then she broached the subject she wanted to avoid. "They won't tell me about Julia. I can get all the information I want about Susan and the girls, but any discussion of Julia and Rose is off-limits."

Drew stood and looked back toward the door to her room as if to see if Dr. Myers was monitoring their conversation. He had to discuss Julia with his wife because he needed her approval to lead his team in any rescue effort.

"Okay, but I need you to stay calm. I don't have all the details yet, but we believe they've been kidnapped."

"What?" asked Abbie as she tried to push herself up. Frustrated, she felt around the bed for the button that controlled the bed's position.

Drew made the necessary adjustments and helped her get propped up on the pillows. He took a deep breath before responding, "Here's all we know. After the attack, witnesses described and security footage showed three black SUVs speeding away from the back of the mall. The Secret Service and the FBI conducted a sweep of the mall, searching for them, but they weren't found."

"So they weren't killed. Right? I mean, there were no bodies."

"That's right. We'd hoped the black SUVs, which were of the same type used by the Secret Service, might have rushed them to safety. However, they confirmed the trucks were not related to any government entity. That leads everyone to the abduction theory."

"By who? Why?" Abbie asked as she shook her head from side to side.

"I don't know. Sarge and the guys were working through that when I left Camp David to come see you."

She patted him on the chest. "Honey, you have to go find them. You're the best there is at tracking people."

"I know, Abbie. But, I mean, I need to be by your side."

"Listen, I'm fine. I'm surrounded by doctors and nurses here. I'm sure they're gonna whisk me away to Walter Reed or some place in DC. I'm confident I'm in good hands."

Drew sighed. "I've already called King and the guys, just in case."

Abbie smiled. "Sarge is a good man. I have no doubt he's putting on a strong exterior. You know, acting all presidential, leader-of-the-free-world stuff. Inside, he's probably out of his mind."

"Seeing the boys will help," said Drew. "I'd like to look in on them."

"You should, but you should also kiss me first. And I mean a good-quality love-you-forever kiss."

Drew did as instructed.

CHAPTER FORTY-FIVE

Evening
Roxborough Memorial Hospital
Philadelphia, Pennsylvania

Drew took a moment to gather himself in the corridor. For years, he'd taken Abbie's safety for granted. In the early part of her first term in office with Sarge, the threats against them were more frequent. Sarge had had a couple of close calls as those loyal to the prior administration blamed him for the division. Once the media was up and running again, without giving any credit to Sarge and Abbie for making it happen, they fell back into their old ways. The president of the Pacific States who seceded was the golden boy. Sarge was portrayed as the villain.

As a result, the threats persisted, and Drew asked to play a larger role in her protection. However, everyone, especially Abbie, said no to the idea. He was too close to the situation, they'd said. As time passed and the nation rallied behind their recovery efforts, Drew became content with the Secret Service protecting his wife.

Today, he'd nearly lost her and their unborn baby. Someone had done their level best to kill them, including the children. Some sadistic, deranged bastard went to great lengths, using a near-unlimited budget, to wipe out the Loyal Nine and their families.

The anger built up inside Drew as he slowly made his way down the corridor to the boys' room. He was confident that Abbie was being properly cared for and that the Secret Service had quadrupled their protective efforts. Fair or not, the day's events would be a black eye on their reputation. The entire intelligence community would be condemned for their failures.

Drew rolled his head around his neck and shoulders to relieve some tension. A deep inhale followed by an exhale designed to expel his intense desire to hurt someone helped him prepare to see the boys. They'd have lots of questions for Drew to deflect. He needed to remember the bottom line. Their family would be together soon.

Drew cracked the door to listen before entering. The kids were still playing a video game. He'd expected them to be passed out. Instead, they were dueling one another in some version of *Super Mario Bros.*

"I see how it is," Drew began jokingly. "You guys aren't gonna play all night, are you?"

"Uncle Drew!" exclaimed Frank. Using fingers that protruded through the bandages on his hands, he paused the game so his brother couldn't gain an advantage in the game. The young boy ran like a middle linebacker in training, headfirst into Drew's legs.

"Hey, buddy! I probably stink."

Frank took a big whiff and laughed. "Very stinky, Uncle Drew." Despite the aroma and the sticky blood on his shirt, Frank hugged his favorite unofficial uncle.

Win was slower to rise out of his chair. He winced in pain as he slowly made his way to get a hug. Frank was keenly aware of his brother's injuries, so he politely stepped aside.

Drew smiled at the young warrior. "How about a fist bump?"

Win smiled and returned the gesture. He, too, needed a familiar face, as the hospital staff had limited their time with Abbie. The kids were filled with uncertainty, and because of security protocols, they'd been unable to talk with their father. Naturally, they were completely unaware of what had happened to Julia and Rose.

"Sorry. I'm kinda sore."

Drew reached out to Win's face and rested his hand on his warm cheek. He bent over at the waist to look into his eyes. "I am very proud of you, and so is your dad. They're calling you a hero."

"Dad's okay?" he asked.

Drew found his question odd. How would Win have any inkling that the hunting party had been attacked?

"Duh. He's your dad and our president. There's nobody tougher in the world as far as I'm concerned."

"I bet you are, Uncle Drew!" said Frank, who promptly slugged Drew in the thigh. Drew looked down at the kid, who almost caused a charley horse.

Drew knelt down in front of both boys. "Guys, toughness is more than being able to take a punch like the one Frank just threw. It also requires mental toughness, bravery, and staying strong during tough times."

"Like the attack at the mall?" asked Win.

"That's right. Neither one of you should ever have to go through something like that. But you did. I came here to see how you were doing but also to thank you for helping Abbie through it all. She relied upon your toughness and love to make it out of the mall. You see, sometimes love can make us average people much stronger."

"Me too?" asked Frank.

"Yes, absolutely. You and Win protected one another. Abbie, too. This inspired her to stay strong while you guys all got to safety."

Win was grinning now. "When do we get to talk to Dad? And where's Mom and Rose? Nobody seems to know."

Drew thought of a quick explanation. He lowered his voice to a whisper and pulled the boys closer to him. He feigned concern by looking around the room as if to confirm they were alone. The looks on the boys' faces led Drew to believe they were buying his ploy.

"Win, when you are President of the United States, you have to be extra careful about what is discussed around others. You know, there's a lot of top secret stuff that can't be said."

"I know," he said. "Sometimes Mom will say 'need to know.'"

"Yes, exactly. Do you realize that everyone in the government works for your dad?"

"Really?" asked Frank.

"Yes, including me. He's our boss. Sometimes, there are reasons that the boss, or his family, have to keep certain secrets from all the other employees. This is one of those times."

Win furrowed his brow. He searched Drew's face. Kids have a pretty good bullshit meter.

"So the guards don't know where they are?" he asked.

"That's right. After what happened at the mall, your dad thought it was best to keep some things secret. He'll be able to explain more when you return home to the White House."

"You don't know where she is either?"

Drew sighed. "No, I don't."

He didn't lie.

PART VI

———

The Trackers
Black Friday, November 2024, late evening

CHAPTER FORTY-SIX

Late Evening
The Oval Office
The White House
Washington, DC

Presidents forge their legacies during a crisis. Crises were moments when presidents can rise above prior challenges during their administrations to redeem themselves in the eyes of voters, or they could sink them deeper into the abyss.

In 2001, President George W. Bush was besieged by below average polling numbers in the wake of his controversial election and the famous Florida recount. However, in the days following 9/11, his approval rating ballooned to ninety percent based on his response.

Throughout history, whether it was Lincoln grappling with a nation divided or Hoover failing to pull a nation out of the Great Depression, America's presidents had faced seemingly insurmountable challenges that impacted the country.

However, there had never been a president who faced the loss of close family as Sarge was on this late Friday evening. He was torn between being a husband and father on the one hand, and the leader of the free world on the other. As president, he owed a duty to his country and its citizens to offer words of reassurance that the nation was not weakened or endangered because of the attacks.

His communications team had been in contact with Donald while they were returning to the White House. They'd suggested that Sarge address the nation, if not in person, at least through a strongly worded statement. The difficulty Sarge faced was the fact that Julia and Rose were in the hands of kidnappers with an unknown agenda. Assassination attempts on his life had occurred not once but twice during the day. He didn't want to make any kind of statement that might trigger the kidnappers into causing harm to his family.

For articulate politicians, it's easy to use profound words to put a nation at ease. During FDR's inaugural address, he famously uttered the line "the only thing we have to fear is fear itself." Until he tempered the profound statement with the warning to Americans that "only a foolish optimist can deny the dark realities of the moment."

For Sarge, the reality was that the nation was not at risk or imperiled. Did they have a right to know? Maybe, maybe not. Could matters be made worse if he said the wrong thing? For now, Sarge decided to err on the side of caution and say nothing. He'd wait until his sons were back at the White House and for some type of demand from the kidnappers.

Donald and Brad joined Sarge in the Oval Office. All three men were exhausted because it had been a long day that was not only taxing on them mentally but physically. Fear, worry, and adrenaline kept them functioning on all cylinders.

After Betty spoke to them about bringing in some food, beverages, and fresh clothes, she politely excused herself. Sarge removed his camo shirt, revealing the blood-soaked thermal undershirt he was wearing. He pulled it away from his body, the dried blood sticking slightly to the hairs on his chest.

Donald and Brad watched him, prompting Sarge to explain. "This is Morrell's."

His eyes became watery, causing him to turn away from his friends. Both men picked up on Sarge's emotions revealing themselves. They rushed to his side to console their friend.

Sarge continued to speak, fighting back the tears. "Dammit, guys. We've been through so much together. It was almost over."

Brad spoke first. "We're gonna pull through, Sarge. We always do. What can I do to help?"

Sarge took a deep breath and replied, "I trust our intelligence agencies, but at this point, I've lost confidence. Are you telling me nobody saw this coming? No terrorist chatter? No threatening letters or emails? No moron jumping over the fence and streaking across the White House lawn? Seriously, what the hell?"

"I know, Sarge. I cannot disagree. After we get them back safely, heads are gonna roll."

"Maybe. I don't know. Listen, for now, Brad, I need you to spearhead their efforts in locating Julia and Rose. I'm not saying it's easy, but the tracking devices in their necklaces should help pinpoint their location."

"As in we should already know," added Donald.

Brad scowled. He agreed, but it didn't help to get Sarge stirred up. "I've already called everyone into the Situation Room, which will act as a central location for gathering information. Let me go there now for an update, and I'll stay in touch with Donald if there is a development."

Sarge managed a smile and patted his top general on the back. "We'll figure out who dropped the ball or might've been involved later. First, let's find my girls."

The two men exchanged a hug, and Brad exited the Oval Office. Betty had a change of clothes waiting for him, which he gladly accepted. She and the Secret Service detail turned their heads while he changed in her office.

Donald closed the door and addressed the public messaging

issue with Sarge. "I've talked to Crepeau and Ocampo. We're not gonna make a statement of any kind. It's too risky."

"Yes, I agree," said Sarge. He quickly turned his attention to the matter of whodunit. "Have the FBI picked up Lowell, Cabot, and Briscoe?"

"They're on their way to the White House. A note about that per the deputy director, who is coordinating this entire effort. Briscoe, of course, was aware of the attack because of his home's proximity to where we were hunting. Gardner Lowell claimed he learned about it as the story broke on CNN."

"Yeah, right," said Sarge.

Donald shrugged. "I'm just relaying the observation of the Special Agent who informed Lowell at his home."

"What about Walter?"

"This is interesting, and I'm using the deputy director's words."

"Okay." Sarge stretched out the word, anticipating some great revelation.

"The agents who picked up Mr. Cabot said he, quote, had no clue about the attack. He and his wife had been watching a movie in their home theater when the news media began to report on what happened. His staff didn't interrupt him until the agents showed up at the door."

Sarge slowly nodded as he wandered around the Oval Office, mindlessly studying the paintings. He came to his partner's desk and picked up a photograph of Julia holding Rose after she was born. Their cross necklaces dangled daintily around their necks. He closed his eyes and sighed.

"Donald, I'm torn between grabbing Gardner by the throat and threatening to kill him. Or I might just start bawling and begging for their lives. I honestly don't know what I'll do when I see the smug bastard."

Donald approached his friend and led him back to the sofas. He encouraged Sarge to sit. "If you are teetering on the edge of murder and emotional breakdown, maybe we should let the FBI question them all? Or I'll be glad to do it although I'll probably hold a gun to Lowell's head until he spills the truth."

"You sound like Steven and not the mild-mannered accountant I once knew."

"Yeah, well, I've been hardened over the years. One of these assholes tried to kill my family, too. There's gonna have to be a reckoning for whoever is behind this."

Sarge wiped the tears off his face and firmly set his jaw. "Count on it, DQ."

Donald's face turned ashen. His initials, DQ, had often been used by Steven Sargent when referring to him. The last time Sarge had called him DQ was the day Win was born after his inauguration. Moments later, Sarge marched into the basement of John Morgan's home and put a bullet in the head of his brother's killer. In that moment, he seriously doubted Sarge would reveal any emotions in front of the men en route to the White House other than the face of a homicidal maniac.

CHAPTER FORTY-SEVEN

Late Evening
The Oval Office
The White House
Washington, DC

In preparation for their meetings with the high-power men, Sarge and Donald changed clothes and continued to rack their brains to consider other potential culprits behind the attack. They believed if they could identify the party behind the attacks and kidnapping, they could better identify a motive, which in turn might help them locate the hostages.

"Don't think for a second I'll forget about what happened on my wedding night," said Sarge. "If it weren't for Drew, I might be dead. Hell, Julia, too, for that matter."

An accomplished assassin had been hired to kill Sarge during his wedding ceremony. Drew's instincts had told him Sarge was in danger. He'd slipped away from the wedding and stalked the killer in the wooded area on the Morgan estate. Proving his nickname, *Slash*, was well deserved, Drew had thrown his blade with deadly accuracy, killing the contract killer.

Just a month before at a gathering of the world's most powerful people, a threat to their very existence had been identified. It was Sarge. Not because the cabals and consortiums who'd gathered at the Grove in Watford, England, feared Sarge would cause them physical harm. It was the way Sarge was winning over everyday Americans with his plans for the collapsed nation's future.

Secretive cabals relied upon their conspiracies with other wealthy, like-minded thinkers to exert control over all aspects of world affairs, both political and economic. Sarge's populist messaging to his fellow Americans was of grave concern to them. Groups such as these sought to control every aspect of human life. They had names like Bilderberg, Illuminati, CFR, Trilateral Commission, and Boston Brahmin.

Sarge suspected one or all of these loosely connected organizations were behind the first attempt on his life. It would not surprise him they were prepared to eliminate him now that he was approaching private life and focusing his full-time attention on the Boston Brahmin's interests.

He was frustrated. The unknown was taking its toll on his psyche. What did they want? Ransom? Some form of accommodation? Complete capitulation over a matter of policy? With no demands being issued, he became increasingly nervous that this was no longer a hostage situation. He fought the negativity that invaded his brain.

They're alive! I'm sure of it!

His brain shouted the words over and over again. He needed to stay calm. Yet Sarge would do anything for proof they were alive.

Betty gently knocked on the door, and Donald let her in. She was smiling with some good news. "Gentlemen, the choppers will be arriving in minutes with the vice president, Susan, and the kids."

Donald's spirits lifted immediately, but he managed to curb his enthusiasm as he understood this was only partial relief for Sarge. He was surprised by Sarge's reaction. Maybe hugging his sons was just what he needed to drag himself out of his melancholy state of mind.

"Let's go get 'em, Donald!" exclaimed Sarge.

The two uniformed Secret Service personnel standing outside the Oval Office heard his raised voice and immediately moved toward the open door.

"Mr. President, I'm sorry. They've instructed us to encourage you to remain in the Oval. We can bring your sons to you."

Donald, the ever-present guard dog, walked up to the men, who towered above him. "Gentlemen, there's nothing on this Earth that will prevent the president from running through the snow to hug his boys. Nothing, including your superiors. Now, you're certainly welcome to join us. However, we're leaving. Come on, Sarge!"

Donald shoved his way past, and Sarge walked between the two flabbergasted agents. He shrugged. "You know. What he said."

Sarge picked up the pace to catch up with Donald, who was hustling through the West Wing to exit onto the South Lawn. Their sudden presence startled the security personnel, who could be seen pressing their earpieces and chattering with one another as the two men raced into the cold night air.

A medical team had already arrived with a small, heated transport to take Abbie inside. The White House Medical Unit provided medical care to the First Family and the vice president. The medical staff of more than two dozen professionals included five doctors and two former combat medics. Their facilities included emergency and trauma capability and, because of the Sargents' two children being born in the White House and Abbie's on the way, a full obstetrics team.

To say the reunion on the South Lawn was joyous would be an understatement. Hugs were exchanged. Tears flowed. And Secret Service agents silently plead for POTUS and the others to return to the safe confines of the White House.

Abbie reluctantly joined the medical team only after Susan threatened to snitch her out to Drew. Win and Frank relayed their conversation with Drew. They told their dad they understood why news about Julia had to be kept top secret. With everything that he'd dealt with, Sarge hadn't formulated a plan when it came to Julia and

Rose's whereabouts. He'd decided that honesty, despite their tender ages, was the best policy.

They reached the lower-level entrance to the West Wing, and the head of the new Secret Service detail slowly approached Sarge.

"Sir, they're requesting your presence in the Situation Room. Well, actually, it was at General Bradlee's request, sir."

Sarge knelt so he could address the boys. "Fellas, I've got to go. I need you to go upstairs and get ready for bed. Win needs to heal, and Frank, it's waaay past your bedtime."

"Okay, Daddy," said Frank, dutifully following orders.

"What about Mom?" asked Win with concern oozing out in his tone of voice.

"Son, we're working on getting your mom home right now. Okay? You guys rest so you'll be ready when she arrives."

The boys nodded and took the hands of two members of the Executive Residence's staff.

Sarge turned to Donald. "You two spend all the time you need. I'll—"

Susan cut him off. "No way," she interrupted. "You guys do whatever it takes to get them back, Sarge. Donald, go with him."

"Are you sure?" he asked.

She took his face in her hands. "I wouldn't have said it if I wasn't. Now, go!"

Donald hugged the Quinn women one more time and then hustled off to catch up with Sarge, who was already jogging down the West Wing Colonnade.

CHAPTER FORTY-EIGHT

Late Evening
Roxborough Memorial Hospital
Philadelphia, Pennsylvania

Drew was pensive as he leaned against the parapet wall overlooking downtown Philadelphia to the east and the bedroom community King of Prussia to the west. He'd managed an hour's worth of sleep in a fourth-floor room of the hospital after Abbie and the boys left for DC. Moments ago, a member of his security detail informed him that the group of men he was expecting were en route from the airport and would be arriving shortly. He requested they be led to the rooftop.

Many years ago, Sarge had provided Drew a vision for the use of Aegis during his years in office. He wanted the team to be made up of accomplished former operators from all branches of the armed services. They needed to be talented without blemishes on their service records. Sarge could not afford to go outside the U.S. military to achieve certain objectives if he had men prone to going off the reservation or who had a record of insubordination, which could come out in the media if a mission was exposed.

Drew discussed Sarge's criteria, and they both agreed money was a big part of the recruiting inducements available to potential operators. Drew put out feelers throughout the ranks of former SEALs, Army Rangers, and Delta Force operators, offering guaranteed six-figure salaries, top-of-the-line equipment, and most importantly, the opportunity to return to the camaraderie and the purpose they loved as elite operatives within the armed forces.

Drew, King, and the other special operators balanced the risks and rewards, then chose to join Aegis. Drew and King led this small group of eight elite operatives to make up the Global Response Team Sarge had envisioned. This group, who named themselves the Elite Eight, had performed admirably when called upon.

They'd saved lives. They'd deterred military coups. They'd foiled assassination attempts. Now, they'd be called upon to rescue the First Lady and her daughter.

King was the first to emerge onto the rooftop. He immediately began complaining. "Man, it's too damn cold up here. They got heat downstairs, right?"

"Yeah, they got heat, asshole." Peter Parker, whose name was the same as the character in the Spider-Man comic series, scolded King for his whining. The tall, lanky operative from East Texas was an avid outdoorsman and therefore used to inclement weather. Despite the obvious correlation with the Spider-Man cartoon character, Parker's nickname was Spidey for his ability to scale walls, climb trees, and his borderline-suicidal lack of fear of heights. "The boss wouldn't have called us up here if it wasn't for a reason. Um, right, boss?"

"Nice Huey," said the third man to emerge from the emergency stairwell. Chris St. Nicholas, nicknamed Santa, was a former SEAL who trained with Drew. The four of them made the core group of the Elite Eight. The remaining members offered logistical support depending on the team's mission. "Is this our ride, Slash?"

Drew greeted his brothers in arms. He gave them a sitrep, quickly explaining what they didn't know. They all offered their condolences for Abbie being attacked and inquired about her health. Now they were ready to get down to business.

"Listen up, y'all. We've got a serious threat to the country coming from an unknown, well-financed group of operators. They took a shot at us while hunting in Maryland. Then, while I was on my way here, a second squad fired RPGs at the president, the chief of staff, and General Bradlee. Fortunately, nobody was hurt, and they're safely back in the White House."

"Abbie, too?" asked King.

Drew nodded. "She will stay there under a doctor's care. Susan Quinn, Donald's wife, and their kids were also at the mall during the attack. They're safe and unharmed."

"So what's the play?" asked Santa.

Drew took a deep breath and blew white, condensed air out of his mouth before he replied. He wandered over toward the wall and pointed his right hand from right to left along the system of highways connecting Philadelphia with King of Prussia.

"The First Lady and their daughter, Rose, are missing. We believe they were kidnapped by people connected to the mall attack who were posing as Secret Service agents."

"Have they made any demands?" asked Spidey. He walked up to the parapet wall and looked down, undoubtedly imagining climbing down the face of the hospital.

"Nothing and it's driving Sarge nuts. Intelligence has been at a loss, but they're using all available resources."

"Blah, blah, blah," King said in his deep, bass voice. "Where were they *before boom?*" The phrase *before boom* referred to the events prior to the attack or event.

"They all missed it," said Drew.

"Wow, that's hard to believe," added Santa, shocked by the revelation. "You'd think they'd pick up some kind of chatter."

Drew agreed. "Listen, these guys were definitely pros. Well funded. Disciplined and coordinated. Also, I believe they were Hispanic, possibly Cuban or South American." Drew went on to explain the facts that led him to that theory.

"Okay, what are our orders?" asked King.

"For now, we're on hold. The city is too big to go knocking door-to-door. NSA is studying satellite recon. The FBI is scouring files, interviewing eyewitnesses, and looking at mall footage in search of suspects."

"We've gotta do something, right?" asked Spidey. "In these abduction situations, every minute counts. I mean, it's been hours so far, right?"

"Correct on both counts," replied Drew. "It's just, well, we don't have a starting point. We could run out of here half-cocked and only end up chasing our tails. I think we need to be patient."

"That sucks," groaned Santa.

"Yup." Drew leaned onto the parapet again, his forearms chilled from the aluminum flashing. "It sure does."

CHAPTER FORTY-NINE

Late Evening
The Situation Room
The White House
Washington, DC

All eyes were on Sarge as he entered the Situation Room. The men and women who monitored unfolding crises around the world and then worked diligently to solve them had never undertaken a task as personal as this one. Their eyes told the story, and Sarge made a point to acknowledge each of them with a nod.

Every president since John F. Kennedy had made use of the Situation Room as the world had become an increasingly dangerous place. After the Bay of Pigs fiasco, President Kennedy was infuriated by the conflicting advice and information provided to him. He ordered the bowling alley built in the lower level of the West Wing to be demolished and renovated. The result was the suite of offices known as the Situation Room.

Over the years, two presidents, Nixon and Ford, never used it. Others, like President George H. W. Bush, a former head of the

Central Intelligence Agency, relied upon it heavily. During Sarge's presidency, as the conflicts with China became more frequent, the staffing in the Situation Room hearkened back to the days of the Kennedy administration when an intelligence analyst staffed the room nearly twenty-four hours a day.

"Good evening, everyone, and thank you for helping me." It was a solemn greeting from the president and very personal. For a man who carried the weight of a nation on his shoulders, he now held a burden the size of Mount Everest.

Cal Stanwick, the deputy director of the FBI, stood at once and addressed the president. "Mr. President, on behalf everyone in this room, and an entire nation, we are sorry for what has happened. More importantly, we are committed to locating the First Lady and your daughter. We will devote all of our resources to bringing them home to the White House safely."

"Thank you, Cal." Sarge had handpicked Stanwick for the job years ago. While the director of the FBI was an administrator, Stanwick was very active in the nation's most pressing law enforcement matters. "Please tell me what you have."

"Sir, we were able to locate and reconstruct the history of their tracking beacons." Cal paused and directed one of his assistants to fill the screens with both street maps and aerial views of metro Philadelphia. "I have omitted travel prior to their arrival at the mall. Please recreate the tracking sequence for the president."

"Mr. President, you will see two red dots on the screens, one for Mrs. Sargent and the other for Rose," said a female analyst. "If you can follow, sir, they are shopping throughout the mall before a long pause near the entrance to Nordstrom. There, we believe, they interacted with Santa Claus before heading toward the Pottery Barn store."

"Santa Claus," muttered Sarge. A wave of sadness came over him. This was to be a happy day for his family. A chance to experience some normalcy before they returned to private life. It had gone very wrong.

"Um, yes, sir. Now, at the moment of the attack, they are located in the center of the Pottery Barn location. They move slightly toward the wall of the adjacent retailer until this happened."

Everyone in the Situation Room followed the red dots moving quickly through the store and then outside.

The screens changed to a combination of mall video and the maps as the analyst continued. "Here's what happened next. You can see three black SUVs approaching from the north side of the mall, forcing their way along the service road through fleeing shoppers. And there, striking a woman and child who sustained minor injuries, we're told."

"They were summoned," Donald opined.

"We believe so," said the analyst. "As you see, the red dots, your family, remained stationary. We were unable to get a camera on them in order to make any kind of identification of the kidnappers."

"Well, actually, we have one angle, but it was inconclusive," added Stanwick.

"What do you mean?" asked Sarge.

"Sir, it was actually an image caught in the reflection of a parked car's window," Stanwick replied. He turned to a second analyst. "Please isolate that footage on the large screen behind the president."

Sarge and Donald turned to watch the footage. It lasted only a few seconds, and it showed Julia and Rose being led past the vehicle toward the service road that separated the mall from the parking areas.

"Only one gunman?" asked Donald.

"Yes, sir," replied Stanwick. "It appears they were being escorted through the utility yard to the approaching SUVs by a single individual."

"It's hard to see," continued Donald. "But, um, I don't see that they're being forced in any way. I don't even see that the person has a weapon raised."

Stanwick paused for a moment. "We reached the same conclusion."

Sarge turned around to the deputy director. "This looks like a Secret Service extraction. Was this person an agent or posing as one?"

"Mr. President, we're exploring all possibilities at the moment. We've studied the footage from the mall security. Overall, it would seem your wife knew the person who was leading them out of the mall, or was at least comfortable with them. In the brief amount of footage at our disposal, there was no evidence of struggle. In that snippet, if anything, it appeared they were readily cooperating."

"So she knew this person?" asked Sarge.

"It is possible. Yes, sir."

Sarge looked at the monitors and then to the aide controlling the displays. "Where did they go next?"

She nodded and directed everyone's attention back to the screen. "The red dots, um, your family remained in the vehicles as they traveled south-southeast away from King of Prussia toward Philadelphia. They came to a stop under a bridge abutment just outside Penn Terminals."

Donald interrupted as he sought clarification. "Penn Terminals? The shipyard?"

"Yes, sir," she replied. She stood from her chair and approached the monitor with the enlarged aerial view that included Philadelphia International Airport on the right side and the Delaware River along the bottom of the image. She circled the location with her index finger. "Penn Terminals is here. At this point, based upon our tracking, it appears the First Lady was separated from your daughter into two vehicles."

Stanwick tapped her on the shoulder and gestured with his head that she should return to her seat. His demeanor turned pensive.

"Mr. President, at this point, we believe your wife and daughter were taken into Penn Terminals and likely placed on a ship."

Sarge's face turned ashen. "What? Like a freighter?"

"Yes, sir. This shipyard primarily caters to oceangoing vessels like container ships. Our investigators are mobilizing to descend upon that location now."

"What happened to their beacons?" asked Donald before adding, "They are tracked by global positioning satellites whether on land, sea or air."

Stanwick grimaced and furrowed his brow. His facial expression silently voiced his concern. "There are several possibilities. One is that they were placed deep inside the steel hull of one of these massive vessels, effectively blocking the signal. The other possibility is that their tracking devices, the necklaces, were discovered and dropped into the Delaware River, resulting in the loss of signal. From there, the First Lady and Rose could've been placed on a ship or taken by car to another destination. Or they are still at Penn Terminals."

Sarge paced the room. He'd relied on their ability to track Julia and Rose. This gave him a sense of comfort knowing they could be found quickly. That had just changed. His palms became sweaty, and he shut down emotionally.

Donald noticed the difference in Sarge's physical and emotional appearance. He addressed Stanwick. "What is your next course of action?"

"Our agents will be ready to conduct a raid of the shipyard. I've instructed them to move quickly, but quietly. We don't want to draw the attention of the media, nor do we want the kidnappers to be tipped off that we're this close to finding them."

Donald received a text. Betty advised him that Sarge's *guests*, as she called them, had arrived and were sequestered from one another as he'd requested.

"We need to return to the Oval," said Donald. "Please keep General Bradlee abreast of all developments."

Stanwick nodded his understanding. Donald led Sarge out of the Situation Room, followed by Brad, who tried to offer words of comfort.

"I know how bad this looks, but the tracking beacons gave us a huge head start on finding them."

Sarge only nodded. He was forced to admit to himself that his hopes and expectations had been higher than warranted. The people responsible for the kidnapping were formidable professionals. It would take time. As helpless as he felt, there was something he could do. Beginning with the three men awaiting him in the West Wing.

CHAPTER FIFTY

Late Evening
The Oval Office
The White House
Washington, DC

Hanson Briscoe was the first to be questioned; however, Donald urged Sarge to relax for a moment before he was called in. Sarge had regained his composure and appeared contemplative as he approached his desk.

When he'd entered the White House for the first time after the National Guard had regained control of the city years ago, he'd presided over the reconstruction of a nation far more difficult than the post-Civil War era. He'd faced turbulent times in his efforts to restore the power grid following the devastating cyber attack.

The nation had rallied behind him. Businesses were given tax and regulations incentives to restart their factories. America's citizens stepped up to help one another, either directly through community-wide efforts, or indirectly by working jobs that might not have been their first choice of occupation but were nonetheless critical to the reconstruction effort.

Sarge was just the leader America needed in those times of turmoil, yet there were always those opposed to him politically who tried to thwart his efforts. And then there were the political powerhouses who were always angling for a bigger piece of the government pie, whether economically or politically.

Donald urged Sarge to take his seat in one of the chairs flanking the fireplace. He offered him a drink before they started. Sarge declined. Instead, he looked his friend in the eye and put him on the spot.

"Give me your honest assessment, Donald. What's your opinion of what Stanwick relayed to us?"

"Number one. Julia and Rose are alive. Please don't consider my statements as callous or insensitive. I'm trying to be detached. At least the best I can, anyway."

"I get it. I am as well but ..." Sarge's voice trailed off as he gripped the arms of the chair. "Dammit, Donald. I need to do something. No, I want to do something. This is killing me to rely upon others to find my family."

"Yes, I agree. You have to know they are still alive. I feel it, and you do too. The kidnappers stand to gain nothing with them harmed. If that was their intent, they'd be dead already. And blunt as it sounds, Abbie and my family were targeted and dispensable. Julia was treated differently. Sadly, I believe Rose is collateral damage in their overall goal, which was to kidnap Julia."

Sarge rose from his chair even though Donald reached out to stop him. He began pacing the floor again, walking over the Presidential Seal rug in front of his desk. He stopped to face the fireplace. He took in the painting of George Washington. The portrait gave him the strength to continue.

"They are alive, and we're going to get them home," he said with a renewed sense of courage. "I'm ready for Briscoe. Bring him in."

Donald exited the Oval Office and spoke in hushed tones to Betty, who'd devotedly manned her desk throughout the crisis. Minutes later, Donald led Briscoe in to meet with Sarge.

"Mr. President, I am so sorry for what happened on my property. I couldn't have imagined anything like that would—"

Sarge wasn't interested in apologies at the moment. "I understand you've spoken to the FBI already." Sarge had wanted to be the first to quiz Briscoe, but Stanwick had ordered a team to confront Briscoe in his home before he left the farm.

"Yes. In fact, when I heard the first explosion, I reached out to their field office in Baltimore to report the incident. I'm surprised they weren't on the scene sooner."

Sarge and Briscoe went back and forth concerning the attack on the hunting party, both in the woods and at Camp David. Because of the media blackout, the incident at the mall had not yet disclosed Julia and Rose's kidnapping.

Sarge paused for a moment as he gathered his thoughts. "Hanson, I've always considered us to be up front with one another."

"Of course, Mr. President," he interrupted. "Know this. George Trowbridge and I have always been in your corner. We've always seen us as rowing in the same direction with you as our coxswain." A coxswain was the member of a rowing team who sits in the boat facing the bow, steering and coordinating the power and rhythm of the team.

"I want to believe that, Hanson. Yet my days in the White House are coming to an end, and some might look at this as an opportunity to end my private career before it starts."

Briscoe leaned forward and stared Sarge in the eye. "Let me assure you, we are your sworn allies, Sarge. Our goals have always melded perfectly with one another. The only difference between us is the name of the school on our diplomas."

Sarge studied the man, who was certainly capable of deception. However, at least this time, Briscoe appeared to be genuine. Sarge suddenly stood and extended his hand. "Hanson, my apologies for dragging you to Washington this evening. We brought death and destruction to your home. For that, I am sorry."

Briscoe took his hand and shook it firmly. He leaned in to Sarge and spoke in a low tone of voice as if he thought someone might be listening. "Mr. President, our resources are vast, as you know. We will stand down unless you request our assistance."

"Thank you, Hanson. I will if necessary."

Briscoe nodded and said before he departed, "Godspeed, patriot."

CHAPTER FIFTY-ONE

Late Evening
The Oval Office
The White House
Washington, DC

As soon as Briscoe had exited the Oval Office, Donald was prepared to bring in Walter Cabot. The oldest living member of the Boston Brahmin, he'd outlived his wife, Mary, who'd died shortly after Cabot's best friend, John Morgan, had passed away. It had a devastating effect on the man who'd continued to grow the world's largest shipbuilding industry. Cabot Industries was now led by his granddaughter, Mary Margaret Cabot. Sarge had only met her once during a family gathering at the Cabot estate. Otherwise, they'd never had any personal dealings although Sarge's activities as president certainly benefitted the Cabots significantly.

Walter entered the outer office and was greeted by Betty when Donald received a text message. He suddenly excused himself and rushed back into the Oval Office, abruptly closing the door behind him.

"What is it, Donald? Did they find them?"

"No, but there's been a development. Well, two actually."

"What?" Sarge walked closer to Donald and stared down at his phone, somehow expecting it to provide the answers.

"Penn Terminals, the shipyard, is owned by a Cabot Industries subsidiary."

Sarge shrugged. "O-kay," he began, stretching out the word. "I'd be surprised if they didn't. Walter's bought up everything he could to squeeze out any competitors. It also guarantees lucrative government contracts for Cabot Industries."

Donald nodded. "Yeah, there's more. The FBI have reported that the ship docked nearest the point where the beacons stopped transmitting was part of the Crowley fleet. They were recently purchased by Cabot Industries."

Sarge ran his hand through his hair. He began pacing the floor again. "Are they saying Julia and Rose were taken aboard this ship? A Cabot-owned ship?" His voice began to express his anger.

"That's still unconfirmed. They're questioning the dockworkers and supervisory personnel. They're also sifting through the security cameras at Penn Terminals."

"Okay, let's give them a little time. But first, I have some questions for Walter. Bring him in."

Cabot walked with the use of a cane. He was now in his late eighties, and the years since his wife's death had taken their toll. Mary had been the rock that held him up when the man who was like his brother, John Morgan, died. Since then, he'd been a staunch supporter of Sarge's until recently when it was apparent Gardner Lowell had been poisoning their relationship.

Sarge had won the vote of confidence he'd sought yesterday afternoon following Thanksgiving dinner. Cabot, while expressing his support, had been wavering. Despite his age and his apparent diminishing capacities, the influence of Walter Cabot over their fellow Boston Brahmin could never be underestimated.

"Henry," Cabot greeted in a heavy Bostonian accent. He'd known Sarge since he was born. Cabot had also been a dear friend of Sarge's father, Henry Winthrop Sargent III. "I've heard about the trouble you've had. I was shocked and outraged at the unmitigated gall of the perpetrators. I trust you've captured them?"

"Not alive, Walter," replied Sarge. That was not entirely true. Donald had received word that a couple of the operatives who had descended upon Camp David had been wounded and taken into custody. Thus far, they were not talking and had demanded lawyers. A laughable request considering where the CIA was holding them and the conversation that was soon to follow.

Cabot shook Sarge's hand, and the two men hugged, as always. Morgan was Sarge's godfather, but Cabot was like an uncle. As boys, Sarge and Steven had both referred to him as Uncle Walter.

The same had not been true of Sarge's relationship with Lawrence Lowell, Gardner's father and the other confidant closest to John Morgan. After several family get-togethers after Sarge's parents had died, he was teasingly encouraged to call Lawrence Lowell Uncle Larry.

After the third such occasion, Constance Lowell put her foot down. "My husband is not the boy's uncle, nor is he a Larry, for goodness' sake," she'd said. That was the end of that. As Sarge looked back on those days, he was not surprised that Constance was such a huge, negative influence over Gardner when it came to Sarge. And, as he and Julia had discussed briefly last night before falling asleep, they saw a similar hostility between Gardner's son and Win. It was a brewing rivalry that had started strictly from one side—the Lowells'.

Sarge approached his conversation with Cabot in much the same manner as he did the prior meeting with Briscoe. While he was intent on quizzing Cabot about his knowledge of the shipyard at Penn Terminals and the Cabot connection to the Crowley container ship, he wanted to determine if Cabot was aware of more than what had been disseminated in the media before he got started.

After several minutes of back-and-forth in which Cabot seemed to know less about the day's events than Briscoe, Sarge got to the point.

"Walter, tell me about Penn Terminals," said Sarge, gauging the reaction of the man he'd known all his life. Cabot was more apt to let his guard down in his later years.

Cabot glanced at Donald and shrugged. "What's to tell? I believe it's part of our shipyard operation, as are so many others. Is Penn somehow related to the attack on you?"

Sarge spoke slowly, focused on any change in Cabot's demeanor, however slight. "Maybe. It might also be related to the attack at the mall."

"What mall attack? Henry, on my doctor's orders, I turn off the television after five in the afternoon. I have difficulty sleeping, and he doesn't want me overly stimulated with the news."

"So you know nothing about the terrorist attack at the King of Prussia Mall?" asked Donald.

Cabot raised his hands and shrugged. "I do not. However, I must ask, Henry. What does this have to with me and one of my many shipyards?"

Sarge did not immediately respond. "How did Cabot come to own Crowley Shipping?"

"Who? Crowley?" asked Cabot.

Sarge wasn't sure how to gauge Cabot's reaction. He'd exhibit remarkable clarity during their meeting with the other Boston Brahmin in the Solarium the day before. Now he seemed somewhat confused and short of memory.

Sarge glanced at his watch. It was after eleven. At this point in time, Cabot would've been sleeping for many hours. Ordinarily, an interrogator might use sleep deprivation to extract information from a suspect. In the case of the octogenarian, Sarge appeared to be fighting through a thick, dense fog to get to the truth.

Donald picked up on Cabot's awkward responses. "Crowley specializes in container shipping from the Atlantic into the Pacific." He'd received a one-paragraph briefing on Crowley from the FBI via text just now.

"I don't know, Henry. It's possible my granddaughter made that acquisition. I am not one to micromanage her affairs at this juncture. I have to trust in her capabilities at some point because I certainly cannot manage her from the grave."

Sarge was perplexed. His gut told him Cabot was not involved in the decision to kill him or kidnap Julia and Rose. There simply wasn't enough of a reason for Cabot to be part of such a drastic move.

Sarge decided to lay out the facts for Cabot that could be discerned from media reports. He also told him about the kidnapping and how it related to his businesses. At first, Cabot was saddened by this news, and then he gradually became angered by it. Like Briscoe, Cabot swore his fealty to Sarge and promised all available resources at his disposal to help if called upon.

After a few minutes of Cabot heaping condolences on Sarge, he was escorted out of the West Wing so Gardner Lowell would be unaware of his presence in the Oval Office. He turned to Donald after the door was closed to provide them privacy.

"Anything new from downstairs?"

"Nothing concrete although they've developed their working theory," replied Donald. He gulped and shook his head in disbelief before he continued. "They're operating under the presumption that you would be assassinated along with the rest of us. The two-phase attack required enormous human and financial resources."

"Have they ID'd any of the gunmen?"

"Yes, a few. All fingers point toward South America and former drug cartel enforcers. A few even have U.S. special forces backgrounds, while others were once part of the Colombian army."

Sarge raised his hands and scowled. "Why the hell would the Colombians try to kill me? I mean, truth be told, we've left them alone down there. I've redeployed DEA assets to the southern border to stop the flow of drugs into the Southwest. If anything, they should be sending me freakin' chocolates."

Donald shrugged. "They think they're hired guns. Offshore assets to avoid the dots being connected to a domestic source."

"Like who?" asked Sarge.

"Unknown at this time because nobody has taken credit for the attacks, and there have been no demand requests from the kidnappers. It's all purely speculation."

"What about news from the shipyard? Anything?"

Donald shook his head. "I'm waiting on a text. If I hear from them, do you want me to interrupt you and Gardner?"

"Only if it's something concrete," Sarge replied as he thrust his hands in his pockets and walked back toward the fireplace.

"And do you still want me to leave the Oval while you speak with that pompous asshole?"

Sarge smiled and patted his friend on the shoulder. "That's precisely why you need to step out. As much as I wanna smack him around, I'm afraid you'll grab him by the throat."

"Yeah, and would that be so bad? You know, whether he's involved or not?"

Sarge laughed. Donald's candor helped lighten the mood so Sarge's judgment in dealing with Gardner wasn't clouded. "There will be a time and place for dealing with Gardner. Count on it. For now, I need to get the girls back safely."

"You're the boss. However, I'll be right outside the door in case you need to tag me into the ring. I'm ready."

Sarge led Donald to the door and opened it for him. "Betty, please have security bring Mr. Lowell to me. Also, Donald needs some coffee. Um, decaf, please."

Donald flipped the President of the United States the bird, drawing a stern rebuke from Betty. Sarge smiled and walked back into the Oval Office. He took a deep breath and steadied his nerves. His discussion with Gardner would be far different than those that preceded it.

CHAPTER FIFTY-TWO

Late Evening
The Oval Office
The White House
Washington, DC

Gardner was an international law attorney who split his time between his New York offices and the Lowell estate on Martha's Vineyard. His law firm specialized in cross-border resolutions—experts in mediating as well as litigating trade and investment disputes between countries. They were also one of the most respected lobbyist firms in America. Lowell, for all his faults and the immense ego that prevented him from recognizing said faults, was a skilled negotiator. Sarge intended to handle him differently from the outsider, Briscoe, and the elderly Cabot. He intended to use a variant of the bully pulpit afforded any president.

Sarge found himself asking *what would John Morgan do* for the second time in as many days. The night before, he'd used tact and détente to maintain his good standing as the head of the Boston Brahmin. Now, he was one-on-one with Gardner. No witnesses.

Lay the cards on the table. Threaten in any manner necessary to get to the truth.

Sarge was ready for Gardner, who, not surprisingly, made it easy for Sarge to play rough. "What's the meaning of this, Sargent? You can't just have the FBI drag me out of my home like I'm some kind of common criminal."

"I can and I did, Gardner. Sit down and shut the hell up!" Sarge's face immediately turned red with anger.

Gardner had never been spoken to like that by anyone other than his mother. Even his father, a well-respected attorney and judge, would never address his son that way. Only Mother, as Gardner called Constance, had that authority.

"Now, hold on, Sarge. I understand somebody tried to kill you today, but why do you think you need to treat me with such disdain?"

"My wife, Gardner! And my daughter! Where the hell are they?"

"What? I have no idea! Dammit, Sarge. I'm at a loss here!"

Gardner stood from his chair and began walking toward the door to exit.

"Where do you think you're going?"

"I don't need this, nor is your attitude toward me warranted. I know you've had a bad day, but know this, I had nothing to do with it, whatever the hell it is, if that's what you're thinking."

Sarge moved to block his exit. He was prepared to get physical if that was what it took to disrupt the master chess player. "You wanna know what I'm thinking? Fine! My wife and daughter have been kidnapped. I think you have something to do with their abduction."

"Come on, Sargent. We may have our differences, but I'm no kidnapper. Nor am I going to arrange for the assassination of the president."

"If you're lying, Gardner, I will find out about it. One word from me and I'll unleash the hounds. CIA, FBI, IRS, and any other three-letter agency I can't think of at the moment. You've made it very clear how you feel about me. I firmly believe you've tried to undermine me within the Boston Brahmin."

"Differences, to be sure, Sargent. I would never consider killing you or involving your family in our disagreements."

Sarge walked away, clearing the exit for Gardner if he chose to leave. He didn't. Instead, he turned around to address Sarge.

"I honestly know nothing about this other than the news reporting. The same is especially true of what has happened to your family. Sarge, I'd like you to hear my words." Gardner paused to allow Sarge to face him before continuing. Sarge's face was no longer flush with anger. His emotional exhaustion was beginning to take over.

"Sarge, we are fellow Brahmin. We stand shoulder to shoulder against all outside threats and enemies. I will help discover who is behind this. Then I will not expect, nor will I accept, your apology for this confrontation. If I were similarly situated, I'd lash out at the nearest enemy I could find as well."

Sarge nodded, forcing himself to continue putting up an angry front. He wasn't sure if he was succeeding.

"Gardner, please don't get in the way or do anything to jeopardize getting Julia and Rose back safely. That's my only priority at this moment. Finding blame is secondary. However, I want you to know that if you are behind these attacks and their kidnapping, the government will be the least of your concerns."

"Your threat is heard loud and clear," said Gardner as he stood a little taller. He'd not backed down under the pressure. "I meant what I said. I will help get to the bottom of this if for no other reason than to clear my name."

With that, Gardner exited the Oval Office. Donald wasted no time slipping past the larger man to speak with Sarge.

"They need us back downstairs. The FBI agents who raided the shipping terminal have provided more footage and a line on where they are."

Sarge didn't hesitate. "Lead the way."

CHAPTER FIFTY-THREE

Late Evening
The Situation Room
The White House
Washington, DC

Brad was waiting beside the watchman's desk at the secured entry to the Situation Room. Before Sarge and Donald entered, he wanted to make a suggestion to avoid any unnecessary delays.

"Brad, what is it?" asked Sarge.

"They're gonna brief you. However, I want to set something in motion to avoid any unnecessary delay and interagency power struggle."

"Tell me."

"I want to dispatch Drew and his team to Virginia Beach. We can provide them details en route and brief them further upon arrival. While they're travelling, I'll have their gear prepared for them." Virginia Beach was the home of the Naval Special Warfare Development Group and the widely known SEAL Team Six. The famed counterterrorism unit was considered the best of the best.

Drew was a former SEAL Team member, as were other members of the Elite Eight.

"So they're alive?" asked Sarge. "Have we received contact?"

"Sarge, please go inside and allow them to brief you. I need to get started."

Sarge swallowed hard and nodded. He'd always trusted Brad's judgment.

Donald led the way into the Situation Room, which was buzzing with activity. Cal Stanwick continued to spearhead the effort. He was bouncing from one analyst to another as they began to receive new information from the FBI field agents in Philadelphia.

"Mr. President," announced one of the analysts who noticed Sarge first. Everyone began to stand.

"No, please keep your seats," he said graciously. He turned to Stanwick. "Cal, what have you got?"

He didn't immediately respond, which reflected his sense of urgency. He instructed his aide to project their new intelligence onto the largest screen in the room located opposite of where the president was normally seated.

"Mr. President, we will be showing you a series of images and video clips that have been spliced together from the security footage at Penn Terminals. Also, to cut to the chase, we are near certain your wife and daughter were placed on an oceangoing vessel. A container ship, to be exact."

The analyst began streaming the images and video onto the monitor. When Sarge saw Rose being carried out of the SUV in a duffel bag onto the ship, his knees buckled, and he fell backwards into his chair. A hush came over the room as everyone helping with the search became emotional. They revered Sarge and were keenly aware of what he'd done to rescue America. All of them were personally invested in finding Julia and Rose.

The series of images and video continued until another SUV arrived minutes later. A lifeless body covered in a raincoat and hat was being dragged up the gangway. It was impossible to confirm it was Julia, but the presumption was a strong one.

Sarge leaned onto the conference table and rested his elbows. For a moment, he stared in disbelief at the images before burying his face in his hands. Stanwick allowed him a moment before speaking.

"Mr. President, I know this may not come as any solace at the moment, but our analysis of this security footage leads us to believe that both your wife and daughter are still alive. Further, we have been able to confirm the ship that left port with them aboard was a Crowley container vessel. We have repositioned an NSA surveillance satellite to track its path."

"Where are they going?" asked Sarge.

"Sir, they are travelling south along the Atlantic seaboard with a direct route toward the Turks and Caicos Islands or quite possibly Cuba."

"South America," Sarge muttered. "Cal, we have confirmation that some if not all of the operatives involved in our attack are from Colombia, do we not?"

"Yes, Mr. President. The route the freighter is traveling would take them into the Caribbean Sea and toward South American ports, including Colombia."

"Cal, if they dock in Colombia, I may never see them again. We cannot trust the Colombians if they are in fact behind this."

"Agreed, Mr. President. At General Bradlee's directive, we are mapping out a rescue strategy that involves an at-sea rescue."

"We can't go in there guns blazing," added Donald.

"That's correct, Mr. Quinn. This will require a special ops team. We've contacted the Department of Defense without providing the specific purpose for the mission."

Sarge interrupted him. "Cal, ask them to stand down for the moment. General Bradlee will coordinate that effort. Just make sure he has everything he needs on this ship, its route, and the number of kidnappers on the ship."

"Yes, sir," responded Stanwick. "Each member of our team is gathering facts and data on every aspect of the kidnapping and the people behind it. We'll forward it to Mr. Quinn and General Bradlee as it is received."

"Thank you," mumbled Sarge, who continued to watch the continuous loop of images and video filling the monitor. Suddenly, he cocked his head to the side and jumped up from his chair. "Stop the images. Please pause it!"

The aide fumbled on the keyboard and finally entered the proper keystrokes to halt the montage of images showing the activity taking place on the dock near the *Crowley*'s gangway. The rest of the investigation team stopped working as Sarge walked slowly toward the monitor, his eyes affixed to the image.

"Please slowly back up the video," he instructed.

The aide complied and reversed the images and video until Sarge yelled, "Stop!"

He eased forward. He pointed toward the monitor. "That person. The woman. Can you center her on the screen?"

"Yes, sir."

The woman had been walking behind Julia with another operative. For just a brief moment, she'd turned her head back toward the parking lot of Penn Terminals. It was directly at the cameras.

"Zoom in on her face," Sarge ordered.

"Yes, sir, However, the image will be grainy and somewhat obscured due to shadows." The aide isolated the woman's face. It grew ever larger on the screen. The aide manipulated the image to sharpen the contrast.

Sarge gasped. He turned to Donald and began to touch his index finger to the screen. "Do you see?"

Donald scowled and approached the monitor. His mouth fell open, but he was unable to speak. Sarge, however, was certain of who was looking directly into the security camera.

It was Katie O'Shea.

PART VII

The Rescue
Saturday after Thanksgiving, November 2024, predawn hours

CHAPTER FIFTY-FOUR

1:00 a.m.
The Oval Office
The White House
Washington, DC

Sarge had called Abbie and Susan to the Oval Office. He arranged for J.J., despite his broken leg, to be included in the hastily called meeting via a secure video feed. All the Loyal Nine were included except for Julia, who unfortunately knew of Katie's involvement before anyone else. A video camera with a monitor had been moved into the Oval Office, allowing the remote attendees to see the group seated on the couches. Sarge sat in a chair near the coffee table, forcing himself to sit still and not wander as he addressed everyone.

"An hour ago, we received confirmation that the woman in the image standing near Julia is in fact Katie O'Shea."

The revelation was a shock to everyone, especially Abbie and Susan, who'd been tasked with consoling Katie after Steven's death. Katie had been exhibiting anger during that tumultuous period of time, and she'd frequently lashed out at the others. However, her ire had been directed at Sarge, not because he'd caused his brother to die but because, in her mind, he'd received preferential treatment from John Morgan and the Boston Brahmin.

The Loyal Nine had come together by fate, and their group was built on a foundation of trust. Lineage was a factor, as Abbie, Julia, Brad, and J.J. were also tied to the Founding Fathers and the Boston Brahmin by blood. Sarge's fate had been determined by the handshake of two powerful men one sunny day on Baker's Island off the Massachusetts coast.

There were the outsiders, brought into the fold because of their friendship to Sarge and Steven. Donald had been a loyal accountant to John Morgan for years, and his wife, Susan, had proven herself to be a tight-lipped confidante of the group.

Finally, there was Katie, who was included because of her relationship to Steven and her extraordinary skills as a spy for the CIA. She'd been a vital asset to the Loyal Nine and the Boston Brahmin before and after the collapse. However, her love for Steven resulted in jealousy of Sarge's success. It caused a rift within the group, and the warning signs of discord were readily apparent to all.

Sarge had to deal with the reality that Katie was privy to information that could tear apart the Loyal Nine and expose the dealings of the Boston Brahmin. Her attitude warranted banishment from the group. Katie had become a liability.

Nonetheless, Sarge gave her the opportunity to come around. He tasked her with finding Steven's killer, which she did. And as a loyal soldier, she brought the man to Sarge, who executed the man himself.

After the collapse, she was given an excellent position at Aegis, running private security details and covert operations. Her supposed death in Berlin was a blow to the firm and was mourned by the Loyal Nine.

Be that as it may, they were facing a problem that should've been dealt with many years ago. Katie was not just a thorn in their side. She was holding Julia and Rose captive while her intentions were unknown.

Sarge took a deep breath. "I believe I made a mistake years ago when I allowed my sense of fairness and loyalty to my brother to overrule what needed to be done. I knew expelling someone from the Loyal Nine would carry great risk to us all. I thought I could rehabilitate Katie and keep her close to be used as a valuable asset. I was wrong, and now my family is paying the price."

"We all agreed, Sarge," said Abbie, who reached out and patted him on the hand. "We analyzed her emotional state and presumed she'd get over Steven's death. Hell, Julia and I discussed this many times. We were convinced that locating Steven's killer would bring her back into the fold. Obviously, she still harbored resentment against us."

"Us is the operative word," added J.J. from his hospital room. "Sarge, there is a bigger agenda here that should not be taken personally. She didn't set out to harm just Julia and Rose. She came after all of us. Her goal was to eliminate the Loyal Nine."

"I agree," added Brad. "She is nothing more than a spiteful terrorist who has partnered with someone with outlandish resources."

"I'm just gonna say it," said Donald. "All fingers point to Gardner Lowell. He wants to exercise dominion and control over Sarge. His jealousy of Sarge's relationship with the Boston Brahmin aligns perfectly with Katie's. Somehow, those two must be connected."

"Maybe so," said Sarge. "I already tried to play heavy handed with Gardner. If I push too hard, I'll never see them again." His voice trailed off, and he looked at his feet as he fought back tears. Sarge had made the right decision to bring the Loyal Nine together. His emotions might cause him to make a mistake.

Drew became the voice of reason from afar. He and his team were ready to pull out to undertake a rescue effort.

"Lowell can be dealt with later. I didn't know Katie all that well, but from what you've told me, she's a loose cannon. They've made no effort to reach out and undertake any form of negotiation. Please excuse my bluntness, but it could be that Julia was some kind of prize awarded to Katie for her efforts.

"We don't know. I do know this about any hostage situation.

With no lines of communication with the kidnappers, every minute leads us closer to a horrible ending. If you push Lowell again, he's likely to give the order out of spite. We need to move now while we still have cover of darkness."

A hush came over the room as they soaked in Drew's words.

Sarge was the first to speak. "He's right. Punishment and revenge can come later."

"Agreed," said Abbie. The others nodded their heads as well.

Sarge looked into the camera. Drew's face was covered in shades of black and gray camouflage paint. He was wearing a wetsuit that covered his head as well.

"Drew, please bring them back to me."

"Yes, Mr. President."

CHAPTER FIFTY-FIVE

1:30 a.m.
Aboard the *Crowley*
Atlantic Ocean
Off the Outer Banks, North Carolina

Katie had slept hard for three hours, more than enough to recharge her internal batteries. In the short time she'd been aboard the container ship, she had a new perspective into sailing the open waters on a vessel as large as an office building.

After boarding and departing the Delaware River, the ship was faced with rolling waves as it traveled in a southerly direction along the Atlantic seaboard. It took her some time to get her sea legs and for her stomach to adjust to the constant movement. When she questioned the captain and crew about the conditions, their response was that this was normal for the open waters.

Her team reported that Julia and Rose had both become violently ill from seasickness. Julia had demanded to see a doctor. That wasn't going to happen. Katie told her crew to give them additional latrine buckets, extra water, and Dramamine.

Only a handful of the crew members were aware of the captives on board. The captain was paid handsomely for his silence and cooperation while his crew dutifully complied with his orders.

Katie's seven-man team traded shifts attending to Julia and Rose. The others either rested or roamed the ship to provide security. The crew was told that the heavily armed gunmen were to prevent pirate attacks, an explanation that puzzled most since they were unaware of such activity off the coast of North America.

She spent most of her time on the bridge, the command center and brain of the *Crowley*. The container ship carried thousands of containers of exported goods destined for the Philippines. Four huge cranes dipped over the containers at different locations on deck like vultures ready to scoop up roadkill. The ship's lighting cast an eerie shadow across the tops of the containers. The cloudy evening coupled with the new moon phase left the ocean dark and mysterious.

Katie wandered through the bridge, scanning the computer screens of the crew and studying the gauges to determine their speed. She drew a nasty look or two when she hovered over a seaman's shoulder for too long. Satisfied that the crew was doing their job and not trying to sabotage her operation, she stepped outside into the cold, salty air to gather her thoughts.

She'd given herself a new life after being declared dead in Berlin. Like any international operative, Katie had multiple identities with money stashed in secretive bank accounts around the world. During her time recuperating from the injuries sustained in the bomb blast, she'd considered her future.

It was time to become a ghost. Not just because she'd already begun to plot her revenge against Sarge and his associates. Her skills would become more marketable, and her invisibility was a plus to employers who needed someone with her capabilities to commit murder or abductions.

For years, she'd made more money than anything Aegis had paid her after she'd been unceremoniously expelled from the Loyal Nine. Sarge had bought her off in order to try to maintain her confidentiality. She understood his motives and couldn't quarrel with them. She was alive.

Then, one fateful day, she was contacted by an old acquaintance. To be sure, she and her new employer were far from besties. They'd only met in passing. Her contacts with his associates were more prevalent, and she assumed he'd become familiar with her capabilities as a result.

Their paths had crossed by accident when the powerful man's fixer had put out feelers on the dark web for special ops personnel to undertake a delicate mission. After several online communications and then a series of phone calls utilizing burner phones, Katie was hired. When she learned the identity of her employer and what the mission entailed, she was shocked at first. Then she could barely control her enthusiasm. Not only could she exact revenge on Sarge and the others, but she could secure her position with a new center of power in America.

As the mission quickly unfolded, Katie was astonished at the information her employer had about Sarge's schedule and that of the First Family. Because Katie had been an insider at the highest levels of the federal government for many years, she was ideally suited to lead the operation.

She was astonished at the intelligence given to her, including details of the First Family's movements. Her employer had access to information only disseminated to members of the Secret Service and the Department of Homeland Security. During her time in the White House, she was keenly aware that staffers who'd professed their loyalty to the president were in fact the biggest leakers of information. Katie knew because she had been one of them, handpicked by John Morgan to spy on the former administration.

As part of her resource materials, she had been provided a list of names and a dossier on each of the hunters and shoppers who were targets. Katie recalled laughing as she scrolled through the information provided. Not only could she have prepared it herself, but she could've also expanded upon it to include the personal idiosyncrasies of each individual.

This background knowledge helped her plan the mall attack and subsequent abduction. She could recall the favorite stores of the women in her sights. She knew nothing of the children and was surprised that Julia would separate from her kids. However, that was an indication her targets had let their guards down. They'd become too comfortable. Soft. Unlike her.

Katie checked her watch and was perturbed that she hadn't heard from the team attacking Camp David. She was aware from news reports that the hunting party had escaped except for the Secret Service man and J.J. They were insignificant in the scheme of things.

She'd tried to reach out to Garcia, the team leader, via satellite phone text messaging. He did not respond. That did not bode well for his fate. Before exiting her quarters, she scanned all available news sources to obtain any information about the attack on Camp David. There was very little except for speculation that the president had survived although there had been no formal statement from the White House.

After several minutes in which she took in the open seas, she placed a call on the satellite phone to her employer at the prearranged time. She'd be giving him an update that would proudly proclaim partial mission accomplished. She hoped that would suffice for the man with the volatile temper.

CHAPTER FIFTY-SIX

1:30 a.m.
Dam Neck Annex
Naval Air Station Oceana
Virginia Beach, Virginia

The 160th Special Operations Aviation Regiment, the 160th SOAR, or Night Stalkers as those in the military call them, were headquartered at Fort Campbell, Kentucky. When called upon by the Pentagon, they quickly assembled their team and necessary equipment to rendezvous with Drew and his team of Elite Eight operatives at the Dam Neck Annex in Virginia Beach, home to SEAL Team Six.

The Night Stalkers were prepared for a mission that would require stealth operations, speed, and daring under pitch-black conditions. Their chosen aircraft was a medium assault helicopter, the Sikorsky MH-60M Black Hawk. It was equipped with a fast rope and a set of rigs that allowed its operators to quickly descend to their drop zone. These same ropes were used to extract personnel under all conditions. As many as eight personnel could be hoisted with a single rope.

As a medium attack helicopter, the Black Hawk was also fully equipped with a variety of weapon systems mounted on its stub wings. Chain guns and laser-guided missiles could provide a force multiplier for the operatives on the ground or, in this case, on a ship.

Drew's team knew the risks. The most dangerous part of the mission would be getting on board the *Crowley* undetected. Death could come in the open waters just as easily as from a bullet.

Aboard the Black Hawk, Drew checked his watch to gauge how much daylight they'd have. In less than ten minutes, they'd pull out from the Dam Neck Annex to intercept the *Crowley*, which was now southeast of their position. At a cruising speed of one hundred forty knots, they'd be in position to drop in the path of the freighter within the hour.

Each member of his team was equipped with identifying beacons to prevent friendly fire from one another and the gunners aboard the Black Hawk. On the helicopter's flight deck, a digital glass cockpit with night-vision displays allowed the pilots to operate in complete darkness to avoid visual detection from their target. They also had state-of-the-art threat detection and defensive countermeasures, including infrared jammers and radar warning receivers.

Drew took a quick glance at his team, who were packed like sardines into two crowded rows. King Dawkins, the bulkiest of his eight operatives, muscled Spidey on one side and Santa on the other for more room on the seat. Both men complained and swore at their fellow team member.

Inside the loud, vibrating interior cabin, the men were mostly silent. Some leaned their heads back and visualized their mission while others leaned forward with their hands clasped together, anxious to perform their duty.

In the cockpit, the two pilots were flying at a very low altitude, barely a hundred feet above the choppy Atlantic waters. Their instruments cast eerie blue and green hues onto their helmets and clothing.

Drew studied his men. He was keenly aware that each of them was going over their role in the rescue of Julia and her daughter, Rose. They thought about their training. They focused on the ship's layout and the probable point of attack. They cleared their minds of any extraneous thoughts, focusing on saving the president's family.

"We're coming up on our drop point!" the Night Stalker chief pilot announced, indicating to the Elite Eight to prepare to be lowered into the ocean.

Drew stretched his legs out and then pulled them back toward his chest. He repeated the action, forcing the blood to circulate through them. Unconsciously, he gripped his UDT fins, the preference of Navy Seals assigned to underwater demolition teams. Their level of rigidity made them ideal for long swims and treading in water. Their winged tips provided them power to sustain a kick speed of one hundred fifty feet per minute.

Drew glanced out the porthole and caught a brief glimpse of the *Crowley*, which was fully illuminated at night to avoid a collision with a yachtsman or other pleasure craft with poor navigational skills.

"Gentlemen, check your gear. Spidey, you and I will be first to attach the suction devices to the ship and secure the grab line."

"Copy that, Slash," said Spidey.

"Three minutes out," announced the copilot.

Seconds later, the pilot came on the intercom. "Jackson, we've got incoming voice for you."

"Is it SOCOM?" he asked, using the acronym for the Special Operations Command communications team.

"No, higher, sir," came the cryptic response.

"Go ahead, then."

Drew took the headset, and it was immediately filled with static. Through the crackling sound, he made out a familiar voice.

"Drew, I know it's last minute. I just wanted you to know that I'd give anything to be riding with you and your team right now."

Drew smiled. He glanced around the cabin at the seven

inquisitive sets of eyes that bored into his mind. He provided them a thumbs-up.

"Thank you, Mr. President," he said formally in response.

"Drew, you've become like a brother to me. I have a hundred percent faith in you and your team to bring my girls home."

"Yes, sir. I feel the same way. We've got this. And if I can, I'll bring that bitch back alive or in a body bag."

"A photo will do," said Sarge coldly. "Be safe, my friend. Out."

Sarge dropped the call, and Drew smiled as he relayed what had been said. He could see the positive effect Sarge's call had on his team. They were all alert, rubbing their hands together as if they were heavyweight prize fighters ready to enter the boxing ring. For Drew, he was shocked Sarge would call him so close to his insertion point, but he understood. He'd be concerned about saving Abbie and would do the same.

The darkened Black Hawk sped ever closer to a rendezvous with the *Crowley* and a resurrected demon who needed to be sent back to Hell.

CHAPTER FIFTY-SEVEN

2:00 a.m.
The Situation Room
The White House
Washington, DC

It was standing room only in the Situation Room at two in the morning. Stanwick had made the arrangement for Sarge to give Drew and his team a few final words of encouragement. Now Sarge was seated at the head of the long conference table, awaiting the rescue effort to unfold. To his right sat Donald, and on his left, over Sarge's objection, was Abbie. He was concerned that the further stress might cause her difficulties with her pregnancy. However, like Sarge, she had a loved one whose life would be in danger, so she insisted on being there.

Other high-ranking government officials were in attendance as well as several analysts, who stared at their computers to monitor various aspects of the operation. Periodically, they'd be made aware of a pertinent fact or development. They'd politely raise their hand until Stanwick approached them and received the information. If it was important enough to relay to the president, he did.

Unknown to most, the conference room widely referred to as the Situation Room was only one of many within the high-security suite of offices. Beyond the four walls were numerous information gatherers monitoring all aspects of the rescue, including NSA satellites data and the results of FBI eavesdropping. Because Briscoe, Cabot, and Lowell had been identified as possible suspects, not only were their phones and computers being monitored, but so were those of their closest associates.

Stanwick unexpectedly announced, "Sixty seconds from the drop zone."

Sarge took a deep breath and nodded to Donald, who'd glanced in his direction. He reached across the table to take Abbie's hand. He gave it a gentle squeeze, and the two shared a knowing glance. There was no reason to hide the personal nature of this mission. Everyone was keenly aware of the ramifications of failure.

Via NSA satellite imagery, the attendees could watch the progress of the Black Hawk as it raced toward the interception point with the *Crowley*. Miles behind, also appearing as two ghostly images displayed on the screen, were backup choppers who would engage the targets if deemed necessary. After the attacks on Camp David, all the Black Hawk pilots were instructed to prepare for surface-to-air missiles. The man portable air defense systems, or MANPADS, would be devastating to a Black Hawk caught off guard.

Sarge didn't regret placing the call to Drew. He did it for himself and Abbie, who'd been nervously fiddling with her hands as they awaited the mission to get underway. Sarge meant what he'd said. He wanted to be alongside the team as they rescued Julia and Rose. He wanted to punish those who caused his family harm. He wanted to look Katie O'Shea in the eye and deliver the deadly blow that ended her life, just as he'd done to Steven's killer.

Sarge forced himself to be patient, keeping his mouth shut to prevent the many questions he had about what was likely happening during the operation. So he watched and waited.

Drew and another member of his team dropped into the water.

They were mere blips on the screen as they positioned themselves in the way of the massive container ship headed directly for them. The Black Hawk veered away to the south and then hovered, the remaining six blips clustered together as if they were one. A team. Also waiting.

The seconds lasted like minutes as Sarge's mind raced back to those days during the collapse. He'd been in the shoes of these operators. He'd taken on an enemy, one who should never have been called onto American soil. He recalled working with his fellow patriots, breathing hard, gripping his weapon in his hand, his body tense as he prepared to open fire and take another man's life.

The circumstances were different, yet they were the same. He was out there. Exposed. Vulnerable. In the line of fire, just as likely to die as the man he was trying to kill. For some, it was exhilarating. To Sarge, it seemed senseless.

Waiting. Waiting to see Drew and his team climbing up the side of the hull, hundreds of feet to the deck of the ship. The muscles in their arms would be burning, screaming for relief. They'd be battered from the wind and waves bashing them against the unforgiving steel of the ship's hull.

Sarge closed his eyes for a brief moment, trying to visualize the team getting into position. He'd been told that from the second they dropped to the time they climbed over the railing onto the deck, their chances of survival were less than fifty percent. He'd shuddered when those words came out of Stanwick's mouth. He'd asked himself repeatedly before giving the green light for the mission whether it was fair to risk the lives of these brave men, including a dear friend and the father of Abbie's baby, in order to possibly save Julia and Rose.

Sarge prayed and begged God for forgiveness in advance in the event the mission went awry. In his mind, it was Sarge's intention to make that last minute phone call to give the team some words of encouragement. Deep down, he was still contemplating calling it off.

Now, on the screen, he observed the figures moving upward. He abruptly stood and leaned on the desk with both hands, drawing the attention of those seated around him. His mouth was moving, yet he wasn't emitting any sound. He silently shouted words of encouragement as he counted the blips.

Abbie and Donald studied one another before focusing on Sarge's face.

A minute later, Sarge managed a smile, and he exhaled as two words came out of his mouth.

"All eight."

CHAPTER FIFTY-EIGHT

2:00 a.m.
Aboard the *Crowley*
Atlantic Ocean
Off the Outer Banks, North Carolina

Katie stepped back into the ship and found a quiet place away from the bridge and curious ears. She found a porthole window and settled against the steel wall. She took a deep breath, and at precisely two o'clock, she placed the call. Unlike her prior contacts with the man years ago, it was different now. He exuded a confidence and power over the phone that was different from her face-to-face encounters.

When he picked up the phone, he dispensed with the preliminaries and got right to the point.

"My people have reconstructed the events in Maryland. You failed."

Katie closed her eyes and gently smacked the back of her head against the porthole window. She was afraid this would be his reaction.

"Yes, sir. I am aware. However, we have the wife and daughter secured. We are traveling now to the rendezvous point."

"Well, let's hope it is sufficient leverage to accomplish my purpose. I know Sargent well enough to see through his ploy. The pocket veto is a powerful tool that is rarely exercised. My loyalists within the administration have leaked his schedule to me. He has no plans to sign the Statehood Act. If he doesn't in the coming week, it will be considered vetoed, and I must start over with a new administration."

"Yes, sir. I understand. My apologies for failing to eliminate the president and vice president altogether, paving the way for a change of leadership. However, I know how precious his wife and daughter are to him. Once he is made aware of what is expected of him, he will comply with your wishes."

"It's not just my wishes, young lady. It's what is best for the country. From this point forward, I will track your progress. There is no further need to contact me, as my associates will meet you at your destination." With that, the line went dead.

Katie confirmed her satellite phone had disconnected the call before slipping it into her coat pocket. She conducted a mental inventory of the benefits to her, both tangible and intangible, to her taking on Sarge and the Loyal Nine. Certainly, her employer wielded power. But could he protect her? Would he?

All these things raced through her mind, screaming for attention from Katie to provide answers. Her brain was so cluttered that she almost mistook the sound of gunfire for yet another unfamiliar sound aboard the oceangoing vessel.

However, the second burst was unmistakable. They were under attack.

CHAPTER FIFTY-NINE

2:02 a.m.
Aboard the *Crowley*
Atlantic Ocean
Off the Outer Banks, North Carolina

In the cold, salty air, Drew dropped to a knee and held his arm high in a cold fist, signaling everyone to stay down and quiet. His eyes scanned the LoLo vessel, the term used for a container ship capable of lifting containers on and off, loading them with their own cranes. This vessel had been chosen by Katie to give her the ability to offload her freight, namely the containers holding Julia and Rose, to a dock without assistance. To accommodate the large cranes bolted to the deck of the ship, the design necessitated wider than normal walkways along the outer perimeter of the ship.

Using hand signals, he pointed to King, Spidey, and Santa to join him. He tasked the other four operatives with clearing the deck of any armed security guards who were roaming the ship at that time of night. During their preparations, they were instructed to interrogate any hostiles if possible, as their goal of locating Julia and Rose on the massive ship was daunting.

Drew suspected the mother and daughter were being held below deck in one of the many holds, which would explain why they could no longer be tracked via the beacons in their cross necklaces.

His team was equipped with communications and cameras. The live feeds were transmitted back to the States and watched by those in the Situation Room. The team assigned to monitor his activities could also relay to him useful information such as activity observed by the NSA satellites or even something detrimental to the mission like the loss of a man.

Drew studied the seven-story bridge castle rising high above the deck. Through the hazy green lens of his night-vision goggles, it almost appeared to be an illusion. A mirage.

Stacked both fore and aft of the main housing structure of the *Crowley* were rows upon rows of steel shipping containers. They were neatly arranged several rows high.

Breaking ranks, his team fanned out, two headed aft while the other two made their way to the bow. They were instructed to clear the ship while Drew and his team invaded the most likely places where the captives would be held.

They rushed along the railing toward the superstructure. Drew was the first to arrive. He slowly tried the handle on the heavy steel door and, confirming it was unlocked, gestured for Santa to man the door. He and King would be the first to enter.

Drew held up three fingers and counted Santa down.

Two. One.

Santa slowly eased the door open. Once it swung open far enough, he and King slipped inside. Within seconds, his radio sprang to life.

"Contact aft. Tango down."

Nice and quiet, Drew thought to himself as he covered Spidey and Santa, who entered the hallway next. He and his team were equipped with suppressed automatic weapons with more than enough rounds in their waterproof utility belts to engage in a firestorm if need be.

They entered the center of the massive structure in search of targets of their own. An unsuspecting member of the crew, not likely one of the kidnappers but an accomplice in Drew's mind nonetheless, suddenly appeared at the top of a stairwell.

With catlike quickness, Drew pounced on the man and wrapped his powerful hands over his mouth. The man tried to struggle until Drew hissed in his ear, "I'll kill you if you fight me. Do you understand?"

The man's eyes grew wider in the dimly lit hallway. He saw three guns pointed at him and eagerly agreed to Drew's demands.

"Good," Drew continued in a low, menacing voice. "Where are the hostages?"

The man, an American, shrugged and shook his head side to side. He was clearly trying to convey that he didn't know anything about hostages.

"Okay, that's fine," said Drew as his grip on the man's mouth strengthened. "Answer this. Is there anyone on board the ship out of the usual? A passenger. Maybe armed security?"

He nodded rapidly. The man was attempting to speak. Drew glanced at King, who'd moved closer to the man in order to point his rifle into his chest.

Drew whispered in the man's ear, "I'm going to slowly remove my hand so you can speak. If you try anything, my friend will kill you. Understood?"

The man nodded vigorously once again.

"Okay, now I want you to whisper. Who is on board who doesn't belong?"

His body relaxed, so Drew took a chance. He eased his fingers away from the mouth of the man, who immediately began to cooperate.

"There's a woman. Pretty, too. She came on board with some guys who were supposedly here to protect us from pirates. We all think that's stupid because there are no pirates where we're going."

"Where's that?" asked Drew.

"Caribbean Sea and down to the canal. From there, we have a stop off in Honolulu, and then we head to the Philippines."

"Okay, tell me about this woman. Does she have a room assigned to her?"

The man shrugged. "I don't know. The only time I see her is on the bridge."

"What about the security? How many are there?"

He shrugged again. "Six. Maybe eight. I'm not sure."

Drew abruptly clasped his hand over the man's mouth again, startling him and striking fear in his eyes. "I'm not going to hurt you. However, I have to tie you up and gag you until we find what we're looking for."

He began to struggle again, making a lame attempt at pulling himself free. This angered Drew, who wrapped his free arm around his throat.

"Listen to me. Would you rather die? I personally don't give a shit one way or the other."

The man stopped squirming, and his body went limp just before he urinated in his pants. King was the first to notice.

"Geez, Slash. He pissed himself."

Drew shook his head in disbelief. He dragged the man toward a utility closet, where the guys helped gag him while binding his legs and wrists with zip-cuffs.

Seconds after they exited the closet, automatic fire erupted on board.

CHAPTER SIXTY

2:09 a.m.
Aboard the *Crowley*
Atlantic Ocean
Off the Outer Banks, North Carolina

Katie wasted no time responding to the sound of gunfire. She immediately pulled her two-way radio and called out to all members of her team to provide her a situation report.

"Sitrep!"

"We have a man down at the back of the ship. Two gunmen."

"We're under fire at the foredeck. Multiple shooters. Suppressed, full auto. Arrrgggh!"

The end of his transmission told the story. She might be down two already.

Katie thought fast. Being outside the bridge did nothing to help defend her hostages. Her first thought was to race down the stairwell to back up her men outside the containers. She rushed toward the stairwell, talking into her comms as she went. She reached out to the guards who were off duty and ordered them to the deck to assist the men guarding Julia and Rose. Then she broke her own protocol and asked the location of the hostages.

She carried a sidearm on her belt, but the other members of her team carried U.S. military-issue machine guns. She drew her weapons and started down the stairs. She'd descended three flights when she had a thought. She knew exactly how to back off her attackers.

It was premature, but necessary. It was time to place a call.

Katie knew Sarge would be in the Situation Room, monitoring the assault on her ship. She intended to call him and order his teams to stand down.

Or else.

The White House switchboard was monitored twenty-four hours a day. The volunteer operators had no knowledge of covert operations or even the whereabouts of the president at any given moment. However, they had procedures to follow, which involved notifying the Secret Service of any threats.

She had one chance, and that was to reveal herself to Sarge. Then she'd threaten his wife and daughter.

A young man answered the phone.

"Listen very carefully to me," she snarled into the phone. "I want you to deliver this message to your supervisor and then to the Secret Service. I have kidnapped the president's wife and daughter. He needs to speak with me immediately. Do you understand?"

"Um, ma'am," the college student stammered, "it's after hours, and I think—"

"You idiot! Pass along the message. Now!"

Katie paced the landing of the all-steel stairwell. She heard the gunfire echoing through the superstructure. Bullets were ricocheting off the bridge castle and the containers as her men engaged in the firefight.

"Ma'am, may I help you?" an elderly woman asked.

Katie was about to respond when she heard footsteps racing up the stairs toward her. She was trapped. She disconnected the call and rushed up the stairs to the floor of the superstructure that contained the living quarters and mess hall.

The dark hallway was full of activity as the ship's crew was awakened by the gunfire. Their panicked voices shouted over one another.

"Are we being boarded?"

"Is it the pirates?"

"What do we do? We don't have guns!"

An authoritative voice ordered the crew back in their rooms. They reacted immediately, rushing back inside and pulling their doors closed behind them. Like a game of musical chairs that left the odd man out, Katie suddenly found herself alone in the hallway.

She looked back and forth and started to run toward the rear of the ship. Appearing out of nowhere was a broad-shouldered man who filled the narrow passage. He was pointing a rifle at her. Frightened by his sudden appearance, she backtracked toward an officer's quarters. She desperately tried to open the door, but it was locked.

She tried an unmarked door and forced it inward. She entered a utility room with a narrow spiral staircase running through the center of it. Katie rushed downward, replacing her gun in her holster so she could use both hands to keep her balance.

She'd almost reached the main deck when she heard a door open. She abruptly tried to slow her progress. Instead, she stumbled and tumbled, head over heels, down the staircase until she landed upside down at the next floor.

A man approached her with his weapon drawn. She reached for her pistol.

"Forget it, lady. You'll be dead before your hand reaches the grip."

Katie pulled her hand away from her gun and tried to sit up. The man brusquely forced her back down, causing the back of her head to hit the steel floor.

Santa moved a little closer. "What's your name?"

"Screw you! How's that?"

"Another time. Another life, I guess. Somehow, I think I found who we're looking for."

He stepped away from Katie and spoke into his comms. "Slash, I've got the woman. Second floor, center of the superstructure, at the bottom of a spiral staircase."

"Roger. On my way."

Katie's mind raced. She'd heard the code name Slash before. He had to be related to Aegis. Or maybe Steven. Seconds later, she found out.

"Thanks, Santa," said Drew as he entered through a hallway on the second floor. "Her people have hunkered down on the foredeck, toward the middle. I guess this piece of crap is holding them in one of the containers. Go help out the rest of the team. I've got this."

Katie thought of another ploy. She shouted into her comms, "Kill the hostages!"

CHAPTER SIXTY-ONE

2:12 a.m.
The Situation Room
The White House
Washington, DC

"Kill the hostages!"

The audio and video feeds coming from the rescue team's cameras had been spotty at best. The steel superstructure caused frequent blackouts, while the darkness made viewing the gun battle on the deck near impossible. However, Katie's cold-blooded, heartless words came through loud and clear.

Everyone in the Situation Room gasped—shocked and revolted by the order Katie had given her men. She'd lost. She'd been captured by Drew's team. Yet her final, ruthless act was to order the death of an innocent woman and child.

"Nooo!" shouted Sarge.

"They have to do something!" said Abbie as she slammed both hands on the arms of her chair.

Drew spoke into his comms. It came across garbled, but his sense of urgency was clear. "Engage! She's ... kill order!"

All eyes in the Situation Room darted from monitor to monitor as the members of the Elite Eight broke cover and rushed directly toward the remaining hostage takers. Their automatic weapons opened fire, some emitting flames from the superheated barrels of the rifles.

Two of Drew's operatives immediately took bullets to the chest. The impact against their lightweight body armor caused them to spin around and fall. However, Katie's men had exposed themselves in order to take the shot. They were immediately killed in a barrage of gunfire from Drew's team.

"They're in the containers!" said one of Drew's operatives.

"I've got two men attempting to open side-by-side containers!" shouted another into his mic.

King, who'd made his way to the deck, urged them forward. "Move in! Hurry!"

The cameras bounced in all directions as the team descended upon the last of Katie's security personnel. One of the men had just turned the latch on the container when a quick burst of gunfire riddled his back with bullets. His body slumped with his fingers stuck in the container's latch.

The other man turned and tried to raise his hand in an attempt to surrender. King refused to accept it, firing several rounds into the man's chest, as the kidnapper had forgotten to lower his weapon.

"All Tangos KIA," King announced into the comms.

The Situation Room erupted in applause, and hugs were exchanged. Sarge remained stoic, his eyes glued to the large screen, where Drew had lifted Katie onto her feet and slammed her against the wall. On the two screens flanking the one containing Drew, cameras showed King opening the door to free Julia, and Spidey doing the same for Rose. Within seconds, mother and daughter had rushed into one another's arms before falling to their knees.

There wasn't a dry eye in the Situation Room as everyone observed the reunion from afar. Abbie eased next to Sarge and hugged her longtime friend, who was trying his best to contain his emotions. Donald approached Stanwick.

"Cal, can we speak with Drew?"

"Yes, of course," he replied before taking the communications headset from one of the analysts. "Slash, Colonel Stanwick here. Stand by, please."

"Roger."

He handed the headset to Donald, who turned to Sarge. "I know you want to speak with Julia and Rose, but we have some business to attend to, Mr. President. May I suggest we clear the room?"

"What? Why?" asked Stanwick.

"No disrespect to you or your team, Cal. This is a matter of national security."

Sarge understood and confirmed the directive. "He's right, Cal. I'm sorry, but everyone needs to leave for a moment."

Stanwick scowled and then nodded. He urged everyone out of the room, leaving only Sarge, Abbie, Donald, and Brad. Susan had to leave because she didn't hold the requisite security clearance, and it would look odd to the others if she didn't.

Sarge walked around the table to get closer to the monitor. He studied the back of Katie's head, as Drew had forcefully pinned her against the wall.

"Drew, this is Sarge."

"Go ahead."

"Get me some answers. I'm going to speak with Julia and Rose. When I come back, we'll decide what to do with this garbage."

Sarge handed the headset back to Donald. While he tried to raise King on the comms, Sarge explained, "Whatever she has to say, it needs to be kept within this room and the Loyal Nine. I suspect there's more to this whole scenario than we realize. Katie has those answers."

"You're right," said Brad. He reached to take the headset from Donald, who continued to fumble with its operation. "Let me help, but first, I need to address Drew."

Brad donned the headset and spoke to his top operative. He

instructed Drew to cut off his communications temporarily while he questioned Katie. Then he turned the dial to find King.

"Sergeant Dawkins, do you read?"

"Roger."

"Dawkins, this is General Bradlee. The comms to Slash have been temporarily disabled, but he is not to be disturbed. Copy?"

"I copy, General."

"Also, Dawkins, the president would like to speak to his wife and daughter. It will be awkward, but would you mind relaying his words to them until they can see one another stateside?"

"It would be my honor, General," replied King, who was in good spirits. He added, "And, hey, say hello to the president for me."

The group laughed. Abbie knew about the operative's sense of humor, as she'd spent a lot of time with his team at the Jackson family farm in Muddy Pond, Tennessee. She turned to Sarge.

"He's all business when he has to be," she said reassuringly.

"I believe my own eyes after seeing him in action. All of them are fearless."

Sarge took the headset, and Brad provided him a thumbs-up, indicating he was free to speak.

"Sergeant Dawkins, I want to thank you and your team for your heroics. Your bravery will allow me to reunite my family."

"It's my pleasure, Mr. President. Listen, I wish I could pass all of this electronic stuff to your wife, but it's kinda, well, wrapped in all of my gear."

"I understand, Sergeant."

"Sir, you can call me King. You know, to avoid confusion. Get it. I'm a sergeant. You're a Sargent. We're both Sarges, sort of. Right?"

Sarge exploded in laughter, as did the rest of the group. The hardened operative broke the tension and caused Abbie to cry again.

"Well, King, you've made a great point there. Maybe we should find a way to raise your rank to avoid confusion, as you say?"

"Sounds like a plan, sir. Let me think on that. Anyway, here they are."

The large man dropped to a knee and positioned his body camera to face Julia and Rose.

"Tell them I love them, and I'll see them as soon as they arrive in the States," instructed Sarge.

King expanded on his words to spruce it up a little, as he told Drew later. "Madam First Lady, your husband, the president, said you two are the loves of his life, and he can't wait to hold you. He said in no uncertain terms these very words, 'I love you.' Now, that came from him, not from me. Okay?"

Now the four most important individuals in the United States government were in tears laughing. The tenseness of the situation had disappeared, and joy had overcome them all. King's words had the same effect on Julia.

"Sarge, I love you and miss you more than you know. We're all right. Your daughter is a real warrior."

"Hi, Daddy!" Rose waved. She looked down at her soiled clothing. "Um, I puked on my dress."

The emotions poured out on both sides of the conversation. Sarge addressed them via King's eloquent mouthpiece. "I love you, sweetie. We'll go shopping for a new dress."

King hesitated before he relayed the message. He took a risk that might not only end up taking away his newly promised rank but might get him kicked out of his unit.

"Your daddy says he loves you very much, and he promises to buy you a new dress online. Would that be okay?"

"Yes. No more store shopping for me."

King paused again and then asked, "Mr. President, anything else you'd like me to relay?"

Donald laughed and made a suggestion to Sarge. "Tell him he's got a job in our press secretary's office when he returns."

Sarge grinned and waved off the thought. "No, King. You've said plenty. Thanks. I will see all of you in Virginia Beach. We've got a loose end to deal with."

"Copy that, Mr. President," he said before turning to Julia and Rose. "He's gonna meet you guys at Virginia Beach. Wave goodbye."

Julia's and Rose's grinning faces filled King's camera. They enthusiastically waved to Sarge and blew him kisses before signing off.

Donald set down the headset and wiped the tears off his face. "Shall we give him a few more minutes?"

Brad nodded.

Sarge moseyed toward the monitor. "Yeah, let's not interrupt Drew while he's working."

CHAPTER SIXTY-TWO

2:22 a.m.
Aboard the *Crowley*
Atlantic Ocean
Off the Outer Banks, North Carolina

Katie would've appreciated Drew being interrupted. He was enjoying his interrogation of her a little too much, but thus far, despite the incredible pain he was inflicting on her, she hadn't broken. Then an opportunity presented itself.

Two members of the ship's crew wandered into the utility stairwell, which momentarily distracted Drew.

"Hey, what's going on here?" one of them shouted.

"Get out of here!" Drew hissed, turning toward them as he spoke. They quickly backed out of the utility room.

This provided Katie an opening.

She'd succumbed to the raw strength of Drew's grip on her as he attempted to beat the truth out of her. The second he turned his attention away from her, she stomped on the top of his foot, trying to break his hold.

Katie forced her body forward into Drew's, causing him to

stumble slightly. His grip loosened just enough for her to twist her body enough to squirm away.

Angered, Drew swung at her, but Katie ducked to the right, the punch sailing wide and leaving him vulnerable to a counterpunch. She caught him in the rib cage, causing him to gasp for breath. Drew's legs buckled. Katie pushed him slightly and lunged for his weapon.

Drew rolled as her outstretched arms grabbed at him. She tumbled forward, and their two bodies rolled until they crashed into the steel support pole of the spiral staircase.

Both of them jumped to their feet simultaneously, only Drew pulled his knife as he did. He slashed at her midsection, tearing open her clothing and slicing open her forearm. Katie screamed in pain and jumped backward to dodge Drew's second attempt.

She jumped and attempted a side kick toward Drew's midsection. He was ready for it. His abs felt like granite as his stomach muscles tightened in anticipation of the blow. Drew dropped back a couple of steps from the impact. He immediately regained his balance and charged toward her.

Katie spun around. In a flash, she ran for the exit leading to the passageway connecting the port and starboard sides of the ship. The two crewmembers who had interrupted Drew were standing in the hallway, mouths open and unsure as to what they should do.

Katie grabbed at them as she ran past. She was out of breath, and her clothing had been torn, helping her sell the ruse. "Help me! Please! He's trying to rape me!"

Drew rushed out after her. The two men attempted to block his path. "Hey! Who are you? Stop!"

The men were nothing more than a brief obstacle for the determined Drew. He pushed them both in the chest, causing them to fall backwards like a set of swinging doors flying off their hinges.

Katie had put some distance between them. Her bloodied hands exited the interior of the ship onto the gangway. She ran aft, hoping to get to the motorized launch that was suspended over the rear deck. However, Drew was too fast.

Just as she reached the deck overlooking the back of the ship, he threw himself into her. The tip of his knife embedded in her lower back near her left kidney, causing pain to shoot through her body. She twisted to free herself and attempted to throw a punch. Drew easily deflected it.

The muscles in her toned arms bulged as she used all her strength to pull away from his grip. Drew was now straddling her, his left hand mashing the side of her face into the cold steel deck and his right holding the knife against the top of her neck, threatening to sever her spine.

"Give it up, Katie," he snarled in her ear. "If you wanna live, just tell me what we want to know."

Blood was streaming down the side of her face and into her mouth. She spit it out and smiled.

"You can't stop what's coming!" she yelled with a malevolent laugh. "He is going to make your lives a living hell!"

Drew grabbed her by the hair and slammed her face into the deck. "Who? What are you talking about?"

Katie twisted and spat blood in Drew's face. "Screw you!" She gathered one more effort to break free, twisting her body and freeing an arm. She swung wildly at Drew, trying to make solid contact. She didn't, but someone else did.

The two men Drew had knocked down in the hallway jumped on his back and knocked him onto his side. Freed, Katie scrambled away toward the motorboat. Chest heaving from exertion, she got to her feet and rushed toward the mechanical arm to begin lowering the boat into the water.

Drew knocked one of the crewmen out with a single punch. The other made a move toward Drew, who swiftly swung his knife back and forth to frighten the man off.

As the mechanical arm whirred to life, it began lowering the launch off the back of the boat toward the water. Katie began running, prepared to jump into it as it began to drop over the side of the ship. Drew gave chase, turning his knife in his hand until he gripped the blade in his fingers. Just as Katie began her leap, he let it fly.

The swooshing sound was muted by the powerful engines propelling the ship. However, the knife's impact was unmistakable as it embedded in Katie's back. The mere force with which it was thrown knocked her forward, smashing her face into the side of the motorboat.

Incredibly, she managed to hold onto the safety rails of the launch. Her body dangled for several seconds as the boat continued to lower past the main deck toward the ocean.

Katie's grip on the stainless-steel railing was slipping. Her arms were weary, and her hands were covered in blood. The entire blade of the knife had embedded in her back, the steel wedged near the vertebrae of her spine.

Suddenly, one hand fell loose from the rail, causing her to flail in an attempt to regain her grip. In the ship's safety lights, Drew could see Katie's face as her eyes grew wide, puzzled in surprise and shock as the reality of death overcame her. Her body suddenly twitched spasmodically until she completely lost her grip.

Katie's mouth was wide open in sheer terror as her body dropped into the churning waters of the Atlantic.

Dead. Once and for all.

CHAPTER SIXTY-THREE

2:40 a.m.
The Situation Room
The White House
Washington, DC

As Sarge and the others paced the floor in the Situation Room, Drew suddenly appeared on the primary monitor that had remained static-filled awaiting his return. After Katie had fallen into the ocean, Drew retraced his steps to retrieve something he'd seen Katie drop from her pocket as she ran from him on the gangway. After making radio contact with King and his team, he returned to the aft deck to check on the man he'd knocked out. His body was gone, so Drew prepared to reach out to Sarge and the others.

"He's back," announced Donald, who rushed for the headset.

Brad gently grabbed his arm. "Let me bring him in through the intercom." After several keystrokes on the computer, all parties to the conversation could speak freely.

"Drew, they rescued Julia and Rose," said Sarge immediately.

"I heard. I touched base with King and my team. One of the Black Hawks is lowering the baskets now to pull them and my injured men aboard. They should be stateside by dawn. I'll follow shortly after I interview the captain and crew."

"I'll never be able to thank you and your team for what you've done for my family. Thank you, brother."

Drew nodded and grinned. Oftentimes, two men who fought side by side, whether in a hot war or a political one, referred to each other as brother. In this sense, he knew Sarge meant it on a more intimate and personal level.

"You're welcome. Abbie, are you okay?" Drew expected his wife had been nervous the entire mission.

"Get your ass home, sailor. I love you more than you know."

"I love you, too, Madam Vice President."

"Zip it, Jackson!" That was twice he'd teased her like that tonight. This time, it was warranted after she'd used an authoritative tone with him.

Donald was anxious to hear what he'd learned from Katie. Despite the rescue, in his mind, a new battlefront had just opened up, and they needed intelligence to thwart the threat.

"Did she talk?"

Drew sighed. "That woman's insane, and I believe part wildcat."

"Apparently, anger has been building up within her for a lot of years," interjected Brad. "She wasn't working alone, was she?"

"No," Drew replied. "Y'all, I really hurt her in just the right ways that would make anyone else spill their guts. I've seen brutal, hardened operatives reveal intel under the methods I used. It didn't help that a couple of well-intentioned crewmembers got in the way by accident. She got away from me, and there was a struggle."

"Where is she?" asked Sarge.

Drew pointed toward the back of the boat. "She tried to escape using the ship's boat launch. I buried a knife in her spine. She was dead before she hit the water a hundred feet below."

"Are you sure?" asked Abbie.

Drew nodded. "Nobody could've survived the fall. The ship was still under power, so the waters alone would've sucked her under.

Plus, if she wasn't paralyzed by the knife in her back, she would've been from the fall."

"Did you get anything out of her?" asked Sarge.

"Two things. One is her satellite phone. Can we do anything with this?" He held it in front of his camera for them to see.

Brad stepped forward. "Absolutely. Bring it here, and I'll put our forensics people on it. They should be able to pinpoint the location of whoever she called by the satellite relays used. We may not be able to identify the individual, but we can certainly determine where they were when they spoke with her."

"Okay," began Drew. "As she was giving up the fight, she said, 'You can't stop what's coming. He is going to make your lives a living hell.'"

"Seriously? Who was she talking about?" asked Donald.

"I don't know," replied Drew. "However, those were her exact words. She never intimated anything else, especially who she was working for. Honestly, I think she was prepared to die to keep the secret."

"Think about it," said Abbie. "She was already dead. After the Berlin bombing, Katie had to live another life in the shadows. Every second of every day, she had to be on edge, hiding the truth. Dying may have been a relief to her, especially if she was able to inflict some kind of torment on us."

"So, who the hell is it?" Sarge shouted his question out of frustration.

Drew responded, "I'll debrief my team to see if they learned anything. We'll also interview the crew of the ship."

"That phone will help, too," said Brad. "There are two parties with the resources to pull this off. Both of them happen to live in the same neighborhood, practically speaking."

"Roger that," said Drew. "If there's nothing else, I'll get to it."

A chorus of thank yous came in response as well as an I love you from Abbie.

The call was disconnected, leaving the group in silence.

Sarge was the first to speak. "I haven't heard anything that leads me away from Gardner Lowell, have you?" He looked everyone in the eyes, seeking their insight.

Donald answered for the others. "Not really. Hopefully the phone calls will reveal something. We also have a couple of their people captured at Camp David. So far, they've only revealed the identity of their team leader during the raid, and he's dead."

"Who is he?" asked Abbie.

"Confirmed as a former security member of a Colombian drug cartel. We have the FBI running his ties to anyone in the U.S."

They were at a dead end, for now, so Sarge turned his attention to meeting Julia and Rose when they arrived in Virginia Beach.

"I'm gonna get cleaned up and get them a change of clothes. Brad, will you arrange transportation for me to greet my girls."

"Absolutely. Um, what about the boys?"

Sarge furrowed his brow. "I think I'm gonna let them sleep. I'd like to downplay what happened, at least at first. I'm not sure how chatty Rose will be."

Abbie laughed. "If I know your daughter, she won't be able to wait to throw the entire episode in her brothers' faces."

"Oh, yeah," agreed Donald. "She'll declare herself to be the family badass."

"No doubt," said Sarge.

PART VIII

The Aftermath
The week after Thanksgiving, November 2024

CHAPTER SIXTY-FOUR

Dawn
Saturday morning
Naval Air Station Oceana
Virginia Beach, Virginia

NAS Oceana was the U.S. Navy's East Coast Master Jet Base and home to the F/A-18 Super Hornets. They operated in a constant state of readiness, deployable for unexpected attacks from America's enemies at any given second. As a result, they were able to rapidly prepare for the unexpected arrival of the president that morning just before dawn.

Sarge was met on the tarmac as he exited Marine One by Captain Carl Beaufort, a twenty-five-year veteran of the Navy and a Cape Cod native.

"Welcome, Mr. President," he said as he saluted Sarge.

Sarge returned the salute. "Good morning, Captain, and thank you."

"It's an honor and our pleasure, sir. If you will join me, we have the Black Hawk inbound as we speak. They will be touching down shortly on the other side of the complex nearest Building 220, our fire station."

"Why not here, Captain?" Sarge asked.

"Purely circumstances, sir. Due to the events of the last twenty-four hours, the Secret Service has elevated our security protocols. Also, we have medics assigned to the fire station who can provide a cursory examination of your family if warranted."

Sarge smiled and nodded. He appreciated the captain's thoughtfulness and the attention to security. He grabbed the duffel bag with clothing and toiletries and followed the armed personnel to three Humvees that would drive Sarge parallel to the runways. He noticed a number of F/A-18s were on standby, awaiting deployment.

Captain Beaufort explained, "This morning, we were to conduct a joint emergency training exercise with the City of Virginia Beach. Frankly, sir, you've provided an element of reality to our training."

Sarge nodded and then grinned from ear to ear as he saw two Black Hawk helicopters landing in tandem on the tarmac near the fire station. He desperately wanted to fling the door open and run to greet them. However, with enhanced security measures in place, Captain Beaufort had to delay the reunion until the rotors had stopped on the choppers and armed security surrounded the entire meeting area.

"Okay, sir. My apologies for the delay. Please enjoy this moment." The door was opened for Sarge.

He was off and running. Not walking briskly. Not jogging. Racing across the tarmac, he opened his arms wide as a rejuvenated Julia and Rose exited the Black Hawk to meet him. The dozens of military personnel remained at a respectful distance as the Sargent family, without the boys, crashed into one another.

They wept tears of joy and hugged one another, stopping only to examine each other to confirm that no physical harm had come to them. Sarge pointed back to the Humvee as he explained he'd brought a change of clothes. He also acknowledged the medical team standing just outside the fire station.

"No, Daddy, we're not hurt. We just wanna go home."

Julia laughed. "Like she said. Can't we just go, or is there some requirement that we—?"

"Nope, there's no requirement unless I say there's one."

Julia looked toward the Humvee. "The boys? King said they were safe."

"They are," he replied. "I thought we might want to talk about what and when we tell them about all of this."

"You're a great dad," said Julia as she planted a kiss on his cheek. "We'll figure it out. Can we go now?"

"Yeah, Daddy. We stink. Don't we, Mom?"

Julia spoke in a faint whisper. "Katie?"

"Dead," Sarge mouthed the word in response.

"Are they sure?"

"Yeah, she's no Michael Myers," he replied, making reference to the character in the *Halloween* series of movies who couldn't be killed. In Sarge's mind, Katie was no invincible boogeyman, only flesh and blood.

Julia winked at her husband and smiled. *It's over.*

Sarge hugged them both again despite their aroma. At that moment, there was no greater feeling in the world than holding them. As they walked to the Humvees, he told them they could change clothes and freshen up on Marine One. He'd already told the staff to hold off on feeding the boys breakfast until they returned. He'd requested mounds upon mounds of pancakes with bananas, strawberries, and Rose's favorite, Reese's peanut butter, as toppings. He'd even brought her blueberry Pop-Tarts as a snack for the ride.

Reunited, their spirits lifted, and just like that, the trauma was shoved into the back of their minds as they made their way back home to the White House.

CHAPTER SIXTY-FIVE

Monday Morning
The West Wing
The White House
Washington, DC

The West Wing was bustling with activity on Monday following the attacks. Sarge entered the West Wing from the West Colonnade. Throughout most of his presidency, he'd make the walk alone after freshening up following his morning jog with Captain Morrell. With his loyal companion in the hospital, recovering from the wounds he'd sustained saving Sarge's life, Sarge chose to get right to work on what was expected to be a hectic day.

On this day, above all that preceded it, he was glad he'd removed the White House Press Corps from their former location behind the windows to his right. The media had enjoyed unfettered access to prior administrations, resulting in intentionally leaked information by staffers or overheard conversations by reporters who inserted themselves into parts of the West Wing where they didn't belong. He was not interested in dealing with them just yet.

Sarge and his communications team would be meeting immediately after his daily briefing in the Roosevelt Room. He'd studied the headlines in the major newspapers and online media sources. Many reporters couldn't hide their dismay at not having all the details of Friday's attacks already. The Sunday news shows were filled with speculation. Fingers of blame were being pointed at the nation's geopolitical enemies. The State Department had to work overtime to dispel any rumors and to mollify incensed world leaders.

As he approached the doorway to the West Wing, uniformed security personnel assigned to the president hustled to open the door for him. Secret Service had notified him early Saturday morning that his protection detail would be stepped up considerably in light of the attack. They would maintain the highest level of security for many days until they were comfortable that the threat had passed.

Sarge didn't argue. In fact, he planned on keeping enhanced security protection for everyone within the Loyal Nine and their families. With only a month and a half to go in his presidency, he wanted everyone to feel comfortable in their surroundings. Once they returned to private life, they'd have the protection of Secret Service and Aegis personnel.

"Good morning, Mr. President," said one staffer as he raced down the hallway with a stack of binders that slipped around in his arms.

"Good morning."

On the one hand, there was an added level of tension in the air following the attacks. Despite the urge to be actively involved in the investigation of Friday's attack, Sarge resisted the urge to enter the West Wing. He'd remained in the Executive Residence with Julia and the kids. All of them needed time to decompress and discuss what had happened. It was time well spent.

After the PDB, he made his way to the Oval Office to meet with Crepeau and Ocampo, his dynamic duo comprising the top positions within his communications team. They'd fended off reporters all weekend and were preparing for the one o'clock press briefing.

"Mr. President, we'd like you to consider making an appearance at the briefing," said Ocampo.

"Really?" Sarge asked.

"Yes, sir," Crepeau responded. "You look well, of course. And very presidential in your suit and tie."

Sarge laughed. "Why do you say that?"

"Well, sir, the last time we saw you, you were in camo and covered in Dave's crusty blood."

Sarge shrugged as he assessed his appearance in a gilded mirror near the exit to his personal study. "I see your point. The nation needs to see their president in one piece, right?"

"Yes, sir," they answered in unison before Ocampo added, "We think it's a good idea and will help dispel any rumors of injuries. You know how conspiratorial the media can be."

"Yes, I do. By the way, what is their theory as to who was behind the attacks?"

Crepeau emitted a wicked laugh. "In a word, dumbfounded. They're so confused at CNN that they're dragging fiction authors on set to get their opinion. You know, if they were writing a book, who would they make the bad guy."

Sarge shook his head and rolled his eyes. "I can only imagine what those people might come up with. Okay, I need to get started with Donald, who's undoubtedly marching toward the door as we speak. I'll see you guys at one."

The dynamic duo hustled out, and his dutiful chief of staff filled the void in the doorway. Brad was hot on his heels. They entered the Oval Office and closed the door behind them.

"Do you have anything yet?" asked Sarge.

"Not yet, but they are making progress," replied Brad. "It's not easy to recreate the source of each transmission. Her phone was very active, and calls were placed from points located throughout the Western Hemisphere."

"Geez," said Sarge as he took a seat behind his desk.

Brad continued. "She traveled to South America twice and even spent time in California. Her calls varied in length, and the people she interacted with were all over the place. It's gonna take several days."

"Has the NSA picked up any chatter to speak of?"

"Not so far," replied Brad. "We have the FBI recreating Katie's life since the bombing that sidelined her in a hospital years ago. We hope that might lend some insight into her frame of mind and possible activities."

"Are we continuing to monitor Lowell and Cabot?"

"Yes," replied Brad. "Sarge, honestly, I don't see Cabot as being any part of this. Lowell is another matter."

"I say we have the FBI pick him up and put the squeeze on him," added Donald. "Maybe he'll make a mistake."

Sarge tamped down Donald's enthusiasm to hang the fellow Brahmin. "Let's give it a few days to see what the satellite phone investigation yields. Then I'll decide how to deal with him. This is bigger than filing criminal charges against him. I have partners, so to speak, that I have to answer to."

"Understood," said Brad. "If there's nothing further, I need to get back to the Pentagon. The Chinese are still pissed 'cause you made them look bad. They've deployed several warships to the South China Sea off the coast of the Philippines. We're closely monitoring them."

"Naturally, they'd use this situation as a means to take advantage of us," added Donald.

"Well, that would be a helluva mistake on their part," said Sarge. "I've got a lot of pent-up frustration." He laughed, but Brad knew he was serious.

Sarge spun around in his chair and stared across the South Lawn. He wondered if anybody understood how complex his job was. Every decision, or moment of indecision, could have deadly consequences for a nation. He vowed to keep a firm grip on the wheel until he turned over the keys to the next president.

CHAPTER SIXTY-SIX

Friday
Camp David
North of Frederick, Maryland

Sarge was used to starting his day before dawn. In fact, he couldn't remember the last time he'd awakened to daylight. It was a force of habit he'd acquired dating back to his years in college. He'd been conditioned to believe the old axiom *early to bed, early to rise makes a man healthy, wealthy, and wise*. The phrase most likely dated back to late fifteenth-century England, but it was Benjamin Franklin who was most associated with the phrase when it was published in his journal *Poor Richard's Almanack*.

He missed his morning runs. Out of respect for his protector-in-chief, Captain Morrell, who was in his final days of recovery from the gunshot wounds he'd sustained at Monocacy Farm a week prior, Sarge had relegated himself to the treadmill in the Executive Residence.

After jogging on the device for an hour, he picked up the phone and called the hospital. Like Sarge, Morrell was an early riser despite the fact he was recuperating. He'd provided good news. He was on track to be discharged on Monday although DHS would not approve him for duty just yet.

Sarge had been meaning to talk to his friend about the future. Every time the subject came up, Morrell had deferred, saying he still had work to do until the day the moving vans packed up the First Family to return to Boston. Despite Morrell dodging the subject, most likely for fear of being put out to pasture, Sarge was making plans for him.

When the Sargent family returned to Boston, they'd be moving into the Morgan estate permanently. Abbie, who was John Morgan's only child, planned on making her home with Drew on the Cumberland Plateau in rural Tennessee. Sarge had agreed to purchase the Morgan estate from her although money was not an overriding factor for either Sarge or Abbie. Sarge was the son Morgan never had, and Abbie thought it appropriate that he should have it. Besides, she said, Drew would go bat-shit crazy living on the ostentatious estate and in Boston, no less.

With that agreement made in private between Sarge and Abbie, he considered what to do with the top three floors of 100 Beacon, the luxury mid-rise condominium building where he and the Loyal Nine had created a preparedness fortress in the heart of the city. After eight years in office, Sarge had an in-depth knowledge of the threats the nation faced, both manmade and naturally occurring. Now more than ever, he found a need to maintain a level of preparedness in the event these unlikely, yet possible, catastrophic events were to occur. He needed someone to spearhead that effort as he and Donald had done in the past. That man would be Captain Morrell.

After his early morning call to the hospital, his family, the Quinns, and the Jacksons made their way to the helipad on the South Lawn for their second attempt to convene at Camp David for the weekend. Brad had arrived a day earlier with the advance team to micromanage every aspect of the security detail at the retreat. To say it would be the most protected three-day weekend since the Camp David accords that included President Carter, Prime

Minister Menachem Begin, and Egyptian President Anwar Sadat would be an understatement. As Brad put it to Sarge before he retired for the night, *I pity the fool who attempts to breach my perimeter,* channeling the eighties television icon Mr. T.

As the sun was rising on a glorious day filled with clear skies, the squadron of Marine One helicopters lifted off as they had a week ago. Only this time, there would be no stops along the way. The air corridor had been cleared by the FAA, allowing only USAF fighter jets to patrol the short distance from the District to Camp David.

Once they landed, any apprehension within the group quickly dissipated. The weather was unusually warm, the snow had melted except for where it remained in the shadows of the nearby mountains, and the group's hearts were filled with love and camaraderie as they descended upon Camp David. Even J.J., with a full cast protecting his broken leg, kept up with the group as they exited the choppers.

Once everyone was settled, the campers, as they called themselves, met on the terrace for lunch. The heated pool was full of children, also known as the Polar Bear Bunch. Their youthful metabolism could easily shake off the cool air once they emerged from the eighty-degree water. None of the adults, except for Drew, dared join them.

It would be a free-for-all, come-what-may weekend for the Loyal Nine and their families with no ground rules except for one— no shop talk. Like any gathering in which the common interest among people was the workplace, it was difficult for conversations not to involve their jobs. They stuck to their promise until later that Friday afternoon.

Julia and Abbie remained at the house to enjoy the children playing and to discuss the joy of giving birth. The Quinn daughters enjoyed playing with the Sargent kids. Sarge, Donald, Susan, and Drew played Camp David's one-hole golf course repeatedly for an hour after lunch. To keep the game from becoming redundant, they made up rules such as playing the hole with only an eight iron or creating two-person teams that had to alternate shots. Side bets were made. Razzing was abundant. Laughs were exchanged.

Brad, who'd enjoyed the interaction with his friends, still kept one hand on the wheel and an eye on the road, so to speak. In his mind, their protection was on his shoulders, and even though he'd make time to spend with everyone, he would also watch over every aspect of their security while at Camp David.

Because he had been in charge of the security detail, it was he who received the phone call from the White House that Gardner Lowell urgently needed to speak with Sarge. Throughout the week, as the White House settled down following the attacks, the intelligence agencies continued to pursue leads, and the analysts attempted to study the phone calls made from Katie's satellite phone.

In fact, Brad was expecting a phone call from the NSA with a preliminary report that afternoon. When his phone rang, he expected it to be the deputy director of Homeland Security. It was, but for a different reason. Gardner Lowell had surfaced.

Brad personally drove out to the one-hole golf course to deliver the news to Sarge. The group called it a day and returned to Aspen lodge. Brad set up a time for the Secret Service to patch Gardner through by video conference to the war room located within Camp David.

CHAPTER SIXTY-SEVEN

Friday
Camp David
North of Frederick, Maryland

Like the Situation Room, this conference room included a large table with seating for twenty-plus. A large television centered on the longest wall was capable of being divided into multiple screens depending on the situation. Above it was a row of digital clocks from major capital cities around the globe.

Donald accompanied Sarge to the war room, and they were the only two people on camera with Gardner. In chairs located on the same wall as the camera sat Abbie and Brad to offer their perspectives on the conversation after the call.

When the call came through, Gardner was sitting in his study at his desk, a cowl-neck sweater pulled tight around his throat. *Almost like a noose*, Sarge thought to himself, who started the conversation by being direct.

"Gardner, this was to be a family getaway. I promised them I'd avoid business of any kind."

Gardner was humble in his approach to Sarge. He was keenly

aware that he was the leading suspect behind the attacks. Even a reporter from *Newsweek* had written an opinion piece pointing out the apparent rift between the two men.

"Mr. President, as you are aware, I have resources of my own within the government and internationally. In order to defend myself against any baseless accusations of wrongdoing, I have called in all my chits."

"Mr. Lowell, wouldn't you agree that any information given under such circumstances would be self-serving and therefore suspect?" remarked Donald.

"Perhaps so. However, I have evidence that I'm prepared to turn over to the proper parties upon your request."

"Evidence of what?" asked Sarge.

"I know about Miss O'Shea's involvement in the plot to assassinate you and kidnap your family. I know little about her and nothing of her personal motives, if any."

Donald leaned in to Sarge to whisper, "He could have somebody within the intelligence apparatus to provide him this information."

Sarge slowly nodded but continued to lock eyes with Gardner through the camera.

Gardner continued. "She was a hired gun. Her role was to recruit an army of mercenaries to undertake the attack."

Sarge took a deep breath. "Gardner, I am going to make you this onetime offer. In order to put this behind us, I am prepared to forgive you for being behind these attacks. However, there will be conditions—"

Gardner leaned forward so his face filled the camera in his study. "Sarge, it wasn't me. The man behind all of it is Barry Sotelo, our former president and the man sitting on the proverbial throne at Iolani Palace."

"Come on!" shouted Donald as he threw his pen on the conference table. He'd never trusted Gardner and was fiercely protective of Sarge. But to accuse the former president?

Sarge patted his right-hand man on the arm to calm him down. He glanced over at Abbie and Brad. Abbie shrugged, and Brad shook his head side to side, followed by a shrug. He took their reactions to be a resounding maybe.

"Gardner, you have proof of this?" asked Sarge.

"I do, and I'm prepared to give it to you under several conditions."

Donald was still fuming. "Oh, I see how it is. Now you're making demands."

"These are not unreasonable requests," continued Gardner. "I want all surveillance removed from my family, my businesses, and associates. Second, I want a seat at the table of the new administration."

"What do you mean?" Sarge asked.

"Treasury Secretary," he quickly responded. "It will suit our mutual interests as well."

If only I could trust you, thought Sarge.

"What is the proof?" asked Donald.

"Sarge, do we have an agreement?" asked Gardner, who now intended to ignore Donald.

"If the information you provide can be confirmed by trusted intelligence personnel, I will speak with President-elect Rawlins about your appointment to Treasury. When can you provide the evidence?"

Gardner stood from his chair and walked toward a large window that was at the edge of the camera's field of vision. He turned to respond, gesturing as he did. "You can tell those men in the gray sedan to come in anytime, and I'll provide them a statement."

Sarge disconnected the call and immediately rose from his chair. He began pacing the floor as he commonly did when processing complex matters. Donald was still fuming, filled with doubt about anything concerning Gardner. Brad placed a phone call and spoke to the other party in hushed tones. It was Abbie who approached Sarge to help him sort through the bombshell statement.

"Hey, listen to me for a second," she began. "We know Gardner has an ulterior motive for shifting the focus of blame elsewhere.

Every criminal defendant uses this ploy to avoid conviction. Any evidence he produces could've been fabricated. We know that because we're capable of doing the same when necessary."

Sarge stopped. "So you agree with Donald? That this whole thing is a ruse. A misdirection."

"On the surface, yes," she replied. She grabbed him by the shoulders to keep his attention. "However, my suggestion to you is this. Forget about his demands. We can do whatever we want, whenever we want, if it's revenge you're after."

"I know, Abbie, after the appropriate passage of time. Plus, I'd need to make the case to the Brahmin."

"Of course."

"But what if he's right? What if Katie was working on behalf of Sotelo? What would he stand to gain by taking me and you out before the end of our term?"

Abbie lowered her eyes. "Because he understands how the pocket veto works. He used it eight times. It didn't get much press coverage except in places like Politico and the Hill, but it happened. His goal was to either eliminate you and me, which would put his pal the Speaker of the House in the White House, or force you to sign the Statehood Act by holding Julia's and Rose's lives over your head."

"Dammit! That makes perfect sense. He's made a move to ensure his return to power."

"Guys! Guys!" Brad rushed toward where Sarge and Abbie were standing.

"What is it?" asked Donald.

"I just confirmed with our NSA analysts. Katie placed two satellite phone calls in the two weeks leading up to the attacks. Their location was confirmed as being on Oahu."

"Bastard," muttered Sarge angrily.

CHAPTER SIXTY-EIGHT

Friday
Camp David
North of Frederick, Maryland

Sarge refused to allow Lowell's revelations to distract from the fun-filled weekend he had in store. They replayed the recording of Lowell's video call. Brad advised the investigative team of the allegations and instructed them to continue following all leads but assign specific, trusted members loyal to the president to confirm Lowell's evidence. Donald, ever the skeptic, insisted that the video be analyzed by body-language experts to assess Gardner's veracity. The man was guilty of something. Donald was sure of it.

Sarge's last words to the group before they exited the war room were ominous.

"If this is true, then it's tantamount to an act of war. However, war does nothing but harm a nation and its people. My goal was to bring the Pacific States back into the Union. Now, I know it must be done without the dictatorial Sotelo as part of the deal. There's only one solution. He has to be eliminated."

They emerged from the war room to the smell of baby back ribs cooking on a large, portable cooker wheeled in for the occasion. Drew was overseeing the meal along with some special guests invited by the president.

Julia and Rose were joking around with King Dawkins, who'd donned an official Camp David apron and chef's hat. He was turning the ribs, keeping them moistened with barbecue sauce. Sarge was handed a Samuel Adams Boston Lager, which he happily gulped down. The full-flavored brew soaked into his body, immediately lifting his spirits.

Several picnic tables had been set end to end on the patio overlooking the pool. The young Polar Bears had been extracted from the water and dressed for dinner. The meal looked like a repeat of their Thanksgiving dinner except turkey had been replaced with the slow-cooked ribs.

Once everyone had been seated, before the food was passed around, Sarge said the blessing.

"Lord God, Heavenly Father, bless us these gifts and bountiful goodness. Dear God, we celebrate this land that's free and the blessing it has provided our families and the families before us. Because of you, Lord, we live a life of peace and liberty while our hearts are filled with happiness and pride. May you continue to bless this great nation and all those who love her so. Through Jesus' name, our Lord. Amen."

"Amen," the group said in unison.

A few tears were shed as the emotions of the past week were still bottled up inside. They were fortunate nobody had died in the attacks. Now it was time to look ahead and enjoy a meal together as friends and family.

Not unexpectedly, King was the center of attention. The brave operative was never at a loss for a quick one-liner to keep the group in stitches. Rose was particularly enamored with the man, who dwarfed her petite frame.

Everyone ate their ribs a little differently. Some liked a lot of barbecue sauce while others used it sparingly. A few preferred the mustard-based Carolina sauce, while the kids, especially, chose the sweetened style. Those with manners employed a knife and fork while Drew's team grabbed a rib and gnawed off the meat.

Then there was Drew, who liked his ribs fiery hot. The Camp David kitchen staff jokingly offered him a bottle of liquid heat called Ring of Fire. They'd made side bets in the kitchen as to whether he'd actually use it on his ribs. He did.

Despite the fact it caused him to open his mouth with every bite to allow the so-called smoke to escape, he continued to gob it on, claiming it was good for his metabolism. Donald quipped that it was good for his sex drive, too, earning him a playful slug from Susan and a *hell-damn-nah* from Abbie.

The weekend was filled with more lighthearted moments like this one. Hearty meals. Old-fashioned board games. Classic movies in the viewing room. Small talk among the guests, filled with laughter.

In the coming days, Sarge and the Loyal Nine would find a quiet moment to discuss their options. Americans had always suspected their nation was run, in part, by shadow governments. It was a notion that actual political power does not reside with publicly elected officials but with powerful individuals who exercise dominion and control over politicians through a variety of means—money, influence, blackmail, and violence.

The Boston Brahmin was one such cryptocracy. Within the Brahmin, another form of shadow government had emerged, one that was currently at the seat of power. A group who could not only dictate the direction of the Boston Brahmin for decades to come, but who could also forge the course of a nation. They were the Loyal Nine.

By Monday, the Washington political elite would wake up to learn that the Pacific Statehood Act had been vetoed by Sarge's inaction. President-elect Rawlins would be informed his Treasury Secretary had been chosen for him. And Sarge would plot his revenge against a despot who never should've been allowed in the White House to begin with.

THANK YOU FOR READING BLACK FRIDAY!

I hope you'll read on as I provide you some thoughts on the story and a few tidbits of note.

If you enjoyed *Black Friday*, I'd be grateful if you'd take a moment to write a short review (just a few words are needed) and post it on Amazon. Amazon uses complicated algorithms to determine what books are recommended to readers. Sales are, of course, a factor, but so are the quantities of reviews my books get. By taking a few seconds to leave a review, you help me out and also help new readers learn about my work.

Sign up to my email list to learn about upcoming titles, deals, contests, appearances, and more!

Sign up at BobbyAkart.com

ACKNOWLEDGMENTS

Creating a novel that is both informative and entertaining requires a tremendous team effort. Writing is the easy part.

For their efforts in bringing you another Boston Brahmin novel, I would like to thank Hristo Argirov Kovatliev for his incredible artistic talents in creating my cover art throughout my career. He and my multitalented wife, Dani, collaborate to create the most incredible cover art in the publishing business. A huge hug of appreciation goes out to Pauline Nolet, the *Professor*, for her editorial prowess and patience in correcting this writer's same tics as we approach publishing sixty novels together. Thank you, Drew Avera, a United States Navy veteran, who has brought his talented formatting skills from a writer's perspective to create multiple formats for enjoying my novels. A round of applause for Andrew Wehrlen who took on the monumental task of taking on this project. He became the voice of Sarge and the Boston Brahmin, providing us a stellar performance as he narrated the audiobook.

As always, a special thank you to my team of loyal friends who've always provided me valuable insight from a reader's perspective—Denise Keef, Shirley Nicholson, Joe Carey, Colt Payne, and Stephen Smith.

Thanks, y'all, and Choose Freedom!

ABOUT THE AUTHOR, BOBBY AKART

Author Bobby Akart has been ranked by Amazon as #25 on the Amazon Charts list of most popular, bestselling authors. He has achieved recognition as the #1 bestselling Horror Author, #1 bestselling Science Fiction Author, #5 bestselling Action & Adventure Author, #7 bestselling Historical Fiction Author and #10 on Amazon's bestselling Thriller Author list.

Mr. Akart has delivered up-all-night thrillers to readers in 245 countries and territories worldwide. He has sold over one million books in all formats, which includes over forty international bestsellers, in nearly fifty fiction and nonfiction genres.

His novel *Yellowstone: Hellfire* reached the Top 25 on the Amazon bestsellers list and earned him multiple Kindle All-Star awards for most pages read in a month and most pages read as an author. The Yellowstone series vaulted him to the #25 bestselling author on Amazon Charts, and the #1 bestselling science fiction author.

Since its release in November 2020, his standalone novel *New Madrid Earthquake* has been ranked #1 on Amazon Charts in multiple countries as a natural disaster thriller.

Mr. Akart is a graduate of the University of Tennessee after pursuing a dual major in economics and political science. He went on to obtain his master's degree in business administration and his doctorate degree in law at Tennessee.

A million-copy bestseller, Bobby Akart has provided his readers a diverse range of topics that are both informative and entertaining. His attention to detail and impeccable research has allowed him to capture the imagination of his readers through his fictional works and bring them valuable knowledge through his nonfiction books.

SIGN UP for Bobby Akart's mailing list to learn of special offers, view bonus content, and be the first to receive news about new releases.

Visit www.BobbyAkart.com for details.

PERFECT STORM, a standalone disaster thriller
Available on Amazon by clicking here

It was the day the sun brought darkness.

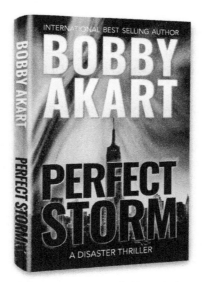

It began as a spectacle like no other.
They called it the Night of the Northern Lights - a
phenomenal light show generated by the power of the sun.
It ended in a powerless world thrust into chaos.

A standalone disaster thriller.

AVAILABLE ON AMAZON

With over a million copies sold, international bestselling author, Bobby Akart, one of America's favorite storytellers, delivers up-all-night thrillers to readers in 245 countries and territories worldwide.

"Akart's uncanny ability to take a topic of what could happen and write an epic story about it is short of preternatural!"

303

The sun gives us life by radiating light and heat. Without this solar energy, the Earth would freeze.

The sun also emits solar flares, eruptions of super-heated plasma that travel through the vacuum of space. When two successive blasts slam into each other, they forge a Perfect Storm so intense that our planet's magnetic field is no match for its fury.

"You are there. Feeling what they feel. Anger, joy, love, mourning. You feel it all. Not everyone can write a book like this. It takes a special writer to make you feel a book!"

This new standalone survival thriller thrusts the most dynamic city on Earth, New York, into darkness as North America is bludgeoned by the sun's ferocity. Scientists promised beautiful aurora providing the city that never sleeps with magnificent hues of blue and green. For three days, New Yorkers took to the streets, parks, and rooftops to enjoy the awe-inspiring spectacle.

"Masterful and suspenseful!"

The city was filled with excitement as the media hyped the rare event as occurring once in a hundred years. It had happened before, and it was happening again.

As the power grid failed, the city of New York collapsed with remarkable speed. The thin veneer of civilization was laid bare as man fought one another for survival.

"No one can research like Bobby Akart and then turn this meticulous research into one exciting thrill ride. "

Bobby Akart delivers intense, up-all-night thrillers that have you whispering just one more chapter until the end.

PREVIOUSLY IN THE BOSTON BRAHMIN SERIES
DRAMATIS PERSONAE

THE LOYAL NINE:

Sarge – born Henry Winthrop Sargent IV. Son of former Massachusetts governor, godson of John Adams Morgan and a descendant of Daniel Sargent, Sr., wealthy merchant, and owner of Sargent's Wharf during the Revolutionary War. He's a tenured professor at the Harvard Kennedy School of Government in Cambridge. He is becoming well known around the country for his libertarian philosophy as espoused in his *New York Times* bestseller —*Choose Freedom or Capitulation: America's Sovereignty Crisis*. Sarge resides at 100 Beacon Street in the Back Bay area of Boston. Sarge is romantically involved with Julia Hawthorne.

Steven Sargent – younger brother of Sarge. He is a graduate of the United States Naval Academy and a former platoon officer of SEAL Team 10. He is currently a contract operative for Aegis Security—code name Nomad. He resides on his yacht—the *Miss Behavin'*. Steven is romantically involved with Katie O'Shea.

Julia Hawthorne – descendant of the Peabody and Hawthorne families. First female political editor of the *Boston Herald*. She is the recipient of the National Association of Broadcasting Marconi Radio Award for her creation of an Internet radio channel for the newspaper. She is in a relationship with Sarge and lives with him at 100 Beacon.

The Quinn family – Donald is the self-proclaimed director of procurement. He is a former accountant and financial advisor who works directly with John Adams Morgan. Married to **Susan Quinn** with daughters **Rebecca** (age 7) and **Penny** (age 11). Donald and Susan coordinate all preparedness activities of The Loyal Nine. They reside in Brae Burn Country Club in Boston.

J.J. – born John Joseph Warren. He is a direct descendant of Dr. Joseph Warren, one of the original Sons of Liberty. The Warren family founded Harvard Medical and were field surgeons at the Battle of Bunker Hill. J.J. was an Army battalion surgeon at Joint Base Balad in Iraq. While stationed at JBB, J.J. saved the life of a female soldier who was injured saving the lives of others. He later became involved in a relationship with former Marine Second Lieutenant Sabina del Toro. He finished his career at the Veteran's Administration Hospital in Jamaica Plain, where he also resides. He is affectionately known as the Armageddon Medicine Man.

Katie O'Shea – graduate of the United States Naval Academy who trained as a Naval Intelligence officer. After an introduction to John Adams Morgan, she quickly rose up the ranks of the intelligence community. She now is part of the President's Intelligence Advisory Board. She resides in Washington, D.C. Katie is romantically involved with Steven Sargent.

Brad – born Francis Crowninshield Bradlee, a descendant of the Crowninshield family, a historic seafaring and military family dating back to the early 1600s. He is the battalion commander of the 25th Marine Regiment of 1st Battalion based at Fort Devens, Massachusetts. Their nickname is *Cold Steel Warriors*. He is an active member of *Oathkeepers* and the *Three Percenters*.

Abbie – Abigail Morgan, daughter of John Adams Morgan. United States senator from Massachusetts since 2008. A political independent, with libertarian leanings. She resides in Washington, D.C. She has been chosen as the running mate of the Democratic nominee for president. She briefly became romantically involved with her head of security, Drew Jackson, aka *Slash*, on the Aegis team.

Drew Jackson – a/k/a *Slash*. Former SEAL Team member who worked briefly for private contractors like Blackwater. Born and raised in Tennessee, where his family farm is located. He has excellent survival skills. He was assigned to Senator Abigail Morgan's security team that works with her Secret Service detail.

THE BOSTON BRAHMIN:

John Adams Morgan – lineal descendant of President John Adams and Henry Sturgis Morgan, founder of J.P. Morgan. Morgan attended Harvard, obtaining a master's degree in business and a law degree. Founded the Morgan-Holmes law firm with the grandson of Supreme Court Justice Oliver Wendell Holmes Jr. Among other concerns, he owns Morgan Global, an international banking and financial conglomerate. Extremely wealthy, Morgan is the recognized head of The Boston Brahmin.

Walter Cabot – direct descendant of John Cabot, shipbuilders during the time of the Revolutionary War. Wealthy philanthropist and CEO of Cabot Industries. He is part of Morgan's inner circle. Married to Mary Cabot.

Lawrence Lowell – direct descendant of John Lowell, a federal judge in the first United States Continental Congress. Extremely wealthy and part of Morgan's inner circle. Married to Constance Lowell.

Paul Winthrop – descendant of John Winthrop, one of the leading figures in the founding of the Massachusetts Bay Colony, his family became synonymous with the state's politics and philanthropy. The Winthrops and Sargents became close when Sarge's grandfather was governor of Massachusetts and his lieutenant governor was R. C. Winthrop. The families remained close and became a valuable political force on behalf of The Boston Brahmin. They have a French bulldog called Winnie the Frenchie. Married to Millicent Winthrop.

Arthur Peabody – Dr. Arthur Peabody is a plastic surgeon in private practice. He is the youngest of the Boston Brahmin at age fifty-five. His wife is Estelle, affectionately called Aunt Stella. They are Julia's aunt and uncle. They're direct descendants of the Hawthorne and Peabody lineage.

General Samuel Bradlee – former general and Secretary of Defense. A direct descendant of Nathaniel Bradlee, one of the key participants in the Boston Tea Party. He is Brad's uncle.

Henry Endicott – great-grandson of former Secretary of War William Crowninshield Endicott. The Endicott family name is synonymous with warfare throughout the world as one of the largest manufacturers of advanced weapons systems in America. His third wife, Emily, is younger than some of his children.

OFFICERS OF 1ˢᵗ BATTALION, 25ᵗʰ MARINE REGIMENT:

Gunny Falcone – Master Gunnery Sergeant Frank Falcone. Under Brad's command for years. A loyal member of the Mechanics. Stationed at Fort Devens. Primary on-base recruiter of soldiers to join the Mechanics.

Chief Warrant Officer Kyle Shore – young. Expert in sniping. Recorded two kill shots in Afghanistan at just over 2,500 yards. Stationed at Fort Devens. Also recruits members of the Mechanics.

First Lieutenant Kurt Branson – Boston native. A loyal member of the Mechanics.

SUPPORTING CHARACTERS:

Agent Joseph Pearson – special agent working for the Federal Protective Services—a division of Homeland Security. He first appeared at Fort Devens to meet with Brad in April. A subsequent meeting at Fort Devens with Brad following the cyber attack became very contentious. He is now the special liaison to the Citizen Corps governor of FEMA Region I—James O'Brien. His office is located on High Street in Boston.

Citizen Corps Governor James O'Brien – former president of the Boston Carmen's Union—one of the oldest and largest public service employees' unions in the city. O'Brien is a staunch supporter of the President and is known to have organized-crime connections. He is a fierce political opponent of Republican

Governor Charlie Baker. He was named the new governor of Region I. His office is located on High Street in Boston.

Governor Charlie Baker – Governor of Massachusetts. First Republican in decades to be endorsed by the left-leaning Boston Globe newspaper.

Marion La Rue – Member of the International Brotherhood of Teamsters. Called upon by union leaders in Boston to undertake special union *activities*, including the orchestrated walkout of MBTA bus drivers during the St. Patrick's Day festivities.

Ronald Archibald – Newly appointed town chairman of the board of selectman in Belchertown, Massachusetts, a small town just to the west of Prescott Peninsula.

J-Rock – Jarvis Rockwell, leader of the unified black gangs of Dorchester, Roxbury, and Mattapan in South Boston. He rose to power after the death of his unborn child during a race riot in Copley Square. He is recruited by Governor O'Brien to loot the wealthy neighborhoods of Boston.

Joaquin Guzman – Head of a Central American drug cartel known as *Mara Salvatrucha*, or MS-13, which predominantly operates in the East Boston ghettos. He is recruited by Governor O'Brien to loot the wealthy neighborhoods of Boston.

John Willis – also known as *Bac Guai John*, or more commonly as the *White Devil*. He is the only Caucasian in Chinatown and the undisputed head of the Ping On gang. Over time he rose through the ranks and became the leading oxycodone importer from South Florida—a three-billion-dollar-a-year industry. He has entered into an alliance with The Loyal Nine.

General Mason J. Sears – descendant of Richard Sears, an early settler of the Massachusetts Bay Colony in the seventeenth century. General Mason J. Sears, USMC, is the current Chairman of the Joint Chiefs of Staff, and has been designated by the President to implement the Declaration of Martial Law. He is an insider for John Morgan and The Boston Brahmin.

Joe Sciacca – *Boston Herald*'s chief editor.

Malcolm Lowe – John Morgan's trusted assistant. Former

undersecretary of state during Morgan's tenure as Secretary of State. He *handles* sensitive matters for Mr. Morgan.

Sabina del Toro – former Marine second lieutenant deployed to Iraq, assigned to the 6th Marine Regiment under the 2nd Marine Division based at Camp Lejeune. The 6th was primarily a peacekeeping force deployed throughout the Sunni Anbar province, which included Fallujah, just west of Baghdad. Sabs, as she prefers to be called, was seriously injured protecting children from a car bomb blast. She lost her left arm and left leg as a result of her heroics. She was in a relationship with J.J. She died in *Martial Law*, book three, during a confrontation with local residents.

ZERO DAY GAMERS:

Andrew Lau – MIT professor of Korean descent. A brilliant mind that created the Zero Day Gamers as a way to utilize his talents for personal financial gain.

Anna Fakhri – MIT graduate assistant to Professor Lau, of Arabic descent. She prides herself on her "Internet detective work." She speaks multiple Arabic languages.

Leonid "Leo" Malvalaha – MIT graduate assistant to Professor Lau, of Russian descent. He is very adept at creating complex viruses, worms, and Trojans used in cyber-attack activities. He speaks fluent Russian.

Herm Walthaus – newest member of the Zero Day Gamers. MIT graduate student. Introverted, but extremely analytical. Stays abreast of the latest tools and techniques available to hackers.

AEGIS TEAM:

Nomad – Steven Sargent.

Slash – Drew Jackson. Former SEAL Team member who worked briefly for private contractors like Blackwater. Born and raised in Tennessee, where his family farm is located. He has excellent survival skills. He was assigned to Senator Abigail Morgan's security team that works with her Secret Service detail.

Bugs – Paul Hittle. Former Army Special Forces medic, who left the Green Berets for contract security work. He owns a ranch in

East Texas, provided to him as compensation for his service to Aegis.

Sharpie – Raymond Bower. Former Delta Force, who now operates a lucrative private equity fund venture with former classmates from Harvard. He resides in New York City.

PRIMARY SCENE LOCATIONS

100 Beacon – Renovated residential building located in the heart of the Back Bay area of Boston. Located on the lower end of the Boston Common, just to the south of Cambridge and the Charles River, the top three floors of the eleven-story building were renovated as a veritable fortress. The top floor housed Sarge's residence, and the Prepper Pantry. The floor below it, was intended to provide housing for The Loyal Nine and The Boston Brahmin. The ninth floor contained an armory, a small medical trauma center, a jail cell, and large storage area. The rooftop provided three hundred- and sixty-degree views of the city, and overlooked Storrow Drive and Cambridge.

73 Tremont – historic building in downtown Boston located at 73 Tremont Street. (Pronounced "trem-mont") Formerly a historic hotel, the building was purchased by John Morgan to house the top floor offices of The Boston Brahmin. 73 Tremont overlooks the gold dome of the Massachusetts State House and Boston Common.

Fort Devens – is a United States military installation located in northern Massachusetts. It is the home to First Battalion, 25th

Marine Regiment, headed up by Lt. Col. Bradlee. It is also the location of a Federal Bureau of Prisons Medical Facility.

Prescott Peninsula (1PP) – The largest land mass in the Quabbin Reservoir, Prescott Peninsula was completely surrounded by the reservoir and was largely unimproved except for an abandoned radio astronomy observatory where the old town of Prescott Center once stood. The observatory was renovated by the Quinn's to create a state-of-the-art bug-out location, known as 1 Prescott Peninsula, or 1PP. Bungalows were built around 1PP to house The Boston Brahmin and the soldiers from Fort Devens who were tasked with protecting 1PP.

Quabbin Reservoir – the largest body of water in the State of Massachusetts. Located in the central part of the state, it was formed by the creation of dams and dikes in the 1930s, and became federal government owned and was largely undeveloped. The largest land mass, Prescott Peninsula, was completely surrounded by the reservoir and was largely unimproved except for the abandoned radio astronomy observatory which was renovated to create 1PP.

PREVIOUSLY IN THE BOSTON BRAHMIN SERIES

BOOK ONE: THE LOYAL NINE

The Boston Brahmin series begins in December and the timeframe of *The Loyal Nine*, book one in The Boston Brahmin series, continues through April. Steven Sargent, in his capacity as Nomad, an Aegis deep-cover operative, undertakes several black-ops missions in Ukraine, Switzerland, and Germany. The purposes of the operations become increasingly suspect to Steven and his brother, Sarge. It is apparent that Steven's actual employer, John Morgan, is orchestrating a series of events as part of a grander scheme.

Sarge continues to teach at the Harvard Kennedy School of Government. He begins to make public appearances after publishing a *New York Times* bestseller *Choose Freedom or Capitulation: America's Sovereignty Crisis*. During this time, he rekindles his relationship with Julia Hawthorne, who is also celebrating national notoriety for her accomplishments at the *Boston Herald* newspaper. The two take a trip to Las Vegas for a convention and become unwilling participants in a cyber attack on the Las Vegas power grid. Throughout *The Loyal Nine*, Sarge and Julia observe the economic and societal collapse of America.

The unraveling of society in America is evident as the chasm between the haves and have-nots widens, resulting in hostilities between labor unions and their employers. There are unintended consequences of these actions, and numerous deaths are the result.

Racial tensions are on the rise across the country, and Boston becomes ground zero for social unrest when a beloved retired bus driver is beaten to death during the St. Patrick's Day festivities. In protest, a group of marchers descend upon Copley Square at the end of the Boston Marathon, resulting in a clash with police. The protestors are led by Jarvis *J-Rock* Rockwell, leader of the unified black gangs of Dorchester, Roxbury, and Mattapan in South Boston. The march quickly gets out of hand, and J-Rock's pregnant girlfriend is struck by the police, resulting in her death and the death of their unborn child.

The Quinn family—Donald, Susan and their young daughters— are caught up in an angry mob scene at a local mall, relating to the Black Lives Matter protests. Donald decides to accelerate the Loyal Nine's preparedness activities as he gets the sense America is on the brink of collapse.

The reader gets an inside look at the morning security briefings in the White House Situation Room. Katie O'Shea becomes a respected rising star within the intelligence community while solidifying her role as a conduit for information to John Morgan.

John Morgan continues to act as a world power broker. He manipulates geopolitical events for the financial gain of his wealthy associates—the Boston Brahmin. He carefully orchestrates the rise to national prominence of his daughter, Senator Abigail Morgan.

As a direct descendant of the Founding Fathers, Morgan is sickened to watch America descend into collapse. Morgan believes the country can return to its former greatness. He recognizes drastic measures may be required. He envisions a reset of sorts, but what that entails is yet to be determined.

Throughout *The Loyal Nine*, the Zero Day Gamers make a name for themselves in the hacktivist community as their skills and capabilities escalate from cyber vandalism to cyber ransom to cyber terror. Professor Andrew Lau and his talented graduate assistants create ingenious methods of cyber intrusion. At times, they question the morality of their activities. But the ransoms they extract from their victims are too lucrative to turn away.

The end game, the mission statement of the Zero Day Gamers, is succinct:

One man's gain is another man's loss; who gains and who loses is determined by who pays.

PREVIOUSLY IN THE BOSTON BRAHMIN SERIES

BOOK TWO: CYBER ATTACK

But who else loses in their deadly game? *Cyber Attack*, book two in The Boston Brahmin series, begins with the Zero Day Gamers testing their skills by taking over control of an American Airlines 757. Throughout *Cyber Attack*, the Zero Day Gamers conduct various cyber intrusions, including compromising a nuclear power plant in Jefferson City, Missouri. But one of the Gamers, in an attempt to impress a young lady, makes a mistake. His cyber snooping into the laptop of Abbie Morgan following the Democratic National Convention is discovered.

Meanwhile, over the summer, the Loyal Nine increase their preparedness activities. Through some legislative maneuvering, John Morgan acquires Prescott Peninsula at the Quabbin Reservoir in central Massachusetts. The Quabbin Reservoir is the largest body of water in the State of Massachusetts. Located in the central part of the state, it was formed by the creation of dams and dikes in the 1930s and became federal government owned and was largely undeveloped. Prescott Peninsula is completely surrounded by the reservoir and was largely unimproved except for an abandoned radio astronomy observatory where the old town of Prescott Center once stood. The entire acquisition encompasses nearly forty square miles. He immediately tasks Donald and Susan Quinn with renovating the property into a high-tech bug-out location for the Boston Brahmin.

While Donald, Susan, J.J., and Sabs focus their attention on Prescott Peninsula, Sarge is making a name for himself on the speaker's circuit as a straight-talk libertarian. His relationship with Julia Hawthorne has grown, and they continue to observe world events with an eye towards preparedness.

After the hack of Abbie's computer, through some excellent cyber forensics on the part of Katie O'Shea, the Zero Day Gamers are located and contacted by Steven Sargent and Malcolm Lowe, acting on behalf of John Morgan. The three orchestrate a ruse upon Andrew Lau and his team of cyber mercenaries for hire.

Morgan has determined that America is descending into collapse, both socially and economically, and is in need of a reset. The Zero Day Gamers are the perfect tool to accomplish this purpose.

Morgan has conducted several private meetings with the President, culminating with a face-to-face discussion in August. The two agree—a reset is necessary, and each will play a vital role in bringing America to its knees only to build the country back in their respective images. These two powerful political players navigate a complex game of chess, not realizing the unintended consequences on the people of America.

As *Cyber Attack* closes its final chapter in early September, Andrew Lau is forced to make a choice. Does he watch his young proteges die by a gunshot to the head at the hands of Morgan's men, or does he push the button that will result in the end of life as we know it?

PREVIOUSLY IN THE BOSTON BRAHMIN SERIES
BOOK THREE: MARTIAL LAW

Lau makes his choice, and his sophisticated cyber attack causes a cascading collapse of the Western and Eastern Interconnected Grid representing ninety percent of America's electricity. Only Texas, whose grid is not connected to the rest of the nation, is spared.

The Loyal Nine are scattered throughout the country. Each faces their own set of unique circumstances and challenges.

John Morgan, despite his meticulous, well-thought plans, makes one critical mistake—he loses track of his daughter's whereabouts. Despite his efforts, Morgan is unable to call off the cyber attack. This leads him to frantically arrange a trip to Florida to extract his daughter and bring her to safety. Just before, and immediately following the grid collapse, he communicates with Abbie's chief of staff to insist that Abbie meet him at Camp Blanding.

Abbie Morgan is in Tallahassee to give a campaign speech. Under the watchful eye of her ever-present protector, Drew Jackson, Abbie addresses a packed crowd at the Donald Tucker Civic Center. Then they are thrust into darkness. Within moments, thirteen thousand people are informed, via text messages and cell phone calls that America has been attacked and the power grid is down.

Drew, Abbie, and some of her entourage attempt to travel several hundred miles east to Camp Blanding, where John Morgan will meet them in his helicopter. First, they have to flee the inner city of Tallahassee, where nearly one hundred thousand people have congregated for the concert and a college football game.

During this night of terror, Drew and Abbie fight their way through looters, marauders, and the throes of Hurricane Danni. Within thirty miles of their destination, they run out of fuel near the small town of Lulu. This small community has been ravaged, not by the hurricane, but by escaped inmates from three of the worst prison facilities in Florida.

Daylight approaches, but the feeder bands of Hurricane Danni continue to obstruct visibility. With a borrowed car from an elderly victim of the inmates' violence, Drew and Abbie make their way to the rendezvous point. Within fifty yards of the helicopter, and safety, they are overrun by a group of attacking inmates. Drew pushes Abbie to the safety of her father, but he is savagely beaten and left for dead. As Drew reaches toward the helicopter, shouting, Abbie and Morgan leave him behind, much to the devastation of Abbie, who had fallen in love with Drew.

In Boston, Sarge and Julia are having drinks on the rooftop of 100 Beacon, having a deep conversation, when the transformers begin to explode. As the lights go out in waves throughout Boston, they immediately recognize this as a possible grid-down collapse event.

They immediately begin to implement their preparedness plan. First, they secure their perimeter. Next, they establish various means of communications and information gathering.

The first call Sarge makes is to John Morgan, who at the time is traveling to the heliport by private car. Morgan's orders are clear: gather up the Boston Brahmin and keep them safe. Sarge knows that this is his call to duty. But something else bothers him about the conversation. Morgan's words weigh heavily on his mind —*widespread, long-lasting*. For the past seven years, somehow Sarge knew this moment would come. What bothers him is the fact that so did John Morgan.

Sarge successfully gathers up the executive committee of the Boston Brahmin, but it does not go without incident. During his last pickup, Sarge is involved in a high-speed chase, with gunfire, through Chinatown. He unknowingly leads them right to the front door of 100 Beacon.

Steven and Katie are in Washington together, enjoying a few beers and shooting pool at a local hangout near the White House. As the grid collapses, they also recognize the need to get out of the major population center and return to Boston. But for Katie, work calls. She ignores her instructions to report to the Situation Room in the White House. She cannot, however, ignore the phone call from John Morgan with instructions to contact General Mason Sears, the chairman of the Joint Chiefs. Katie makes a choice to remain with Steven and loyal to her friends.

Katie is prepared for a bug-out scenario, and the two embark on a road trip through the Poconos toward Boston. They quickly learn that bugging out isn't easy, even when you are armed and prepared. They are attacked near a toll-booth exit and Steven is almost killed. Katie repels their assailants and nurses a badly injured Steven back to health.

But now their car is destroyed. Their gear and communications are lost. They only have their handguns and limited ammunition. They have to enter survival mode in a world without rule of law. Finding a car dealership, they commandeer a Range Rover and begin their trip northward. But another unexpected confrontation occurs.

Within miles of the last encounter, they see a young girl running in fear from a group of men who are chasing her through an industrial park. Steven and Katie give chase and save the girl, leaving four dead bodies in their wake.

At various junctures of their trip, the two meet people familiar with Sarge and his book. Some have tattoos of the Rebellious Flag— five red and four white vertical stripes. Several use the phrase *choose freedom* as a way of showing solidarity. Steven begins to see that Sarge's message is resonating throughout the country.

Finally, driving a FedEx delivery truck, the two make their way to Boston and the safety of 100 Beacon only to find it under assault by four Asian men. Steven, who quickly morphs into *Nomad*, despite his injuries, takes out the four attackers. The only thing standing between them and the top floors of 100 Beacon is a group of frightened residents firing wildly out of the front entrance. Not a problem for Nomad.

At Prescott Peninsula, the detailed preparedness plan implemented by Donald and Susan Quinn is on full display. They had successfully built a state-of-the-art bug-out facility on the old radio observatory site. J.J. and Sabina had grown close over the past several weeks and were officially a *couple*. Along with the Quinn's young girls, the four are enjoying a quiet Labor Day weekend away at the Quabbin Reservoir facility.

When the power goes out, the four are enjoying drinks and dinner in front of 1PP. Because of the lack of surrounding, ambient lighting, they don't realize the grid is down. Once they discover the situation, they begin to implement their preparedness plan.

Their first arrivals come in the form of the Morgan Sikorsky helicopter. Abbie is still upset over the loss of Drew and mourns for several days. As she calms down, Donald introduces Abbie and John Morgan to the sophisticated 1PP facility, which includes a gold and silver vault worth hundreds of millions of dollars.

Brad beefs up security at Prescott Peninsula. After a visit from a representative of Homeland Security, he senses that the President is about to declare martial law. Brad goes rogue and rallies the Mechanics led by Gunny Falcone, Chief Warrant Officer Shore, and First Lieutenant Branson. They systematically divert assets and like-minded troops to Prescott Peninsula. They are nearly at company strength in gear and numbers.

In the process of building up the military assets at Prescott Peninsula, Brad has to send a platoon to Boston. He gathers up the Boston Brahmin from 100 Beacon to take them safely to 1PP. Sabs, over J.J.'s objection, takes up the slack and joins the security detail at the gated entrance to the Quabbin Reservoir complex. In a confrontation with locals, she is shot.

J.J., with the assistance of Susan and Donald, tries valiantly to save his new love, to no avail. Sadly, Sabs dies on the table, together with his unborn baby, of which he has no knowledge. Susan and Donald wrestle with telling him, but the arrival of the Boston Brahmin and the upcoming address by the President puts the issue off for another day.

On the fifth night following the collapse, the President is set to speak to the nation through whatever means of communications are available. Susan overhears a conversation between two of the Boston Brahmin that leads her to believe there is something nefarious going on. Abbie, who has been having nightmares, finally comes to the realization of what happened the morning they left Drew behind. He was shouting, "He knew, he knew." *What did that mean?*

The President addresses the nation, but not with an uplifting message of hope and perseverance. It is divisive, condemning, and declarative. Through executive orders, the President quickly sets up a massive militaristic occupational force called the *Citizen Corps.* In conjunction with regional FEMA governors, the Citizen Corps will establish local Citizen Corps Councils that will fall under the control of the President and FEMA.

Then the President instructs General Sears to read the Declaration of Martial Law, which suspends the constitution and essentially revokes all freedoms guaranteed to American citizens by the Bill of Rights. *Freedom, liberty, and independence are lost.*

After General Sears reads the declaration, he receives a phone call from John Morgan. The four words that General Sears hears from John Morgan are plain and simple—yet chilling.

The end begins tomorrow.

PREVIOUSLY IN THE BOSTON BRAHMIN SERIES
BOOK FOUR: FALSE FLAG

As book four, False Flag opens, Sarge stands atop 100 Beacon alone, reflecting on the President's Declaration of Martial Law. In just a matter of days, the country was rapidly descending into collapse. He was surprised at how rapidly the President reacted to the events, and the level of governmental overreach contained in the Declaration.

But Sarge's thoughts were interrupted by a series of massive explosions as the Kendall Station Power Plant malfunctioned. The blasts rocked the city, and caused the collapse of the Longfellow Bridge. The deaths and casualties were numerous.

Julia insisted on helping the injured by volunteering at Massachusetts General Hospital. Unknowingly, she and Sarge assisted with a severely burned patient—Andrew Lau. Later, Katie and Steven discover that Lau is alive.

Prescott Peninsula, and 1PP, was now inhabited by The Boston Brahmin and their wives, the Quinn family, Abbie, and a platoon of Marines dispatched by Brad. J.J. was still distraught over the loss of Sabs, and insisted upon going back to 100 Beacon. News of the Kendall Station explosion gave him an excuse to leave.

As part of the President's Declaration of Martial Law, the former

FEMA regions were re-designated to fall under the purview of the newly created Council of Governors appointed by the President. With the expansion of the Citizen Corps, the President named former Carmen's Union President, James O'Brien, as the new governor of Region One, which consisted of Massachusetts, and upper New England. His offices were in the FEMA location at 99 High Street overlooking the Boston Harbor.

O'Brien is thrilled at his new appointment, but not out of pride. He is an opportunist. He sees the collapse as an opportunity to enrich himself, and his friends. He also intends to right many perceived social wrongs. He surrounds himself with men willing to work outside the law to achieve this purpose.

The White House assigns for Federal Protective Services Agent, Joe Pearson, to be the liaison between O'Brien and the President. Pearson, who has had heated conversations with Brad on two prior occasions, is prepared to assist O'Brien achieve his goals.

However, for the more nefarious jobs, O'Brien enlists the employment of an old friend, and notorious Union thug, Marion La Rue. La Rue orchestrated the walkout of the union transit workers during the St. Patrick's Day event last March. The walkout inadvertently led to the death of a black man named Pumpsie Jones, which caused social unrest throughout the city.

Pearson is tasked with training forty-four of O'Brien's trusted union associates. The first order of business is to raid all of the Massachusetts Guard Armories across the state. Via inside information, The Loyal Nine are aware of the details of the raids, and provide a surprise for O'Brien's men. Throughout the night, Steven and Katie coordinate ambushes of O'Brien's men using The Mechanics. They apprehend O'Brien's men and imprison them at Fort Devens under Brad's watchful eye.

O'Brien, thinking the men betrayed his trust, looked for an alternative to carry out his plans. He instructs La Rue to arrange a meeting with Joaquin Guzman, head of the El Salvadoran MS-13 gang, and Jarvis Rockwell, a/k/a J-Rock, heads of the unified black gangs in Boston. Their task is a simple one — loot. They are provided assurances that no one under O'Brien's command will impede them as they enter the wealthiest neighborhoods of Boston and take what they want.

Meanwhile, The Loyal Nine seek out an ally of their own to counteract O'Brien. They meet with John Willis — The White Devil, head of the Asian gangs in Chinatown. A celebrity of sorts, having been interviewed extensively by Rolling Stone magazine, Willis is hesitant to to deal with Sarge, Julia and Steven at first. But an alliance is formed for the purposes of thwarting MS-13 and the black gangs of Dorchester, Mattapan, and Roxbury.

The Loyal Nine also begin to organize their modern day insurgent arm — The Mechanics. Meeting under cover of darkness at the location of the original Liberty Tree, 630 Washington Street, Sarge and Steven rally their trusted militia. Steeped in historic precedent as the predecessors to the Sons of Liberty, The Mechanics are ordinary Bostonians who are answering the call of duty to protect and defend the Constitution and the United States.

At 1PP, Morgan, who is exhibiting signs of stress, grows concerned that the President is ignoring his phone calls. Morgan advises the President that it is time to consider rebuilding the country but he is rebuked by the President, who responds "You'll make your money now let me finish what I started." The President is surly and combative, prompting Morgan to contact General Sears suggesting the nation was in a constitutional crisis. He seeks to remove the President from office, but Sears refuses such drastic action as a coup d'état.

Following the shooting death of Sabs at the front gate, the residents of Belchertown, located just west of Prescott Peninsula, became enraged. They insisted their newly appointment Chairman of the Board of Alderman, Ronald Archibald, take action. For Belchertown, supplies are quickly running out and there haven't been any new provisions from the Federal government in weeks. They are panicking. Partly out of revenge for the death of their neighbor, but mostly out of need, they concoct a plan to attack the inhabitants of Prescott Peninsula and confiscate their provisions.

O'Brien begins to suspect that Brad is working against him. After a brief period of mistrust (courtesy of Brad) in Agent Pearson, O'Brien enlists Pearson's support in contacting the White House for reinforcements in the form of a United Nations occupying force. Along with La Rue and Pearson, O'Brien watches as tanks, and artillery, together with thousands of U.N. soldiers roll off the ships lined up in Boston Harbor. "Boys, now I've got my army," he quips.

The Loyal Nine come together at Prescott Peninsula for the first time since the cyber attack. Their first order of business is trade notes on the events which led up to the power outage, and to make a determination of who is responsible. The conclusion becomes obvious — John Morgan.

Without notice to Abbie, Sarge is tasked with confronting Morgan with these facts. While Abbie and Steven watch, Morgan and his godson, Sarge, engage in an epic debate about the use of the cyber attack as a means to reset America from its downward path into economic and social collapse.

As the argument intensifies, Morgan suffers a stroke. J.J. is called in to assist and is successful in savings Morgan's life. After surviving the ordeal, and contemplating his future, Morgan calls in his trusted friends, Cabot and Lowell. Then Sarge is summoned to Morgan's bungalow. The conversation went like this:

"Come, sit with me, Henry," said Morgan, who took a deep breath before continuing. "I promised your father that you would do great things. I promised to be your guardian, your mentor, and protector. For all of these years, I have ushered you through life, keeping a watchful eye over you as if you were my son."

"Yes, sir, I know," said Sarge, who was welling up with emotion.

"I am not a dying man, but I am tired. A tired man can do nothing easily, and we still have work to do, Henry." Morgan attempted to push himself up again, and he was assisted by Sarge.

Morgan continued as he addressed the room. "I thank God that I have done my duty in upholding the ideals and vision of our forefathers. I've done all of the business I am capable of doing on this earth." He turned his attention to Sarge.

"Patriotism is not enough, Henry. I see compassion in you I never had. You recognize that our fellow man must not be forgotten."

Morgan again looked into the faces of the Boston Brahmin. "I intend to live, my friends. You can't dispatch me that easily.

"We must finish what we started, but it requires a younger man. It needs a different vision, one capable of looking beyond the creation of wealth, but to the creation of a new nation. My role now is that of teacher—the grand master to the student." He turned his attention to Sarge and struggled as he reached out to grasp his shoulder.

"It is time for me to step aside. The Boston Brahmin must be led by the next generation of patriots. Henry, I am entrusting you to take the reins and accept your destiny as the new head of the Boston Brahmin."

PREVIOUSLY IN THE BOSTON BRAHMIN SERIES
BOOK FIVE: THE MECHANICS

How do the weak vanquish the powerful?

Sarge takes the reigns and immediately decides to take the fight to Governor O'Brien and his new friends—the United Nations occupying forces. But first, they face the residents of nearby Belchertown as Ronald Archibald, the appointed Citizen Corps leader of the town, undertakes an ill-fated attempt to assault Prescott Peninsula.

Experience and preparation wins the day as Steven Sargent leads a gun battle on the waters of the Quabbin Reservoir which displays the benefit of planning and superior firepower. Brad's men are efficient in their ability to defend the shores of Prescott Peninsula and repel the three pronged attack. A valuable prisoner in the form of Archibald's son, is taken into custody and plays a pivotal role later.

With 1PP once again secured, The Loyal Nine now face the bigger threat posed by the tyrannical O'Brien and the UN *peacekeeping force*. Sarge is firm in his resolve when he announces to a secret meeting of The Mechanics, "Gentlemen, it's time to start poking the bear."

Using resources from Fort Devens, Brad and Steven undertake a two-pronged attack. The first was designed to distract the UN troops, as well as eliminate their superior firepower in the form of two assault helicopters. Brad retrieves Stinger missiles which were supposed to be used for a training exercise and decimates the air power of the UN.

During the attack at the Seaport District, UN troops are called away from their post at the Greater Boston Area Food Bank where Governor O'Brien was hoarding relief supplies for his own benefit. Steven liberates the food and hauls it away to be disbursed throughout the city.

Once again, The Mechanics prove themselves as a force for freedom, but there is still work to be done. Sarge, in his newfound position as head of The Boston Brahmin, begins to learn from the master—John Morgan. Morgan imparts his knowledge and experience upon his godson who learns the extent of The Boston Brahmin's wealth and power.

Morgan's intricate planning is paying off for his friends as he reveals to Sarge that The Boston Brahmin now control seventy percent of the gold mining operations in the world. With the collapse of the dollar and the world's economy, gold, coupled with political influence, will assist Sarge in his endeavors.

In the meantime, sitting Governor Charlie Baker attempts to reconvene the legislature. Men and women from across the state arrive at the Massachusetts State House, including Sarge and a security detail. Shortly into the Governor's speech, the detail notices something is wrong. They alert Sarge and barely escape as O'Brien and the UN troops storm the State House. Governor Baker and the legislature are taken hostage.

O'Brien proposes a swap. He offers the legislature and State House in exchange for his forty –four men being held prisoner at Fort Devens, which he wants as well. The proposed trade is to take place on November 8, Election Day.

After Sarge's announced *promotion* to head of The Boston Brahmin, a festering sibling rivalry began to form between Sarge and Steven. This conflict between the brothers was fueled in part by

Steven's envy, but largely due to the inciting rhetoric of Katie. As Steven took the reins of The Mechanics, he formulated a plan to double-cross Governor O'Brien without Sarge's knowledge. It was going to be his opportunity to show John Morgan his worth.

On the day of the prisoner exchange, Steven covertly led his team into the State House with the intention of freeing the hostages. Unfortunately, two members of his team had ulterior motives. Isaac Grant and Rory Elkins conspired against Steven and during the mission, the cowardly Elkins stabbed Steven in the back.

Grant is killed, but Elkins slithered away into the bowels of the State House. Sarge reached Steven in time to hold his brother in the midst of a firefight. Fighting for his life, Steven managed to speak with Sarge.

"*Steven, I can't do this without you. Can you hold on?*" asked Sarge.

"*Fuck me. I can't feel anything.*" He coughed up more blood and grimaced. "*It's karma, you know.*"

"*What is?*" asked Sarge.

"*My whole life has been in the shadows. I killed, and they never saw it coming.*"

He coughed again and his eyes began to roll back in his head.

"I love you, brother," said Sarge, ducking as a rapid burst of bullets sailed over his head. "*Hold on for me.*"

Steven was whispering now. "*You know what they say?*"

"*What's that?*"

"*Karma is just a polite way of saying ha-ha, screw you.*"

And Steven slipped into the darkness.

Choose Freedom begins now ...

Following the death of his brother, Sarge buries him at sea and vows to avenge his murder. He addresses the issue of Katie's admitted betrayal by assigning her the task of hunting down the two men who betrayed the trust of The Mechanics.

The loss of Steven left a hole in Sarge's heart and also a gap in the group's operations. Sarge steps up as the leader of The Mechanics against everyone's protests, but he promises to rely heavily upon Donald as his chief advisor and Brad for military strategy.

As John Morgan recovers from his stroke, he and Sarge become closer. Morgan has mellowed and Sarge is anxious to take the reins of The Boston Brahmin. The two men discuss how to use the considerable resources of The Boston Brahmin to facilitate the recovery of America. They both agree, however, that any approach to making a better post-collapse world starts at the local level, which means they most deal with the tyrannical Governor O'Brien and the United Nations occupation forces.

With the assistance of Drew Jackson who returns to Prescott Peninsula to the delight of Abbie, the Battle for Boston begins. By coordinating the resources of the New England states, Sarge marshals the regions assets to mount an offensive against the UN.

To her credit, Katie has stepped up and found the hideout of the elusive Gov. O'Brien. A surprise in the form of Andrew Lau was also uncovered and the two men were quickly placed in the stockades below 1PP. O'Brien was later exiled to Campobello Island in the frigid North Atlantic. Lau was give the option of death by firing squad, or joining The Loyal Nine in their fight against the President who has convinced four states to secede from the Union — Hawaii, California, Oregon, and Washington.

After the rest of the Zero Day Gamers were rounded up and provided a work space, every aspect of Sarge's plan was implemented. First, the United Nations forces were driven out of Boston. Next, Drew leads a team to recapture Logan Airport from the brutal MS-13 gang. This opened up New England to receive relief supplies from around the world via Sarge's efforts.

With New England under control, Sarge looked to the next aspect of the recovery effort — How to take the movement nationwide? He hopes to spread the success attained in New England to the southern states. This became a team effort and once again, it was successful with Sarge being given full credit for the turnaround.

The mid-Atlantic states of Virginia, Pennsylvania, and New York were a tougher nut to crack but by reaching across the political spectrum to the son of the deceased Vice President, Sarge successfully created an alliance which resulted in the tyrannical Mayor of New York being ousted.

Sarge's successes in the recovery effort did not go unnoticed by the President in Hawaii. Once easily manipulated by power and money, the President hoped to carve out his own fiefdom in the Pacific States. He also chose to use the military power at his disposal to silence Sarge and quell the uprising led by The Loyal Nine.

He ordered a drone to destroy Prescott Peninsula. As the Predator was in route, Lau and the Zero Day Gamers discover the threat. After a brief debate, they jumped into action and diverted the drone into the ocean.

The recovery success spread into more states and Sarge's name became synonymous with the effort. At the Constitutional Convention in St. Louis arranged by Sarge, the majority of the states adopted sweeping reforms and the set the country on a new course. The Convention delegates were not able to keep the nation together as the Pacific states left to form their own nation under the leadership of the President.

An election was held in May and Sarge won an overwhelming victory as President. Two weeks later, he married his nine month pregnant love, Julia, in a ceremony at the Morgan estate which was also disrupted by an assassin.

The story closes with Julia giving birth to the Sargent's son, Henry Winthrop Sargent V, nicknamed *Win*. His trusted aide and protector, David Morrell, advised the President that it was time for him to perform another task.

The final excerpt from Choose Freedom ...

Sarge paced the floor and circled Elkins, who could only follow Sarge's movements with his eyes. Sarge began to pepper him with questions, despite Elkins's inability to respond.

"You didn't have to kill my brother. You had no cause to. Did you do it for money? To gain favor?"

Elkins didn't move or attempt to speak. He sat there, his eyes growing wider as Sarge became more agitated. Sarge became angry. He'd waited so long for this opportunity to confront his brother's murderer.

From all sides, Sarge circled the solitary chair and began screaming at Elkins.

"You're a traitor! A coward! You betrayed us all!"

Sarge continued to circle.

"You killed my brother!"

Then, as quickly as the anger rose, it subsided. Sarge exhaled as he put his hands in his pockets. He stared at Elkins for another moment, then turned and walked toward the door. He reached for the metal handle and then caught himself.

He looked through the small glass window at his security detail, which waited outside. He shrugged his shoulders and chuckled to himself.

Sarge's family was upstairs—Julia, his loving wife and their newborn baby. He was in the home of his mentor—John Morgan—the man who helped guide him since the death of Sarge's dad.

His brother, Steven, was killed in cold blood by this treacherous murderer.

Sarge unbuttoned his jacket, reached for his shoulder holster, and removed Steven's gun, which he'd retrieved from Katie. As he gripped the handle, Steven's voice swirled through Sarge's mind. *Screw it.*

"*What the hell,*" muttered Sarge as he turned and shot Elkins between the eyes, unceremoniously toppling his dead, worthless soul to the concrete floor.

With that, Henry Winthrop Sargent IV started day one of his presidency.

PREVIOUSLY IN THE BOSTON BRAHMIN SERIES
BOOK SEVEN: PATRIOT'S FAREWELL

In politics, nothing happens by accident. If it happens, you can bet it
was planned that way.
~ Franklin D. Roosevelt

With Patriot's Farewell, the Boston Brahmin saga was accelerated through the two terms of Sarge's presidency. The election of his successor was held, the Brahmin's man was chosen by the people and Sarge prepared for his last days in office.

It was Thanksgiving week and the family was preparing to host a dinner at the White House for the Boston Brahmin and their families. However, the world never sleeps and the demands upon America's president are endless.

Congress is debating a critical vote on the proposed Pacific Statehood Act. The law would pave the way for the four seceding states—California, Oregon, Washington, and Hawaii, as well as parts of Nevada, to return to the original fifty United States.

Sarge's predecessor in office, a man who'd conspired with John Morgan to initiate the cyber attack designed to reset the nation, was left angry by Sarge's actions at the Constitutional Convention. He rallied the four seceding states to create their own nation.

Throughout the Sargent presidency, he tried to bring them back into the fold without conditions. Once the former president saw that the political winds blowing in his favor, he made demands that, in Sarge's opinion, would result in the nation tearing itself apart once again.

Sarge and Donald carefully tracked the votes in both the House and the Senate. They thought they had the loyalty of lawmakers sufficient to kill the bill. However, they were outmaneuvered by a fellow Boston Brahmin, the son of Lawrence Lowell—Gardner Lowell.

Wielding his influence and spending his mother, Constance's money, Gardner was successful in getting the law passed over Sarge's objections. His goal was to diminish Sarge's stature within the Brahmin in hopes of ascending to the head of the powerful group's executive council.

With Sarge battling backroom politics at home, he sent Drew Jackson to Taiwan to rescue the U.S. Ambassador who'd been abducted. It appeared that China was behind the effort, in part, as they began to make a move against Taiwan who'd maintained their independence from the powerful Communist country.

Not only did Sarge and Drew rescue the ambassador, but in a show of strength, the U.S. Navy challenged a potential invasion by China by forming a blockade across the Taiwan Straits. Whether this bold act would be tolerated by Beijing was yet to be seen.

And, whether Gardner Lowell would continue to undermine Sarge and his authority within the Boston Brahmin would reveal itself within days.

As Thanksgiving Day came to an end, Sarge had triumphed on many fronts. However, would the feeling of accomplishment last. Black Friday is next.

SIGN UP

SIGN UP FOR EMAIL UPDATES and receive free advance reading copies, updates on new releases, special offers, and bonus content. You can contact Bobby directly by email (BobbyAkart@gmail.com) or through his website www.BobbyAkart.com

OTHER WORKS BY AMAZON CHARTS TOP 25 AUTHOR BOBBY AKART

New Madrid (a disaster thriller)

Odessa (a Gunner Fox trilogy)

Odessa Reborn

Odessa Rising

Odessa Strikes

The Virus Hunters

Virus Hunters I

Virus Hunters II

Virus Hunters III

The Geostorm Series

The Shift

The Pulse

The Collapse

The Flood

The Tempest

The Pioneers

The Asteroid Series (A Gunner Fox trilogy)

Discovery

Diversion

Destruction

The Doomsday Series

Apocalypse

Devil's Homecoming

The Boston Brahmin Series

The Loyal Nine

Cyber Attack

Martial Law

False Flag

The Mechanics

Choose Freedom

Patriot's Farewell (standalone novel)

Black Friday (standalone novel)

Seeds of Liberty (Companion Guide)

The Prepping for Tomorrow Series

Cyber Warfare

EMP: Electromagnetic Pulse

Economic Collapse

Made in the USA
Las Vegas, NV
06 September 2022

54792626R10218